The Widow Makers

Road's End

Novel Publishing

ISBN
978 0 9575730 1 7

Novels by Jean Mead

The Other Famous Five
A novel for children

The Widow Makers
1st Book in Historical Fiction Trilogy

The Widow Makers: Strife
2nd Book in Historical Fiction Trilogy

The Widow Makers: Road's End
3rd Book in Historical Fiction Trilogy

Freya 800 AD
Viking Era Fiction

Kate's Secret
Contemporary Psychological Mystery

Dedication

Edward and Jane Newby

Great, great, great grandchildren of Joe and Emily Ollier

1875

Chapter 1

It was John Bellamy's fortune gained from the sugar plantation of Jamaica that brought the beautiful mansion, Plas Mawr, into being. Designed by the architect Morgan Cross of London, its splendour can only be matched by a handful of grand mansions in England and Wales.

The descendants of John Bellamy found it neither necessary nor desirable to alter or extend the house and so it remains four-square, solid, and seemingly impervious to the storms spawned on the crests of the Snowdonia mountain range.

In the mid-eighteenth century, Lancelot 'Capability' Brown was engaged to re-design the grounds and extensive park. Many exotic trees were imported from abroad. Maples, poplars, and Italian alders were planted and flourish amidst native oaks, beech and elms.

The half-mile long avenue is now as Brown envisaged it, and the twin lines of mature lime trees are spectacular, the leaves an intense spring-green in summer sunlight, and as the year expires the falling foliage blazes honey-gold and amber. At winter's approach, the trees laid bare, a parade of skeletons, stark against a colourless sky.

The entrance to the avenue is guarded by huge ornate ironwork gates, meticulously maintained to the original specification. The Bellamy family crest emblazoned across a sweeping decorative arch.

Italianate gardens are the most recent addition to the grounds;

the stepped terraces lead to the shores of the Menai Strait. At every level there's a perfect vista across the Strait and to Puffin Island. Rooted on the rocky headland, Trwyn Du lighthouse stands sentinel between the verdant isle of Anglesey and the turbulent rolling waves of the sea running into the fierce tidal water.

For generations the house had remained in the Bellamy family, until the advent of Tommy Standish. Desiring to own the mansion above any other thing on God's earth, he deceived Henrietta Bellamy, Bertram Bellamy's only daughter, into marrying him.

Following Henrietta's death and that of her parents, Plas Mawr, Garddryn Quarry, and the thriving enterprises abroad became his to command entirely.

The ruthless pursuit of riches and grandeur, begun so early in his life, came to fruition before he reached twenty. Now his business interests are vast and require Madoc, a solicitor specialising in devious business practice, to ease him through the tangle of consortiums, real and fake. Madoc is clever and invaluable, but that doesn't make him a man that Tommy trusts utterly.

As he had an appointment with Madoc that day, Tommy rose early, enduring a close and meticulous shave from his valet, before taking a quick bathe in the hipbath.

Wearing dark grey trousers, a white silk shirt, and grey necktie, he came down the carpeted wide staircase into the grand hall, and made for the breakfast room, the leather soles of his shoes clacking on the mosaic floor.

Entering through the open door, he glanced at the two footmen standing at the large oak sideboard. Though the glimpse was fleeting, he checked their personal appearance carefully. Recently, yielding to modern fashion, he had decided that dark tailcoats and trousers, worn with white shirts and black neckties, were appropriate. A far cry from the previous livery of red coats braided with gold, white stockings, and buckle shoes, harking back to the previous century.

The second footman reached the table before Tommy crossed the room. Pulling out a chair for him, the servant gave a small bow. Ignoring the man, Tommy sat down and instantly a pristinely white damask napkin was placed across his lap.

Glancing to the silver domed dishes on the sideboard, the footmen said, 'Cook has sent kidneys, lamb cutlets, smoked ham, eggs, and also kedgeree, made with smoked haddock, sir.'

A distinct aroma of hot kidneys stirred Tommy's appetite. He spoke brusquely, as was usual when addressing an underling. 'I'll have kidneys, cutlets and two fried eggs. Bring hot toast immediately, and coffee.'

Familiar with the master's rudeness, the man gave hardly a noticeable nod of his head, before going to the sideboard. As he passed the first footman, bringing a coffee pot to the table, their eyes met, and in the mute communication both saw irritation in the other's face.

As Tommy's cup was filled with steaming coffee, the other servant carried his breakfast to him on a white porcelain plate.

Tommy sniffed the aroma appreciatively. Taking the silver knife and fork he sliced open a kidney. Biting into the succulent meat he found it cooked to perfection but didn't comment on it; instead he forked the cutlets around the plate remarking that they were overdone, and cook must be told. The footmen shared another tense glance.

The meal passed in silence but for the clinking of cutlery on porcelain. The servants standing perfectly still, with their backs against the sideboard, were both hoping that the master would not require a second helping. What remained on the silver platters went to the servants table, and although they had risen before five o'clock they had yet to break their own fast.

With the plate removed and another put before him, Tommy helped himself to fresh toast and peach preserve, made from last year's peaches grown in the orangery. After taking a sip from the coffee cup, he wiped his hands on the napkin, and then put it beside his plate.

Pushing the chair back from the table, he stood. With his hands in his trouser pockets, he went to the open French window to look out onto the sunlit garden.

At the far end of the gently sloping lawns, an ancient gardener was dead-heading roses and placing the full-blown heads into a Hessian sack. The magenta and intensely white blooms in the rose-beds were spectacular this year. Later, he would walk down and take a closer look, and smell the glorious perfume.

Sensing that he was observed the labourer looked up and caught a glimpse of the master at the window. As Tommy came out onto the sun-warmed terrace, the gardener picked up the sack and disappeared out of sight.

Trusting no one to do a job properly, Tommy scanned the lawns for a stray leaf or blown petal, a dropped flower-head to mar the perfection. As there was nothing to complain about, so no need to send a minion chasing after the gardener, he sat down on a beech bench, an involuntary sigh of tiredness escaping him.

Closing his eyes, he turned his face to the glaringly blue sky. Warmed by the sun, a sense of tiredness swept over him, and he was close to dozing. Last night he had endured vivid dreams and had slept fitfully.

That morning, for no particular reason, he took a careful look at his reflection in the looking glass, discovering new creases had appeared at the corner of his eyes, and the twin folds between his nose and mouth had deepened. There were now two distinct lines drawn across his brow which made him appear older than thirty-five.

Thankfully his hairline was still intact, and the dark colour stayed true, but for a few grey strands. His father, Joe Standish, had hair as grey as the slate he quarried at the Garddryn, but it had not receded or thinned significantly, which augured well for his own head of hair.

It was about the only thing about the old saying *like father, like son* that bore any truth, for in every other respect he was totally different from his father. Joe Standish, for all his years of toil, was still a down-trodden quarryman, living in a homebuilt cottage at the far side of Garddryn village.

Despising his father and his ideals, Tommy's thoughts were disparaging. What self-respecting man would work as a labourer at Garddryn Quarry where his son was master? Joe Standish, the *union* man! What an accolade for a man who had recently achieved his sixty-second year.

Sixty-two years were more than a lifetime by quarrymen's standards, he was lucky to have survived on the high galleries of the Garddryn. Tommy grudgingly acknowledged that the old man was wearing fairly well, given the weather conditions he and all quarrymen endured.

This filial thought brought him back to what he had seen in his shaving mirror earlier. He acknowledged he looked older than his years, but what man wouldn't age fast given the responsibilities he was forced to bear? An image of Henrietta, his late wife, only daughter of Bertram and Louis Bellamy, came into his mind.

Henrietta had been addicted to opium. The scenes she'd created had been ugly. On more than one occasion it had been necessary to restrain and chastise her. Though not for one moment would he accept that his brutish behaviour had been excessive. Henrietta alone had been responsible for her eventual demise.

Crossing one leg over his other knee, he listed past woes. George, Henrietta's brother, was a dribbling imbecile. Irrevocably brain damaged in the attack that had occurred outside Plas Mawr gates years before. Thankfully he was now housed in the asylum at Denbigh. This without doubt was the best place for him. 'Good riddance,' Tommy mouthed almost silently.

As a boy, George had been a menace, and as a young man with a penchant for gambling he'd become a threat to the Garddryn, Plas Mawr and the Bellamy fortune. It had been the right thing to do to get rid of George, but the subsequent threat of the hangman's noose upon his own neck had been a strain hard to bear. Was it any wonder that the looking-glass revealed that he looked older than his years?

The reflection overlooked the good times. The little creases at the corner of his eyes may be laughter lines! Sadie, his buxom peasant mistress, servant at Penrhyn Castle, had given him happiness and her love.

He closed his eyes, and in a moment he slipped into the dark hollow of sleep and he was dreaming of the past, and Lady

Isabelle, dressed in a flame red gown was walking across the manicured lawn of her London mansion towards him. Though the years of her prime were behind her, a shadow of her former beauty remained. The sway of her slender hips was sensual, her smile provocative, and he was reminded of her proclivity for masochism. Aroused, he returned her smile, but her expression changed to one of sneering contempt.

He woke with a jerk, the corners of his lips wet with spittle.

The dream, limpet like, clung to him, and he wondered if a scent in the garden had brought Lady Isabelle to mind, but the only fragrance on the air was the vaguely metallic perfume of the red pelargoniums.

The last time he saw Isabelle she was with her husband, Lord Harvey, boarding a dilapidated trawler taking them from the shore of Caernarvon to Dublin. He had no wish to see either of them again. If it became common knowledge that he had duped the pair into giving up Ruby Quarry, it could lead to a court case. It hadn't been difficult to make a fortune from Lord Harvey; the man was a walking financial hazard, and his own worst enemy.

He wondered what had brought the couple into his mind. He hoped to God it wasn't a premonition of their imminent arrival at Plas Mawr. The idea was preposterous, but he still jumped up, as if to make a hurried escape.

Seeing the master stir, a footman approached quietly. 'Is there anything I can bring you, sir?'

Without glancing at the man, Tommy replied abruptly. 'Tell Price to order the brougham. I am going to Ruby Quarry.'

'I do believe the first footman, Price, has already ordered the carriage, sir.'

Unaccountably ill tempered, Tommy snapped, 'I know who

Price is, you fool. Just refer to him by name in future, not his blasted label.'

The man's expression remained impassive. 'Very good, sir,' he said, backing away.

Still scowling, Tommy went back into the breakfast room. The table had been cleared. A young housemaid was brushing toast crumbs off the polished surface of the sideboard with a soft rag. Nervous at being in the same room as the master, her small face flushed pink, and eyes on the Turkey rug, she bobbed a curtsey.

The master passed by without noticing her. Reaching the door before the footman had fully crossed the carpet, Tommy pulled it open. Once through, he shouted for Roberts.

John Wright, Tommy's personal valet, on hearing his master call for the footman, hurried down the dim corridor of the servant's quarters. He could see no chink of light to indicate the door the staff used to enter the hall was slightly ajar, and for a heart jerking moment he couldn't remember unlocking it on his rounds earlier. It would mean retracing his steps, and losing precious minutes if it was the case.

Reaching the door, grasping the knob, feeling it turn in the palm of his hand, he let out the breath he wasn't aware he'd been holding. Relief brought a smile to his lips, and with this pleasant expression he came into the hall. The master's light grey cashmere frock coat draped over his arm.

Tommy's shoes clacked on the mosaic floor as he walked quickly down the wide hallway. His eyes hadn't completely adapted from the morning sunlight in the garden to the darker interior of the house, and coming into the massive hallway he was momentarily blinded.

On the sweeping staircase, a maid fluttered a feather-duster around the opulent chandelier suspended in the stairwell between the first and second storey, and the crystals chinked.

Tommy shouted, 'Take care!'

The chandelier was a great source of pride to him. It was splendid. Not even Penrhyn Castle had one half as exquisite. On special occasions it blazed with the fire of a hundred candles. It took two men an entire week to polish it afterwards.

The sound of a carriage on the driveway drew his attention, and he went through the door and down the stone steps to the waiting brougham, his valet following.

The brown hood of the vehicle was down, concertinaed on the back of the coachwork. Climbing aboard, Tommy got a whiff of warm leather and wax polish. Arranging the tails of his suit jacket, so as not to crease the lightweight material, he settled into the seat.

The coachman glanced over his shoulder, checking the master was settled before facing ahead again. Lifting his whip he tapped the rump of the grey mare. The wheels turned immediately, scrunching on the pebbles.

Though the figure of the driver partially blocked his view, Tommy looked down the avenue to the twin lines of lime trees now in full leaf, the acidic green spectacular against the blue of the sky. There was hardly a breeze coming off the sea to stir the foliage.

The brougham came to the end of the of the half-mile avenue. A gateman dressed reasonably tidily in Plas Mawr livery saluted it through the open gates.

Once through, the vehicle made a sharp right-hand turn onto the roadway, the leather suspension creaking as the body of the carriage rocked between the high wheels.

Hanging onto the strap beside the door, Tommy glanced to the mature rhododendrons growing on the verge opposite the gates. At this time of year the high bushes were heavy with mauve blooms and sticky leaves, the flowery show a reminder of the night he crouched beneath the branches waiting for George to come home to Plas Mawr. After he had remained there for what had seemed an eternity, he saw George coming down the road, lurching drunkenly. Caterwauling a bawdy tune, and swigging from a gin bottle.

Watching from his hiding place, the sickly fragrance of the rhododendrons in his nostrils, and insects crawling over his flesh, Tommy remained still, and silent, clutching a stone as big as his fist to his chest.

George paused for a moment to take another swig from the bottle. Finding it empty he cursed and slung it in the direction of the ditch, the glass shattering. Muttering, he staggered on.

With only a few steps separating them, Tommy leapt out of the shrubbery like a wild animal, the branches snapping back with a crack.

The shock sobered George and for a split second he was aware that he was in mortal danger. In a flash Tommy raised the stone and brought it down on George's head, hitting him with such force it split his skull. Warm blood sprayed out, splattering Tommy's hands and face.

Even in the darkness, George lying in the roadway, it was easy to see that the wound was horrendous. For a second Tommy considered hitting him again, but to repeat the violence and feel the skull give way for a second time was too grotesque and he had hurled the stone as far away as he could.

Terrified that he would be discovered by a passer-by or

someone coming from the mansion, he'd fled the scene, running towards a nearby field.

It was the same field his carriage was now passing, and he turned his head to look at the broken gate he'd dashed through on that fateful night. The wooden bars were now in a worse state, lying in the long grass, rotting away. Beyond the gate's stone pillars lay the brook where he washed George's blood off his hands and face.

It surprised him that his mind sometimes harked back to the incident, for he didn't hold himself responsible for the attack. George would have ruined the Garddryn Quarry and Plas Mawr. It had fallen on him to save the Bellamy fortune from ruination. If he hadn't taken matters into his own hands, all would be lost by now. Of that he was certain.

The carriage swept past a trimmed hedge, and he caught sight of Garddryn village. Though he had no interest in the place his workers lived, Tommy still glanced towards the grey straggling cottages clinging to the hillside.

His mother, father, and Frank his brother, lived at the far end of the village, in the very last cottage. Though he didn't mean to, Tommy looked in that direction and caught a glimpse of washing on the clothes line. It was a reminder of his humble beginnings, and he turned his eyes away in abhorrence and embarrassment.

Unlike the village, it wasn't necessary to see the Garddryn Quarry to know its location. From early morning till dusk a flow of noise swathed the entire area, like turbulent rivers running down a rocky mountainside. He didn't mind the racket, every clatter and clamour heralded an increase in his personal fortune.

The quarry came into view. Tommy looked towards the

topmost terraces. A red flag was flying. A moment later a siren wailed, warning of an imminent detonation. Tense, he waited for the explosion. When it came it rocked the air.

The mountain, already blasted to the spine, thundered as tons of slate crashed down the sixty-foot precipice to the gallery below. A cloud of grey dust rose from the rocky yield and slowly climbed the mountainside like smoke.

Above it, at the summit, a jagged grey pillar, the height of the local church, teetered, as though reluctant to part from the mother site. Every quarryman had his eyes upon it, and every breath was held fast. Very slowly the column appeared to move slightly to the right. The men gasped in unison, and the sound was like lazy ocean waves. Then the ragged column tilted precariously and its sheer weight tore it from the cliff-face, ripping out tons of slate and debris on its crashing slide to the quarry floor.

A strange silence followed, with only the rattling of solitary stones falling down the newly made cliff-face. A haze of grit and slate dust rose in a cloud. Men coming from shelters to inspect the harvest protected their faces with their tanned, dirty forearms.

As the dust settled, and normal quarry din returned, Tommy was aware of the beat of the mare's hooves and rattle of the carriage wheels. The office building came into view and he gathered his few belongings together, preparing to alight.

The quarry manager, Iwan Rees, imported from Parys copper mine on Mona to replace the former Garddryn manager Oakley, came to the entrance door of the quarry office on hearing a vehicle approach.

He was a tall, slim man, with skin the colour of boiled

oatmeal. His mat of receding grey hair was brushed back from his high forehead and held in place with a liberal coating of palm oil. Narrow shouldered, he was inclined to stoop a little to reduce his height. He looked weak and insubstantial, as though a gust of wind could blow him over. The impression was far from the truth; Iwan Rees was iron-willed, unforgiving and obstinate.

Tommy Standish, recognising that these characteristics would be effective in governing the quarrymen, filched Rees from the Parys copper-mines, and paid a significant rent on a handsome house on the outskirts of Garddryn village for the man and his family. The price of employing the manager was high, and in return Tommy expected blind obedience from him.

Iwan Rees had come to despise Tommy Standish intensely and it took all his self-control to suppress his opinions and keep on the right side of the master of the quarry.

The wheels of the vehicle clattered on the cobblestones at the entrance of the building. Familiar with the routine, the horse came to a standstill without being pulled up by the reins. The animal stood still, one foot tipped forward, neatly balanced on the rim of its shoe.

The liveried driver climbed down from his seat, and pulled open the door, touching the brim of his hat as Tommy Standish alighted. Ignoring the man, Tommy walked across the dusty cobbles to the open door.

Iwan Rees stood in the shadows, immaculately dressed in a fashionable black suit with short tails, a white silk shirt and black necktie. He appeared calm and efficient, and the slight smile on his mouth could be taken for welcoming, but it was a façade to hide his animosity. Wrapped up in his own emotions, he was quite unaware of the flutter of activity going on behind him, as clerks tried desperately to look busy as the master approached.

With the cashmere frock coat over his arm, Tommy strode into the vestibule, and quite mindlessly passed the garment to the manager. Lately this had become part of the early morning office routine.

Glancing over his shoulder, Iwan Rees clicked his fingers at the nearest underling. Instantly a lanky youth jumped down from the high stool where he was working, and crossed the floor hastily. Afraid to make eye contact with either man, the lad took the coat carefully and scurried into the cloakroom with it.

With this small but aggravating daily ritual of the coat dealt with, Iwan turned on his heel to follow the master to his ground floor office, passing through the open door a step behind Tommy Standish.

The heavy door clunked closed behind Iwan. His eyes went to Tommy making himself comfortable behind his newly acquired mahogany desk; the leather of the chair creaking with the master's shifting weight.

Glancing down at the diary lying open before him, Tommy saw that he had an appointment with Madoc, his solicitor, scheduled for eleven o'clock. For the moment he couldn't recall the purpose of the meeting.

Iwan broke into his thoughts. 'Garddryn quarrymen gathered outside the Halfway Inn on Saturday night to hold a union meeting.' He wished for a calm discussion, so didn't mention that Joe Standish, Tommy's father, was the main orator of the evening.

Tommy's eyes darkened dangerously. 'Do you have a list of the names of the men who took part?'

'Mostly,' Iwan answered steadily.

In a moment of silence, Iwan heard the ticking of the tall-case clock; the brass pendulum clicked on the downward swing.

Tommy stretched out his hand, fingers beckoning for the list to be passed to him.

Reluctantly, aware that there would be dire consequences for many, Iwan withdrew a sheet of paper from his coat pocket, and passed it over.

There was a long silence, like the eye of a storm, and Iwan tried to focus on the ticking clock and not what could happen in the next few moments.

Tommy read through the list twice, a smile coming to his lips as he read his father's name. Then taking up a pencil, he wrote a number down on the open page of the diary. Lifting his eyes to Iwan, he said coldly, 'Beginning with the man at the top of the list, I want every other man sacked, today.'

Iwan first impulse was to shout, 'No! It's ludicrous!' It took all his will-power to say calmly, 'There are more than sixty men named. Thirty workers out of the quarry will make a difference to output. The men you intend to put out of the quarry may be union men. We could have the union on our backs.'

'I'll take that chance,' Tommy said coldly. 'Not many Garddryn men are union members. They're too afraid of losing their jobs if they join up.'

Carefully, as though filching dinner from a hungry hound, Iwan put out his hand to take the paper, and was mortified to see the tremor in his fingers.

Though he knew the list verbatim, Iwan still read the first name there, Frank Standish. Frank was Tommy's younger brother. Iwan didn't look up, but he was aware that Tommy was watching him closely. If the master's orders were followed to the letter, Joe Standish would retain his job. Why sack the brother, and not the father? It didn't make sense.

Tommy guessed what the manager was brooding on. 'I don't intend to make it easy for my father. He will find it difficult to accept he has work and his youngest son has none, especially when that son is on a blacklist and banned from working for every other employer in the district.'

'But...' Iwan foolishly interrupted.

Tommy eyed him menacingly. 'If Frank Standish desires to work, he'll have to leave the district and his home comforts to do so.' His voice lifting with amusement, 'I believe he's hoping to marry at the end of the month.'

Sensibly, as his own job could go in a stroke of a pen, Iwan kept his anger under wraps.

'See to it, now!' Tommy snapped, dismissing the man with a flick of his hand.

Treated no better than a lackey, Iwan Rees's face reddened with indignation and he turned quickly towards the door, once through, and out of Tommy Standish's hearing, he spat a barrack room oath.

Passing the clerk's office, he glanced in and saw Elias Hubbard's back, his cheap grey coat wrinkled across bony shoulders. The clerk was sitting on a high stool, the toes of his black boots hooked beneath the struts. Stooped over the desk, engrossed in whatever he was doing, Elias was oblivious to the manager in the doorway. Iwan Rees barked the clerk's name, taking pleasure in watching the elongated figure unfold awkwardly as he jumped.

Coming quickly to his feet, Elias wondered how long the

manager had been watching him, and if in that time he had done anything untoward, embarrassing, like wiping his nose on the sleeve of his coat. Painfully shy, terrified of authority, especially Tommy Standish, Elias's face reddened slightly, and he sniffed wetly. 'What can I do for you, sir?'

'You can send someone to find the quarry steward, Horas Jones. I want him in my office immediately.'

Elias, suffering from what seemed to be a slight but perpetual head-cold, suppressed a sniff. 'I'll fetch him myself.'

Iwan Rees turned and made his way to his office. Once inside he stood with his back to the door, his chin touching the starched collar of his white shirt. How he wished he had never laid eyes on Tommy Standish, and become so dependent on the generous salary he earned as manager. Hogtied, that's how he felt, hogtied. For his wife would never give up the splendid house, or the status that went with being the wife of the manager of the Garddryn Quarry.

Delighted to be out of the hot office, the windows closed against the dust of the quarry, Elias bolted across the cobbles as though he meant to go as fast as he could to the steward's shack. But out of sight of watchful eyes, he sauntered along the pathway, stopping to pluck a strand of grass from the embankment. Glad to be playing truant, and enjoying the sunshine, he sucked the green blade, his ears pricked for the sound of boots on the path.

Coming to one of the cutting sheds, a long building with both ends open to the weather, he took a furtive look inside. Fifty or so men and boys were sitting on low trestles splitting slates into marchionesses, duchesses, and ladies. The roll call of royalty always amused Elias, especially when he was making out the

21

invoices for Broad Countesses. The image it conjured up made him smirk.

When he came in sight of the steward's shack, he chucked the chewed strand, and began to trot. If he dawdled for too long, there was always a chance that someone would spot him and report back to the office.

The shack door stood open to the sunshine, Elias saw a lad inside but no sign of the steward. Going to investigate, he shoved his hands into his trouser pockets and sauntered in. An odour of wood-tar, greeted him, strong enough to prick at his nostrils. Making the most of a rare chance to talk down to a lad employed in an inferior position, other than the boy in the office, Elias was officious. 'Where's Jones? He's wanted in the office, immediately.'

Unperturbed, the lad batted at a fly buzzing around his face. 'He's not here.'

'I can see that. Where is he?'

The boy sniffed, wiping the end of his nose with the back of his hand. 'He's gone off to Nazareth gallery. A chap's fallen, or summat. The stretcher was ordered. The steward went with it, to help.'

Though hungry for the gruesome details, Elias wouldn't stoop to asking. 'You'd better tell him to come to the office, sharpish. The boss wants him.'

The bothersome fly settled on the wooden table-top. The boy slapped the palm of his hand down, squashing the insect. Grinning, he wiped the mess onto the leg of his trousers.

Elias's nose wrinkled in disgust. 'I'll wait for a minute, and see if he shows up. Then I'll have to get back to the office.'

Eventually bored and afraid that he may have overstepped the mark in being away from the office for so long, Elias reluctantly made his way back there.

Horas Jones missed Elias's departure by only a few minutes. Listening to the message, relayed indifferently by the lad, Horas sighed. A summons could only mean more work, or trouble. Reluctantly he started out towards the office.

On seeing the steward hurrying towards the building, Elias took it upon himself to meet him at the front door. Ushering him towards the manager's office he asked about the accident and the state of the fallen man.

Anxious to know the reason he'd been sent for, speculating on every conceivable reason but the correct one, Horas missed the question.

On reaching the manager's office door, Elias rapped upon it lightly. At Iwan Rees's command to enter, he slipped in.

Horas Jones stood waiting obediently, anxiously clutching his black hat with both hands. A dull drone of conversation was just audible, and he heard Elias explaining the reason for the long delay.

Interrupting him, Iwan was brisk. 'Send Jones in, and then get back to your work. An account of the accident is better coming from him, as he was there, at the scene.'

Aware of the dust on his clothes, and clump of his ungainly boots, Horas went into the carpeted room. As he wasn't invited to sit, he stood in front of the desk, his hat circling in his hands.

Iwan remained seated. 'I hear there was an accident this morning.'

Horas gave a small nervous cough. 'A quarryman slipped.' He didn't offer any further explanation.

'Is he badly hurt?'

'Leg's broken, that's all.'

Iwan Rees wondered if the injured man was on the infamous list, it would save sacking him if he was.

'Name?' he asked, a little too sharply.

'Tyler, John Tyler,' Horas said, wondering at the sudden interest.

Iwan checked the list in his hand. There was no Tyler there.

Turning his attention to the steward, he frowned. 'What do you know about the meeting last Saturday night?'

Of course Horas had heard about it, there had been sixty or so men there, hard to hide that from the villagers, and someone would always talk.

'I wasn't at the Halfway on Saturday night,' he said simply. It wasn't a lie; he never went to the alehouse. The men that drank there wouldn't make him welcome. Behind his back they called him Horas Jones, the traitor.

Iwan waved the sheet of paper he was holding. 'This is a list of the men that were there.' Rising, he pushed his chair back and went to the window, and looked out onto the ruined ground.

The steward ran through the names on the list, his lips moving as he read.

Iwan's thoughts were dark. In the days ahead there would be bitter repercussions. Tommy Standish's order would immediately create a strike, and very soon there would be a lock-out, and it would probably be as notorious as the last one, when workers died at the quarry gates.

Turning around he faced the steward, but found it almost impossible to meet the man's eyes. 'The man at the top of that list is to be let go, along with every alternate man.'

Shocked, Horas bellowed, 'Surely not.'

'I'm afraid so.'

Enraged, Horas reddened. 'The master is a mad man. The consequences will be terrible. Men will not take this lying down.'

'You would be wise to curb your tongue,' Iwan counselled. 'The master is quite at liberty to sack whoever he pleases.'

Horas brandished the paper. 'Even his brother?'

'Yes. If need be, and certainly if the brother has been disloyal.'

Horas saw that there was no point in arguing with the man, he was too firmly under Tommy Standish's thumb to listen to reason. It took all his will to keep his voice level. 'The lad is getting married at the end of the month. He mightn't be able to do that now.'

Iwan Rees sighed. 'The master has decided, and I'm sorry to say that a wedding will not make any difference to his order.'

Horas saw a repeat of the strike and lock-out that had brought his family to destitution and near starvation. Tommy Standish had flung a bucket of shite over them all. Frank would be out of work, and robbed of the wedding he was so excited about. No man deserved a brother that would put him through the wringer like that.

Horas felt tears prick at his eyes, and he wanted to quit the room before he embarrassed himself.

In the corridor he shoved the paper into his trouser pocket. For a mad moment he thought of destroying it, and taking the consequence, but dread of what his wife would say brought him back to earth.

Crossing the quadrangle, his boots clacked on the cobbles. The noise roused Elias Hubbard, and glancing out of the window, he was curious to know what Iwan Rees had wanted with the steward.

Hearing Tommy Standish's office door open, Elias bent his head to the paper lying on the desktop.

Horas went towards the head of the quarry in search of Joe. The climb was hard, the soles of his boots slipping and sliding on the dusty earth. It was only mid-morning and already the heat blanketed the grimy air.

A group of noisy quarrymen came clattering down the path, sending a small avalanche of stones and shale before them. Coming upon the steward they refused to give way, and Horas was forced to stand against the rough embankment to let them pass. Eye contact was sparse, but that didn't surprise him; what the quarrymen thought of him was no secret. But if their team leaders wanted good *bargains,* the best and most profitable slate to work, then those men had to kowtow to him. How they hated raising their hats to the traitorous strike-breaker, as he was still known in Garddryn village.

When the men passed by, Horas brushed gritty slate from his clothes, and carried on climbing. He had about nine minutes to reach a shelter before the next explosion.

Talking to himself, a habit that was steadily growing, he muttered, 'With luck, and a following wind, I'll have found Joe by then.'

Joe Standish was a man most quarrymen looked up to. Horas Jones would not listen to a word against the man. Joe had saved the Jones family from starvation during the black days of the quarry lock-out. Horas never forgot that it was Joe and Frank, risking prison with their dangerous poaching that had put meat on his table when money for food was sparse.

Joe had stood by him, even protected him from a mob when he turned blackleg and returned to work, breaking the long strike. There had been no other choice; his children were literally starving to death.

Rounding a hillock of waste slate, he saw Joe hoisting a dirty canvas bag onto his shoulder.

Glad to have found him, Horas shouted his name.

'Now what brings him here?' Joe muttered under his breath, pointing to the newly bored hole stuffed with a reddening Bickford fuse. 'This thing is going to blast us to kingdom-come if we don't get out of here.'

Joe was already moving, sprinting up the hillside towards a stone shelter, the sound of Horas slipping and sliding on the loose scree in his ears.

Harrumphing, Joe dug his boots into the shale and raced back down, grabbing Horas by the arm he hauled him up, both men grunting with effort, and perspiration popping out of Joe's brow like beads.

The small windowless building at the top of mound seemed ridiculously far away, impossible to reach in time, and Joe kept his head ducked anticipating the blast he was sure would catch them out.

Miraculously they reached the ruined path at the top, and Joe sent a prayer to his favourite saint.

Making a leap for the door, grasping the brass knob in his sweaty hand, Joe turned it, and pushed Horas inside; following fast on the man's heels he slammed the door closed. They stood in complete darkness, with their backs to the wood, panting.

In an instant the explosion boomed out of the rock. The shelter shook, and they felt the flag-stones quiver beneath their boots.

Several shards of rock hit the roof with a clack, and rattled down the slates.

'That was close!' Joe laughed with relief.

Horas was breathing hard, his voice wheezed, 'Too close, Joe. Sorry you had to help me.'

'I like to live dangerously,' Joe said, still chuckling.

Opening the door, he peered out. A dust cloud, lit by the noon sun, was floating above Bethlehem gallery.

Horas slumped down on a wooden bench. He looked done-in, and depressed. 'We're living close to danger right now.'

Joe came back into the bare room. 'How do you mean?'

Horas sighed deeply. 'Tommy Standish has decided that certain men have stepped out of line, and they should be punished.'

Joe was used to trouble from his son, expected it even, but when Tommy's name was linked with the quarry and quarrymen, his stomach clenched, and invariably the contents of his bowels turned to water.

'What's the bugger done now?' he said, his mind running down the rat-path of Tommy's previous delinquent behaviour.

Horas drew the sheet of paper out of his pocket and handed it to Joe. 'Read this.'

Joe took a moment to scan the list. 'These are the men that came to the recent union meeting at the Halfway.'

'Aye, they are,' Horas said with a sigh. 'Iwan Rees gave it to me earlier.'

Joe looked up quickly, his grey hair damp with perspiration falling onto his forehead. 'It's not the first time they've got hold of details of a meeting. So what is special about this particular list?'

Horas rose from the bench, his limbs already stiffening from the unaccustomed exercise. 'I'm supposed to sack every alternate man, starting with your Frank.'

Incapable of standing still, Joe crossed the flagstones to the far wall, and then turned and came back to Horas. 'What is the bastard playing at?'

Horas looked into Joe's eyes, and then down at the floor.

Joe spat a curse. 'I swear I'll kill that bloody son of mine. If it's the last thing I do, I'll wipe the sanctimonious smirk off his face once and for all. I'll whip his arse, just as I should have done when he came to me with his crack-pot idea about going for lessons at bloody Plas Mawr.'

His voice was weighted with self-reproach. 'Jesus! Why didn't I see what a viper I was raising?'

'What's to be done, Joe?'

Joe flung round. 'You mean, what's to be done besides killing the sod?'

His chest tight with anger, he turned his back on Horas and stood in the open door to breathe air, warm sunlight washing over his face as he gazed over the quarry.

Below there was a disturbance; raised voices of men aggravated by heat and dust. Here near the summit, a cats-paw of breeze whispered, echoing in the torn slate beds, as though dead quarrymen were weeping.

An image of the workers crushed and killed at the quarry gates came to him; the men had died because of his son's arrogance and contempt. Now there was to be more trouble, men out of work, and Frank amongst them and just before the lad was to be wed.

Behind him Horas spoke. 'Short of murdering the bugger,

what else do you suggest, Joe?'

Joe stood aside for him and they stood on the slate step, Joe smoking his pipe.

'Go and spread the word to the men, Horas. Tell them to be at the Jerusalem caban at noon.'

He was content to let Joe take charge. 'Aye, that's the best thing, Joe. I'll just say there's trouble brewing, and to come to the caban.'

He stayed to finish his pipe, and to watch Horas scrambling down to the quarry path, and then closing the door, he headed in the same direction.

Tudor, an old friend and workmate, stood in the middle of the narrow track to intercept him. He shouted Joe's name three times before Joe heard him and took his eyes off the ground.

The hobnails of Joe's boots raked the dirt as he slowed his stride to come alongside.

Tudor spoke first. 'Is it true? Are more than thirty men to be let go before the end of the day?' He had left the job of clearing away a pile of rock to catch Joe, and his gingery beard and hair were thick with dust. Dirt was permanently ingrained in the calluses on his broad hands.

Joe lifted his eyes and looked out over the working. 'Aye, it's true. Horas Jones found me earlier, showed me a piece of paper with a list of names on it, every other man on it is to be sacked, starting with our Frank.'

Tudor's eyes blazed with anger. 'You can't be serious, Joe. Surely to God the bastard would not go that far.'

'The bastard did,' Joe said, heaving a sigh. 'The men are likely to strike. Then there'll be a lock-out.'

'Christ! It'll be like last time. Families were split up, and some went to workhouses.'

Joe glanced down at men walking towards the caban. 'We had better get a move on if we're to catch them up.'

Two hundred men were outside the caban, nearly all had abandoned their hats and fustian coats in the heat; their dusty shirts were as grey as the surrounding slate.

The cat would be amongst the pigeons when news of the meeting reached the quarry office, Joe thought, but hardly cared.

The men fell silent as he approached with Tudor. Although he was an Englishman and the father of the quarry master, the men had respect for Joe. At the time of the lock-out, Twm Tomas, president of the caban, had told them to hold Joe in high regard. Twm's judgement had never been questioned. Now he was gone, the men listened to Joe, and generally followed his advice.

The murmur of the men's voices ebbed away as Joe and Tudor approached. In the fragile quiet, Joe felt the weight of the problem settle on him.

Pitching his voice for all to hear, he said 'I don't bring good news. So I'll tell it to you straight. Most of you probably know that the master has decided that some of the men that attended a union meeting are to be sacked.'

A roar like a vicious sea swept through them. It was impossible to continue and Joe remained still, searching for Frank in the crowd.

Someone shouted, 'What about the union? Why don't they support and protect us?'

Joe brushed his hair off his forehead. 'There's not enough of us belong to the union. We have a choice. We can strike!'

There were too many present that remembered the last strike to shout for a new one, and Joe's words fell like stones.

A man Joe recognised as a union member spoke out. 'If we strike, the management will threaten a lock-out, and the Irish tinkers will be back for our jobs.'

An angry roar ripped through the crowd.

Joe raised his arms for silence. 'I know it will go against the grain for most of you, but the other way is to let the sacked men fend for themselves. The rest of you will keep your jobs. There'll be no lock-out.'

Someone shouted, 'Why are they getting the sack?'

Joe was afraid that the embryonic union would wither when the men realised the sackings were the consequences of joining or even holding a meeting.

Joe caught the eye of one of the men on the list. 'The men to be let go are some of those at a meeting last Saturday night.'

An angry voice shouted, 'A union meeting?'

'Yes! Until we have enough men committed to a union of quarrymen we will face this problem. We must unite. Get behind the idea,' Joe said determinedly. 'A strike and lock-out will affect every man and his family here. The alternative is negotiation. I, or someone of your choosing, can go to the office and ask the master to capitulate.'

Someone laughed. 'Tommy Standish, capitulate.'

'We have to stand by our comrades.'

'What! And all starve,' someone called back.

A man from the splitting shed shouted, 'What about the union, can't they help us at all?'

'There's not enough of us in the bloody union, is there. If we had joined, we'd be black-legged, and there isn't an employer in the district that would give us work. Talk sense man.'

Joe called for calm. 'I suggest that we at least talk to Iwan

Rees.'

'Who's to go?' Tudor shouted.

'We all do,' Joe said seriously.

Heeding Joe's advice they arrived at the office building in a fairly orderly fashion; the first to arrive stood on the quadrangle waiting for Iwan Rees or Tommy Standish to appear.

It took Tommy Standish less than two minutes to come bounding through the open door. Marching up to his father, he yelled, 'There's no point coming here to beg me to change my mind. The men are sacked and they must get off my property immediately.'

'I'm not begging,' Joe said, sounding reasonably calm. 'All I ask is that common-sense prevails.'

Iwan Rees hurried out of the main door. Crossing the cobbles he came to stand beside the quarry master.

Tommy's face flushed with anger. 'Common-sense wasn't in evidence when you, and some of these men, decided to hold a meeting to discuss the union.'

Joe's temper boiled, but outwardly he looked calm. 'We have every right to discuss matters. There's no one here that can hold our tongues.'

Tommy forced a laugh. 'Rights, what rights? Peasants don't have rights, they have labour. And if they don't labour, they don't eat.'

Taking a step closer to the men coated in grey quarry dust, Tommy bawled at them, 'If you buggers strike, I'll lock you out of the Garddryn. There'll be Irish tinkers in your places within days. If you have any sense you'll not listen to this union warrior,' he glanced at his father, 'but get back to work, there's a half-day left to dig slate.'

Tommy's chin came up defiantly. 'Get back to work, before you have no work to get back to.'

Most of them remembered the last lock-out, and the terrible hardship it brought to their families. Tommy Standish wasn't a man to threaten and not validate his words with action.

There was a shift of mood. Protecting those to be let go would cost them too dear. The men at the rear started to peel off, leaving the crowd. The tide turned and in moments every quarryman but Joe and Frank were shambling away guiltily.

With his eyes on their grey-shirted backs, Tommy chuckled.

Wanting to wipe the smirk off his son's face, Joe closed the gap. His hands bunched into fists, he was ready to strike. 'So it comes to this. You threaten to starve them, and then steal what dignity they have. God in heaven, how did I come to raise such a bastard?' Fighting the urge to strike his first born, Joe turned away.

Frank's anger was simmering and ready to erupt. Not since quarrymen had been crushed to death at the Garddryn gates had he held his brother in such contempt. Back then he had been too young and built like a sapling tree to do anything but cry about it. But the tide had turned, and although Tommy was taller, and the elder, his life was sedentary. His own days had been spent labouring, swinging an axe, digging the foundations of his home. The sleeves of his shirt concealed a hard and fit young man. Lifting his right fist he punched Tommy's sneering face. The next clout landed in Tommy's middle and the master of the Garddryn went down on his knees, clutching his belly.

Without looking at the damage to his hand, Frank walked away. In moments he caught up with his father and they walked on together in silence.

It was the time of the mid-day meal and although the men had gathered at the caban to drink tea, brewed in the great urn, and eat the snap they had brought from home, nobody had made a start on it. Abandoning workmates to their fate didn't come easily, and there wasn't a man who wasn't shamed by the decision to stay in work. It was harder still to meet the eye of a betrayed comrade. Some sat sullenly on the benches, others stood around with hardly a word to say. It was this funereal atmosphere that Frank and Joe walked into.

It was no surprise to Joe that they should feel as they did, and a part of him thought they deserved to, but the sense prevailed and he saw they had little option but to work; families were relying on the wages. Starving children for ideals was not only wrong; it was against everything a father stood for.

'Hard as it is,' he said pitching his voice so everyone could hear, 'You have made the right decision. The health and lives of an entire community are at stake. A strike and the inevitable lock-out would destroy us all. But whilst the majority of us are in work, we must contribute a portion of our wages to the unfortunate men that are to be let go, until they can get on their feet again. The rest of us must combine and look to the union, build on it, make it strong and powerful, and then terrible days like today will become a thing of the past.'

For all his hope, beating of the familiar drum for a union with clout, Frank knew that his father's pride was damaged, not beyond repair, but enough to keep the events of today on his mind for some time to come.

The afternoon passed slowly, Frank was in two minds about staying at work and seeing the day to the bitter end. Unable to afford to lose a day's pay, he stuck it out, wishing to God that he could just walk away, sit by the brook, and figure out what he was going to tell Nora.

The interminable afternoon came to an end and the siren rang out, and the hope that someone would arrive from the office with a retraction, died. Despondent, hot and dusty, shirts sticking to their sweaty backs, the men packed up tools and began to make their way to the quarry gates. Usually the noise of their departure was heard across the village, but this evening talk was subdued. Thoughts were with the men about to be laid off. Rumour and counter rumour had been rife throughout the afternoon, but now everyone knew the names on the list. Hardly anyone looked at Frank as he passed with his father. What could a man say to another when he was being sacked by his only brother?

Horas Jones was standing at the gate handing out slips of paper to the unfortunate men. Ignoring him, Frank kept his eyes to the ground and kept walking. Joe took the paper from Horas's hand, and stuffed it into his trouser pocket. Glancing at Frank's face, Joe remained silent, as there were no words to comfort the lad, or himself. So he lit his pipe, blowing a cloud of smoke, a pillow between their heads.

The front door of Corn Cottage was open, a clay flowerpot propped at the bottom corner. During the hottest part of the day a faint scent of the pink and white stocks growing in the patch of garden drifted in, eventually vanishing on the aroma of meat and potato pie baking in the bread-oven.

Although the front and back doors were propped open, the kitchen-cum-parlour was stifling. The fire in the range had a bed of brilliant red embers, and steam from the pan of potatoes simmering on the hob created a domestic smog.

Emily glanced into the looking glass over the mantle,

patterned with condensation from the rising stream, and reinserted a hairpin that had come loose in her dark hair, now streaked with silver.

Hearing Joe and Frank approach she put the already warm kettle to the hob. Joe liked to sink the quarry dust in his throat with a mug of tea the moment he came in.

Joe was first through the open door, and as he didn't remark on the aroma coming from the bread-oven, or mention his supper, Emily knew that something was wrong. Frank's face was as long as a wet weekend and he looked close to tears.

Suspecting Tommy of causing an upset, Emily's face fell. 'What's up, Joe?'

Remaining stubbornly silent, he sat in the chair beside the fire. Pulling off one boot he dropped it to the floor. He started to untie the laces of the other then abandoned the job.

'A whole lot of things are up,' he said crossly. 'Tommy's sacked over thirty quarrymen.'

Flabbergasted, Emily sat down heavily on the wooden chair at the table. 'Who's been let go?' The inevitable strike was already in her mind.

Joe threw the boot aside, and it landed on the fender with a clack. 'Our Frank is top of the list.'

'Frank!' Her eyes went to her son still standing near the open door. 'Tommy can't do that.'

The pan on the hob boiled over, water hissing on the hot embers. Jumping up, Emily seized a cloth off the table and set the pot to the back of the range.

The heat of the fire on her face was scorching, and she wafted the cloth like a fan. Close to tears, she opened the oven door and pulled out the pie. To her dismay the crust was as dark as mahogany. Cursing the pie, and Tommy, she slammed the door closed with the sole of her boot.

Turning her cross face to Joe, she said, 'Are you going to tell me what happened properly, or do I have to work it out myself from the dribs-and-drabs you're giving me?'

Joe's eyes blinked open in surprise. 'No need to get feisty with me, Emily.'

So caught up in his own thoughts, Frank was oblivious to the brewing disagreement. Until this day it had never occurred to him that he might be forced to leave Corn Cottage. It was the home that he and his father had built from the rocks rooted in the small field. By his own toil, from digging the foundations, to lodging the last slate on the roof, he worked to fulfil the dream of owning a cottage free from a Garddryn Quarry mortgage. With Nora moving in after the wedding, everything would have been perfect. Now there may not even be a wedding.

If he was to earn a wage he had to go to Parys copper, or Merthyr, and come home when he could afford to. The good things in life, climbing the mountain slopes, playing in the chapel band, walking with his sweetheart on a Sunday afternoon, would be a rarity.

Only one good thing had come out of today, he had clouted Tommy. That was worth scuffing his knuckles.

'I'm going to get washed,' he said, disappearing into the scullery.

Sighing loudly, Joe turned to Emily. 'Our Tommy got wind of last Saturday's union meeting. Some bugger gave him the names of the men who were there.'

Staring blankly at the floor, Emily said sadly, 'I despair of Tommy. Whatever did we do to make him hate us so much, especially our Frank?'

Joe stood, reaching for his best pipe on the mantel. 'Plas Mawr, that's what we did. If we hadn't allowed him to go for his lessons with George Bellamy none of this would have happened.'

Remembering how Tommy begged to be allowed to go, her voice rose passionately. 'He wanted to go so much, Joe. We couldn't deny him a chance to better himself.'

'Oh aye, and now the bugger thinks he has the right to lord it over us, and every bloody quarryman. I rue the day I agreed to let him go there. It's been nothing but disaster, and not only for us, but his poor wife Henrietta, Bertram Bellamy, and George. I swear our Tommy had something to do with that poor bugger ending up an imbecile.'

Emily's eyes filled with tears. 'You can't say that, Joe. Tommy can be evil, but surely he would never have attacked George Bellamy. What reason could he possibly have had? George and he were friends.'

'They were never friends. Tommy hated George. He was jealous. George was the boy with everything, Plas Mawr, Garddryn Quarry, a rich father. Whereas,' Joe sneered, 'our Tommy had bugger all.'

'We gave him a good home, don't forget that, Joe.'

It was impossible not to raise his voice. 'It's not me that's forgotten, it's Tommy. But even as a child he didn't want to acknowledge us. Or have you forgotten?'

Past shame made her blush. 'I haven't forgotten.'

He snorted scornfully. 'Neither have I. He didn't want us at his wedding, his wife's funeral, our grandson's christening. When he was nowt but a lad, he banned us from the Christmas service where he was being presented with a prize.'

'Don't go on, Joe. I don't want to be reminded.'

Joe hit the palm of his hand with a closed fist. 'Now it's our Frank he wants to knock down. What has the lad ever done to deserve this?'

Emily was close to tears. 'Poor Frank, what is he going to do about the wedding?'

'What can he do but tell Nora that the marriage will have to wait.'

'He can't do that, Joe. Everything's arranged, the church service, the guest list. Nora has been making fruit cakes for weeks.'

'Emily, what else can he do?'

She shook her head from side to side. 'God knows, Joe.'

As he wasn't interested in eating his appetite had fled hours ago, Frank left the cottage and made for Nora's home. If he delayed telling her the awful news, her father would return from the Halfway Inn and spill the beans in his own fashion.

Chapter 2

'The wedding's off,' Frank said, coming from his bedroom into the kitchen-cum-parlour early next morning. Joe was standing beside the range making tea for Emily. She was dozing in bed after a near sleepless night.

Joe was taken aback. 'Off, definitely?'

'Aye, what else can I do? I'm out of work and on the scrap heap,' Frank said despondently, slumping heavily onto the chair by the fireside.

Joe stirred the tea in the pot briskly. 'Don't talk daft lad. You're twenty-six years old. Not done for at all.'

Frank sighed. 'I feel done for.'

Joe chucked the spoon onto the table where it left a tiny wet mark. 'Aye, I suppose that's natural enough, considering.'

Frank didn't look up, but gazed at the steam rising from the spout of the kettle.

Joe chose his words carefully. 'You will find work, lad. You're blessed with common-sense and resourcefulness and it'll get you through this bad patch.'

Frank didn't share his father's optimism and he heaved a despondent sigh. 'I'll catch the ferry to the island tomorrow. There may be work at Parys Mountain.'

Joe's belly clenched. He'd heard tales of the copper works that would make grown men cry.

'I don't want you working there,' he said sharply. Images of molten copper exploding in wet moulds flitting through his mind. 'It's just another Hades, with too many accidents. If one of those hasn't got your name on it, the sulphur fumes will ruin your lungs. Think again, lad.' A picture of Frank's flesh burned to the bone made the hairs on the back of his neck prick up. 'I don't want you going there, our Frank. It's not safe.'

'Mam's tea's going cold,' Frank said to deflect the promise he was about to be asked to make.

Joe had forgotten about the tea. Sighing, he touched the side of the pot. 'It's hardly warm. I'll brew another.'

In the scullery, he chucked the tea through the open door and the dregs splashed the pale blue asters sprouting in an ancient hip bath.

Hardly waiting for the next pot to brew properly, he poured it, and carried a steaming mug to the bedroom.

Frank found it impossible to contain his restlessness and he paced the floor. Coming back to the chair, he kicked the leg with the toe of his boot, not hard enough to mark it or even make much noise, which summed up how powerless he felt. Slumping down on the seat, a fog of despondency and worthlessness settled on him.

His misery didn't allow for curiosity and he was only vaguely aware of the cupboard door in the back room slamming closed. When his father came back into the room wearing a decent white shirt with the collar attached, and black trousers, Frank in a distracted way connected the noise with the hunt for clean clothes.

Wordless, he watched his father roll the shirt sleeves up to his elbow, revealing weather beaten flesh the colour of old rosewood.

Joe gave his son a quick glance. 'I'm going to Plas Mawr to see our Tommy,' he announced.

Unravelling his limbs, Frank rose. 'I'll come with you.'

'No lad! You've already battered him once. Not that I hold

that against you. The bugger deserves a lot more than a clout from his younger brother. But you know our Tommy, he won't listen to reason if there's a witness. It's not in his nature to risk losing face.'

As though the weight of his body was too much for his legs, Frank flopped back down into the chair. 'Lord knows, I want to come and wipe the smirk off his face, but I'll stay here, if you think that's for the best.'

'It is, lad.' Taking his work-boots off the fender, Joe slipped his feet into them and bent to tie the laces. Straightening, he stamped twice on the rug to settle his feet into the stiff leather. The boots were in need of a polish, but he wanted to go to the big house as a workman, a quarryman, with his dirty boots clacking on the shining floor. Immature, but he didn't care.

He turned his face to Frank. 'Talk to your mother. She's in need of comfort too. It's hard on her when Tommy behaves badly. Poor Emily must wonder how she's going to look friends in the eye.'

The idea outraged Frank. 'Surely they wouldn't blame Mam?'

'Nowt as queer as folk, our Frank. Who knows what might be in their heads.' He was searching in the kitchen drawer for a handkerchief; finding a blue and white striped one he stuffed it into his trouser pocket.

Frank needed something to do. 'I'll make Mam another brew, and then I'll go and feed the pigs.'

'You do that, lad.' Joe patted his pockets checking he had his pipe and baccy. There was no doubt he would need both on departing Plas Mawr.

Leaving the cottage, he walked down the short pathway to the gate, catching a whiff of scent of the white roses. The garden gate clacked closed behind him.

On the roadway, Joe's thoughts turned to how he was going to deal with Tommy, and get the sacked men reinstated. Thrashing Tommy wouldn't get him anywhere. It was too late for that now. It should have been done long ago. If he'd known then what he knew now, things would have been very different. Tommy would not have been educated with George Bellamy at Plas Mawr. The local school and church would have been good enough for him. If the correct route had been taken when the lad was young, Tommy would have become a quarryman, and not the blasted master of the Garddryn, and an expert on ruining lives with his evil-minded conniving.

The sound of wheels turning and the beat of a solitary horse on the roadway broke into his thoughts. It was possible the vehicle was from the mansion. If Tommy was aboard he would ride by without slowing, arrogant imp that he was. He remembered the disastrous day when Tommy had deliberately ridden a mare at him on the driveway at Plas Mawr. By God he'd thrashed him that day, pulled him from the mare and nearly beaten the living daylights out of the bugger.

The rumble of the wheels grew close, and considering that Tommy was just as likely to try something again, the hairs on the back of Joe's neck rose.

Just ahead, a double row of beech trees formed a vibrant arch over the lane; some of the branches were low, drooping with the weight of summer leaves. Joe looked through the greenery and saw a grey horse and loaded cart coming into view. As it didn't look as though it belonged to Plas Mawr, he sighed with relief.

Stepping back onto the grass verge, dried like hay after weeks of hot weather and peppered with the white campions, he waited for the vehicle to pass. *'Bora da,'* he called, lifting his hand in greeting.

The horse clopped by. The driver looked ahead dourly, steadfast in his determination to ignore the English man, father of the English quarry master.

Irked, Joe shouted, 'Good day, anyway.' Muttering under his breath, he walked on.

The elaborate entrance gates of the mansion were open. Walking under the arch of the intricately worked iron, Joe threw his head back to admire the construction. A while ago he knew the original cost of it, but the details escaped him now. As a child Tommy knew the exact amount. Even then he had an eye for the splendid, the cost of everything outweighing the artistic merit.

Joe sighed, not for the child with his flawed ideals, but the man his son had become.

With his hands buried in his trouser pockets, Joe walked purposefully towards the magnificent house, his work boots kicking up the neatly raked gravel.

The double row of lime trees were in full leaf, shading the half-mile avenue from the morning sun, the light breeze drifting off the water of the Menai Strait hardly stirring the leaves.

The birds were silent, perhaps startled by his presence. The sparrows in Emily's patch of garden never ceased flitting from the rhododendrons to the holly tree.

Worried that Tommy may soon leave the house, he picked up his step. It was in his mind that however sanctimonious Tommy chose to be, he had to keep a tight rein on his own temper. Rowing would scupper the jobs of the men he was trying to get reinstated.

A gardener was working close to the terrace, picking leaves off the pristine lawn and dropping the debris into a sack. An easy task in itself, but with Tommy in charge watching every move, the man probably had a hard time of it, Joe reckoned.

The self-same eyes were probably watching him walk up the avenue, critical and judgemental of his working class origins. It went against instinct not to scan the panes of glass for that all familiar face. Determined not to give the watcher satisfaction, he kept his gaze firmly on the gravel until he reached the stone steps at the entrance and looked up to the sturdy closed door.

'It's like a bloody fortress,' Joe muttered under his breath, giving a passing thought to the enemies Tommy had collected over the years.

Mounting the steps, he pulled the bell-chain and heard a clanging within the house. Fully anticipating being told by a pumped up flunky that Tommy refused to see him, Joe's jaw was tight and he was prepared to clout someone.

The door opened. A man he vaguely recognised from a previous visit as being the head footman stood in the opening, his hand on the door ready to close it again swiftly.

Joe took in the cut of man's ebony tail-coat, and the razor sharp creases in his immaculate black trousers. His mind went to the quarrymen who wore strips of flannel beneath inadequate coats to keep out the draughts of the atrocious mountain weather. The hardships of the quarrymen paid for elaborate and costly uniforms for flunkies. Quarrymen didn't grow paunches like this cosseted man had either.

'Tradesmen's entrance is at the back,' Roberts said arrogantly, beginning to close the door.

The flat of Joe's hand slammed into the wood, and he pushed

hard, meeting little resistance.

'I'm here to see Tommy Standish. Tell him Joe Standish is waiting. He'll know who I am.'

Roberts's top lip drew up slightly as he stood back to let Joe enter. Omitting to give a perfunctory bow, he turned on his heel and went silently down the long hallway towards the library. He was braced for an angry reception when he entered the room With a long, drawn out, but virtually silent sigh, he rappe gently on the door.

Tommy Standish was standing at the long arched window. passed through Roberts's mind that the master already knew father was in the house.

Turning towards the servant, Tommy's expression reve nothing.

'Mr Joe Standish wishes to see you, sir. He is waiting ir hall.'

A shadow of a smirk passed across Tommy's face. 'Shov in.'

'Shall I bring coffee? Or would you prefer a tray of sir?' Roberts asked, avoiding the master's eye.

'Refreshments will not be required. Joe Standish will here for a moment.'

Waiting, standing with his hands linked behind his b looked up to the immense chandelier hanging in the stairwell of the sweeping staircase. It had always contention that it was the sheer magnificence of this a had turned Tommy's head, when the boy was barely guest at Henrietta Bellamy's birthday party. On that fa money and grandeur became his idol. The dazzli spawned an evil in Tommy which was present to

Mouthing a blasphemy, Joe turned his eyes away.

The library door opened and the footman came out of the room. Without moving from the threshold, he beckoned. Joe didn't doubt that the casualness of the summons was uncommon.

Stepping out of the circular shimmer of crystal reflected in the mosaic floor, Joe went towards the footman, the clack of his boots resonating in the Great Hall, but Joe was too pent-up, and afraid that he would fail to get the men their jobs back, to take pleasure in the clatter.

Brushing passed the footman, he entered the library. The green baize-lined door, closed with a soft clunk.

Tommy was standing at a long window, his body half-turned to the room.

The clock on the mantel of the marble fireplace, struck the hour.

Joe glanced at the brass dial, and then his eyes came back to his son. 'No point beating about the bush,' he said more starkly than he intended. 'I have come to discuss the problem that has arisen at the quarry.'

'What problem?' Tommy said superciliously. Taking a step away from the window he perched on the corner of the desk.

The restraint Joe had imposed on himself vanished, and he barked loudly, 'The problem that will be yours if the quarrymen cease to work and the Garddryn falls silent.'

Tommy's jawbone tightened. 'Are you threatening me?'

'I would, if I thought it would do any good.' Joe saw that by losing his temper he had probably cost the men their jobs, and for that he would never forgive himself.

Changing tack, Tommy said calmly, 'Save your breath. I've

already decided to bring back all the men, but one.'

The announcement, given so blandly, was a complete surprise. The relief was immense, and Joe experienced a rush of elation. Just when he thought all was lost, the men were given a chance to take up the thread of their lives.

Tommy folded his arms, his expression fathomless.

With a terrible sense of foreboding, Joe ran his son's exact words through his mind: 'all the men, but one.'

Tommy's right foot swung back and forth like the pendulum of a clock. 'Well, are you not going to thank me for being so generous? Thirty men chose to ignore my request that they should not meet to discuss a union, but I have decided not to punish them, as they deserve to be punished.'

Joe felt sick to the pit of his stomach. 'The man you have decided not to take back is your brother?'

Tommy's face broke into a smile. 'Well done Pater. You see, you can think clearly, when you put your mind to it.'

Joe's eyes flamed. 'I'd call you a bastard, but God help me, I was there at your conception, though I wish by every ounce of my being that I had not put the seed into your mother's body.'

Tommy came off the desk, his body taut with anger. 'I can still change my mind. I am not obligated to take the men back.'

Ignoring him, Joe barked, 'Why Frank? What has the lad done to you that would make you hate him so much?'

Tommy's features darkened. 'Frank is supporting the new union. In my book he's betraying me. I'm the master of the Garddryn, he should trust me to take care of the workers and their families should anything happen to a man whilst he's working on the terraces.'

Joe was dumbstruck. Surely Tommy didn't believe the drivel

he was spouting. The man was mad, deranged. Quarrymen at the Garddryn were being worked to death, their families left destitute when a man met with a fatal accident. The tame doctor Tommy employed blamed the over-brewed tea for the belly sickness they suffered and certified the cause of death as pneumonia when a man broke every bone in his body falling from a terrace. To add insult to injury the same doctor preached that slate dust was good for the men's lungs.

On top of all these sins against his fellow men, Tommy still wasn't satisfied. It needed the ruination of his brother, the lad's unhappiness, to make his own world complete.

Joe's spirit sank. There was no point fighting for Frank's job. If he tried, Tommy would retract his offer. The quarrymen that depended on the quarry for their survival would lose their jobs.

Risking a glance at Tommy, seeing the set determination on his face, Joe knew that however ball-breaking, he had to kowtow to him, and promise that all the men, but one, would be back at work on Monday morning.

Though he felt he may choke on the words, Joe was placatory. 'I can see that you have made up your mind, Tommy. I'll tell our Frank that he'll have to find employment elsewhere. I'll speak to the men, and make sure that they're on the next shift.'

Tommy interrupted him. 'They'll have to make up the lost time.'

'Lost time?'

'Well of course.' Tommy smiled thinly. 'Weren't you all at Jerusalem caban discussing your difficulties yesterday noontime?'

Joe sighed. 'It was noon, the hour the men eat the midday meal and drink tea.'

Tommy smiled thinly. 'They'll be grateful to have work so they won't mind an extra hour or two.' He stood, brushing imaginary fluff of his immaculate coat. 'Now I really must get on with things that are important. Good day Father,' he said with a condescending smile.

Joe's hands itched to clout him and wipe the arrogance from the young pup's face. But the cost of the fleeting violence would be paid by the quarrymen. For a long moment he stood rooted to the carpet, a threatening look in his china-blue eyes. He had the satisfaction of seeing Tommy turn his face away. It was a small, but significant victory.

The door was to his back. Turning, he grasped the polished knob; sweat slicked his palm and for a second the door held. Wrenching it open he went through. A footman waiting in the grand hall jumped to attention. Joe made it to the main entrance and the heavy oak slammed shut behind him, rattling the long windows either side. Seething with rage he strode across the turning circle, making for the avenue.

Although he knew that Emily and Frank would be waiting, and anxious to hear the outcome of the encounter, Joe went to the little churchyard on the mountainside where his beloved Chloe, his pansy-eyed three-year-old daughter, rested in perpetual childhood.

Anticipating where Joe's footsteps would lead him, Emily busied herself in the garden, weeding the ground between the fruit bushes. Frank kept appearing at her side, hands in his trouser pocket, fretting unmercifully, only adding to the turmoil in her own mind.

Mid-afternoon, digging out a plant that had passed its best, she heard Joe's footsteps on the lane. Quickly she pushed the tines of the garden fork deep into the soil. She had slept badly, and worried all day, and there was no doubt in her mind that every wrinkle on her face had deepened to a new level. For Joe's sake, she tried to lighten her expression with a welcoming smile, ready to pour oil on troubled waters.

The clatter of garden tools ceased, alerting Frank to the arrival of his father. Dashing out of the house, he took three quick strides to open the garden gate.

Without noticing the greyness of his father's face, he blurted out, 'What did he say?'

'Let me get into the cottage, lad,' Joe said, dreading meeting the lad's eyes.

Emily slipped her hand through the crook of Joe's elbow and pulled him close. On tiptoe she kissed his cheek. 'The kettle's simmering on the hob, there'll be a cup of tea on the table in no time,' she said with false calm.

Too agitated to return the kiss, Joe went indoors, Emily and Frank following.

Stooping down to the cupboard at the bottom of the dresser, Joe pulled open the door and laid his hand on a bottle of whisky.

Unable to wait a moment longer to hear the news, Frank groaned.

Touching the lad's sleeve, Emily spoke gently. 'Let your father sit down, and take the weight off his feet. He's walked all the way from our Chloe.'

Joe's eyes widened. 'How do you know that?'

She smiled faintly. 'It's the place you always go to when your mind is troubled.'

Joe pulled the cork out of the bottle. 'Do I?'

Frank held his hands together, as though praying. 'Da, tell me what Tommy said. Have the men got their jobs or not?'

Joe looked everywhere but at Frank. 'It's not quite that simple.'

Frank's eyebrows arched. 'Not simple?'

Joe poured the whisky, and swirled the golden liquid around the sides of the glass.

'Tommy has given all the jobs back, but one.'

Emily had a rush of tears. 'Oh Joe, you are a miracle.'

'No, I'm not,' he said forlornly. 'The job he's held back is our Frank's.'

Frank slumped onto the kitchen chair. 'So it's just me that's lost a job? Why?' His eyes filled with tears.

Joe looked at Emily. 'You know what our Tommy is like.'

Emily's face reddened with rage. 'Aye, I know he can be vicious. But this time I'll kill the bugger. I'm going to Plas Mawr and giving him a piece of my mind. It's no good you trying to talk me out of it, Joe. I'm going, and I don't care how many of his fancy servants hear me when I take the lad down a peg or two.'

Holding her, Joe felt the tremble in her body. 'It won't do any good, Emily. He's hell bent on not giving Frank work. If you go up there and rile him, he'll not give the other buggers their jobs either. Many people will be put on Queer Street. You can't go, Emily. Regrettably, for the moment, we are forced to accept Tommy's ruling.'

Lifting the glass to his lips he took a mouthful of the spirit, feeling warmth in his throat instantly.

'Well, there is something I can do,' Emily said steely with determination. 'Frank, go and get Nora. Bring her back here for a bite of dinner. We can talk about the wedding, and decide how we are going to manage it. I'll not have our Tommy breaking another lass's heart. The wedding will happen. And if I have my way it'll be right under our Tommy's nose.' Picking up the kettle, she put it down forcefully on the hob. 'I'll show the bugger who is boss.'

Joe grinned for the first time in days. 'That I don't doubt, Emily.'

Frank flung his depression off like an old coat. Almost leaping from the chair, he dashed across the room and through the open door before his father could add a word of caution.

A wave of envy swept through Joe; what he wouldn't give to have Frank's energy and vitality. 'Lad's got magic fluid instead of blood running through his vein.'

Joe's mind went to the library in Plas Mawr, to Tommy sitting on the corner of the desk, swinging his leg. Delivering the news that Frank wasn't getting his job back there had been a nasty smirk on Tommy's face. Joe thanked God that Frank's mind, as well as his body, was healthy too. Tommy's soul was warped. It was the Devil's work. He hoped to God that it wasn't his own.

'I'll go and check on the pigs,' he said, already half-way out of the door.

Emily gathered the ingredients together to make pastry. The neck of mutton would go further and feed four instead of three if it went into a meat and potato pie. Rubbing lard into the cold flour, she thought of the immediate future. Somehow they would manage, they had always done so. 'But there's managing and managing,' a little imp at the back of her mind warned. 'Four mouths to feed, and only one wage. Joe's job is uncertain. Only as safe as Frank's had been.'

Sprinkling flour on the table top, she slapped the pastry dough down, and attacked it with the rolling pin. Two images played in her mind, Tommy as a loving toddler, and Tommy as he now was. She didn't like the latter, and feared he would be the ruination of the Standish family. Spreading the pastry into the bottom of the pie dish, she experienced a moment of terror; money was scarce, and she had added to the problem by insisting the wedding went ahead, and now Nora would move in within a fortnight.

She was mentally moving the furniture around to accommodate another person, when she heard the familiar rattle of the slop bucket outside the back door.

Joe gave his boots a cursory wipe on the mat, and put his head around the kitchen door.

'I'll leave the bucket on the scullery step, ready for the peelings.'

He dropped a dark green cabbage into the stone sink, and plucked a pale caterpillar off it, tossing the creature out into the back yard.

Coming into the kitchen, he sat on the wooden chair near the table, and pulled off his boots.

'Frank's coming down the lane with Nora.'

Emily put the finishing touches to the pie lid, and wiped her hands on her apron. 'How does she seem?'

'It's hard to tell.'

Emily slid the dish into the hot bread oven.

Frank dropped Nora's hand before they came through the garden gate, and they walked Indian file down the path and trailed into the cottage.

Nora was looking somewhat belligerent.

Emily supposed the young couple had shared words, as was to

be expected when a wedding was on, and then off, and back on again. 'Come and sit down, lass. Dinner will soon be ready,' she said, with an understanding smile.

Glad the girl was settled, Joe reached around the back of the chair for his boots. Slipping them on, he tied the laces. 'Me and our Frank are going to the Halfway. We'll bring back a jug of ale to have with our dinner.'

He planted a kiss on Emily's cheek. 'We'll only be a half-hour. It'll give you and Nora time to talk about the wedding, the church an' all that.'

'Don't be any longer, or the pie will be ruined.'

With the men out of the way, Nora confided that on the previous day, Frank had insisted that the wedding be postponed. Angry with him, Nora had suggested that they put it off entirely.

Emily tut-tutted sympathetically. 'Everything is all right between you now?' she asked, wondering if worrying about the future had been unnecessary.

Nora was plaintive, 'Yes, I think so. Frank said he's going to Parys Mountain to get work, so we can be married as we arranged.' Fresh tears gathered in her eyes.

Joe will have something to say about Parys, Emily thought tersely.

She tried to sound cheerful. 'Now stop fretting. Everything will work out, Nora.'

Sniffing back tears, Nora smiled weakly. 'Thank you, Mrs Standish.'

'You must call me Emily. It'll be too confusing when there are two Mrs Standishes in this old place.' In truth, Emily didn't want the young woman calling her Mam. Chloe was the only girl to call her that, in the past, and now in her mind, and Emily wanted to keep it that way.

Nora was draining a pan of potatoes, looking much more cheerful when Frank came into the scullery. Thankful that the tears were finally over, he kissed her mouth.

'Let me carry that back in,' he said, lifting the hot pan from the draining-board.

Joe was pouring ale into glasses, adding Emily's homemade lemonade.

Emily dished the pie and vegetable, and the usual silence fell as they began to eat.

After the first few mouthfuls, Emily said 'We should talk about the wedding, and decide how we are going to get over the problem of work for Frank.'

Frank speared a chunk of mutton. 'I'm going to Parys.'

'It's not what I want you to do,' Joe said seriously.

Frank put his fork down on the plate with a clatter. 'I know that. But I'm short of options.'

Emily glanced between the two men. 'The lad must do as he sees fit. He'll soon be a married man.'

Joe started to interrupt, but Emily went on, 'When you and Frank built Corn Cottage it was decided then that when Frank got wed he and his wife would live here. Frank's made a grand start on another parlour. I realise that putting the roof on will have to wait a while. Until it's finished, we can manage here.'

'It'll cost money to finish it,' Joe said practically.

Emily touched his hand. 'Yes. But the lad will get work.'

Frank glanced uneasily between his mother and father. 'Nora's father won't allow us to marry unless I'm in work.'

Emily was hurt to think that Mr Williams didn't trust Frank to find a job and take care of Nora. 'You take whatever you can get, Frank. You can find a better position after the wedding.'

Joe was adamant. 'I don't want him to go to Parys Mountain. It's a filthy place.'

Emily picked up the knife she had cut the pie with. 'Have you finished, Joe? Or would you like another piece?'

'I'm finished, thanks.'

The conversation wrangled on until it was time for Frank to walk Nora home.

In bed, unable to sleep, Joe went over the discussion more than a dozen times. Worrying that he may not have done the right thing agreeing that Frank would take whatever job was available, so the wedding could go ahead.

That Frank would be forced to move away, coming home when he could afford it, troubled him greatly. He would miss his younger son like buggery, and he didn't care who knew it. Frank had rarely been out of his sight since he burst forth into this life on that wonderful Sunday all those years ago.

There has to be another way, he thought, fingering the frayed edge of the bed-sheet. The lad's good at laying stones and he could make a reasonable house-builder. Perhaps there's a farmer that would take him on. Anything, but please God, not Parys Mountain.

When the idea struck him, it was impossible not to grin. 'Fitting retribution, Tommy lad,' he muttered softly. He didn't know where the idea came from, but it was a bloody good one. The best!

His old colliery mate, Frank, killed in the Galloway so very long ago, came into his mind, he was laughing loudly, his rust-red hair shimmering like a halo around his head.

'Hello, me old cocker,' Joe muttered into the darkness.

In moments he was asleep, and dreaming of the slum alleyways of his childhood home, Frank running beside him, chasing girls with pigtails to pull.

Chapter 3

Joe woke to a cloudy sky. The wind was blowing from the south, heralding the end of the hot spell that had baked the earth for long, airless weeks. He lay for a moment, eyes on the thin crack running across the greyish ceiling.

Fragments of the dream lingered: the smell of rain falling on the black filmed cobbles of Rotherman Street. Frank running alongside him toward the canal, legs pumping with vitality and youth. Frank laughing fit to bust at some prank.

Moving his legs, Joe felt a stab of pain in his lower back. 'Bloody old age,' he muttered crabbily.

The events of the last couple of days, Parys Mountain, and the postponed wedding, came flooding back, and he gave an almost silent groan. Everything that had gone wrong was all down to Tommy's malevolence.

With another sigh, he swung his legs from under the bedclothes. Perching on the edge of the thin mattress, elbows resting on his thighs, he thought of Tommy and how best to thwart his ridiculous scheme to oust his younger brother.

The idea that had come to him during the early hours resurfaced. He smiled. If the concept worked, and there was a very good chance that it could, Frank would be spared the copper mines. Tommy would get what was coming to him. It would be nothing short of splendid! He smiled again. With renewed energy, he rose, and tossed an old coat over his flannel nightshirt.

It was important that he got moving, and preferably before he had to explain himself to Emily and Frank.

Glancing at Emily, checking she was still asleep, he slipped out of the room. In the parlour he threw bone-dry kindling onto the hot embers in the range, and put the kettle onto the hob. Braving the early morning chill of the scullery, he washed in cold water. The kettle was barely warm when he emptied the water into the enamel bowl for his shave.

In the mirror over the mantle, he combed his damp hair. Wearing the same shirt and trousers he'd worn yesterday to go to Plas Mawr, he slipped his stocking feet into newly blacked work boots.

Eager to get going before Frank rose from his bed, as he didn't want to raise the lad's hopes needlessly; Joe hurried to make a pot of tea for him and Emily.

Emily, still dazed with sleep, took a steaming mug from him.

Standing in the half-light created by the closed curtains, he said, 'I've some business to attend to in Caernarvon. Expect me when you see me.'

He passed through the bedroom door quickly before she had time to reply.

Suddenly wide awake, Emily listened to the front door opening and closing, and the clack of his boots on the garden path. The gate swung closed with a familiar clunk. Thoughtfully, sipping the tea, she wondered what bee he had in his bonnet.

For the first time in a month the sky was overcast and the air cool. Joe was relieved that the hot dry spell had come to an end, the cracked earth needed rain. The baking sun had turned the crater of the quarry into a furnace, hell to work in. Everything looked more familiar today; the outline of the destroyed mountain and the terraces softened with the mist of impending rain. Beyond Snowdon, the faraway mountains were lavender-grey and ethereal.

Rain would raise the level of the mountain stream at the back of the cottage. The water was as low as he'd ever seen it. The straggle of quarriers' homes built alongside the flow had privies perched like little bridges over the water. The bed of the stream needed a good sluicing; it stank, and encouraged flies.

It was too early to catch the peal of chapel bells. For company there was only the sound of his boots kicking up dust, and the chirrup of sparrows in the dusty hedgerows.

As it was Sunday he didn't expect to get a lift on a farm cart going to Caernarvon, but villagers and preachers would be on the road, so there was a good chance that his legs would be saved the entire eight miles there, and back again.

Passing the turning to Plas Mawr, he glanced down the lane praying that he wouldn't meet Tommy on an early morning jaunt. He listened intently but didn't catch the sound of a horse, rider, or carriage.

Reaching the centre of the village, Joe found Owain Williams piling a couple of old chairs and a child's wooden cradle onto a cart outside Maisy's shop. Learning that Owain was taking the furniture to Maisy's niece, living on the outskirts of Caernarvon, he offered Owain money in exchange for a lift. Recently married, Owain was grateful for the bit extra towards the housekeeping.

Throughout the journey Owain's conversation centred entirely on his new wife. Reaching Caernarvon, Joe wondered if there was anything he didn't know about her family, upbringing and religion.

It was with some relief that he alighted in sight of the castle. Standing on the pavement he watched the horse and cart round the corner of the street, and breathed a sigh of relief that he'd heard the last of Mrs Owain Williams for the day.

It began to rain fat drops of water, soaking into his shirt. Almost instantly the dirty pavement gave off a whiff of rotten mushrooms.

It took him several minutes to reach the terrace house on New Street, the two up, two down, which had recently become the local quarters of the quarrymen's union. The ground floor was now an office. Lloyd Parry, fund raiser and organiser of this branch of the union, lived in the two rooms above.

Lloyd opened the door at Joe's first knock.

'Well, I'll be darned. What brings you here?' Lloyd said, shaking Joe's hand heartily.

It was the first time Joe had called at the office, and he was impressed by the organised room. The shelves were stacked with office paraphernalia. Against a wall there was a large table, the surface covered with freshly printed leaflets, still smelling of ink. Several account books lay open on a desk.

At the far end of the room, where once there had been a kitchen, there was a small black-leaded range; a small fire in the grate was heating the hob.

Lloyd filled a kettle from a jug of water on the window sill. 'You'll take a cup of tea?'

'Aye, it'd be welcome.'

Whilst the kettle came to the boil they talked of the union, and how the numbers were growing, the members mainly coming from Penrhyn Quarry near Bethesda.

'So what did bring you here on a Sunday morning, Joe? Not to listen to me bragging about how many men have signed up for the union, that's for sure.'

Joe gave a long sigh. Then began to explain the recent problems at Garddryn Quarry and how Tommy had sacked young Frank. It embarrassed him to talk of his own visit to Plas Mawr and the reception he'd received from his son.

Lloyd listened intently, without interrupting.

When Joe got to the end of the tale he fixed his eyes on his old friend. 'So I have come up with an idea. If you don't agree with it, just say so. I will not be offended.'

Lloyd smiled. 'Let's hear it then.'

'I want a job in the union for our Frank. He's a smart lad, knows the quarry trade and understands the problems quarrymen face every day. His reading and writing are good, and his sums are more than adequate.'

Lloyd shifted in his seat, and frowned thoughtfully.

Joe thought he was going to refuse. With Frank's future hanging in the balance, he became earnest. 'I know it's a lot to ask. But the lad will work hard. I reckon he could recruit Garddryn men. He's one of them, a quarryman, they would trust his word.'

'I don't doubt that Frank would give the job his all. He's a hard worker. But there's a problem. The union can't yet afford to pay very much. But we could offer him a small wage and top it up with commission for every member he signs up.'

Relief flowed through Joe. 'That's fair for beginners.'

Lloyd smiled. 'You see this son of yours rising to the top in the union?'

Joe matched his smile. 'Cream always rises to the top, and my Frank is cream. Give him this chance and the lad will not fail you. He's a union man through and through.'

Lloyd nodded in agreement. 'Tell him to come here tomorrow

morning. I'll explain the ropes. Then he can get back to Garddryn village and start organising meetings, and get recruiting.'

'Thank you for this, Lloyd. Frank will not let you down.'

Lloyd's expression became serious. 'Tommy Standish won't like this. It'll split the brothers irrevocably.'

Joe met his gaze. 'I'm banking on it!'

'No doubt you know what you're doing, Joe.'

'Aye, I do,' Joe said seriously.

Lloyd changed the subject. Checking the clock, he said, 'What do you say to wetting the enterprise with a glass of ale at the Black Boy?'

Joe grinned. 'What a good idea. I've talked up a thirst.'

It was mid-afternoon when Joe departed the public house, too late for a lift back to Garddryn village on a church goer's cart. He walked the entire way. The excitement he felt for Frank, glee that at last he had got one over on Tommy, meant the eight miles were easy to travel. As he neared Corn Cottage he saw a window bright with lamplight, and he quickened his step.

Emily heard the clack of the gate, and jumped up out of the one comfortable chair. Crossing the room quickly, she opened the door. Joe came in bringing the smell of rain and fresh air, and a slight whiff of the ale he'd downed at the Black Boy.

'I was starting to get worried,' she said, reaching up to kiss his cold cheek.

'I told you to expect me when you saw me.'

She tucked a strand of hair behind her ear. 'Well you're here now, and looking mighty pleased with yourself, Joe Standish.'

He rubbed his chilled hands together. 'Aye, I am. And I'm famished too.'

'I've kept your dinner warm. It'll be on the table in a moment. But not until you tell me the reason why you're lit up like a Christmas tree, Joe.'

His grin widened. 'Where's our Frank? I'll tell you both at the same time.'

Emily looked to the back door. 'He's just gone out to the privy. He'll be back in a moment.'

The back door opened, a waft of cool air disturbed the lamplight, and the shadows on the walls moved. The door closed, the latch clicking into place. Unaware that his father had returned, Frank was surprised to see him.

'Come and sit down, Frank,' Emily said patting the back of a wooden kitchen chair. 'Your father has something to tell us. And by the size of his smile it must be good news.'

The rain started again, pitter-pattering on the window panes.

Joe had Emily's full attention. Frank looked too despondent to show much interest. It amused Joe to know that in a few moments his son would be hanging onto his every word. Impatient to reach that point, Joe didn't recount the journey with Owain to Caernarvon but began the story with his arrival at New Street.

Frank's head came up when he mentioned the union, and his dark eyes showed curiosity.

Emily guessed correctly what Joe was leading up to, and the tension in her stiff shoulders ebbed away. She leaned her head back, and two tears slipped from beneath her closed eyes.

'So,' Joe said, stretching out the word. 'Lloyd has offered you a job with the union. You're to be at New Street tomorrow morning first thing.'

Opening her eyes, wiping the tears from her cheeks, Emily

saw Frank spring up from the chair. It fell back and clattered noisily to the floor. Grabbing his father, he held him in a bear hug, and laughing and crying, he planted a smacking kiss on Joe's cheek.

His excitement was too big to hold in; releasing Joe, he caught his mother in his arms, and lifting her off her feet, he swung her around.

Giddy, Emily shouted, 'Mind the furniture.'

Carefully he put her back on her feet. Standing in the centre of the room, legs apart, Frank grinned widely.

'I take it you're pleased,' Joe laughed.

'Pleased! Thrilled is more like it, as Mam would say, thrilled as a bride on her wedding day.'

Emily touched Joe's arm. 'You are a wonder, Joe Standish. Why do I bother to worry about the future when I have you?'

'What about some dinner then? Rabbit stew will be a just reward for the hike I had getting back.'

Frank leapt to the range. 'I'll get it. You just sit down and rest your legs.'

'I could get used to this,' Joe said, picking up a knife and fork off the table-top in anticipation.

In awe of his victory, Emily and Frank were silent whilst Joe ate his dinner. Frank began to fidget; a dozen questions had surfaced in his mind.

Emily put the kettle to the hob. 'Tea, Joe?'

'No thank you lass, me and Frank will have a whisky. We'll sit beside the fire for a while and exchange some information.'

'I'm off to bed,' she said, putting the kettle to the back of the range. 'Don't stay up too late, our Frank. You must get to Caernarvon early tomorrow.'

He grinned, the like of which she hadn't seen for days. 'Don't worry about me, Mam.'

Braving the rain, she made a quick trip to the privy. When she returned, Joe was sitting in the comfortable chair, legs stretched out, stocking feet on the brass fender. Frank perched on a kitchen chair, legs curled up beneath him, looking like a coiled spring.

'Sleep well, you two. See you in the morning,' she said, passing through.

In the bedroom, in the half-light of an oil lamp, Emily knelt on the rag-rug at the side of the bed, hands clasped together in prayer. She thanked God for the past day, and asked for his blessing for the following one.

In bed, she allowed her mind to roam through the doubt niggling her; Frank was spared the copper mines, for which she was grateful. But there was another side to the same coin. A great rift would develop between the two brothers. Joe would be at the centre of it, seen to be siding with one son against the other. A giant chasm would grow in the family, irreparable and permanent. She was afraid. Terrible trouble lay ahead. She wondered how they would all weather the brewing storm.

She was still awake when Joe came in and turned down the lamp. The bed jiggled as he climbed in. She heard his sigh of satisfaction as he relaxed. A moment passed before he slept, impossible for her to do the same.

Chapter 4

Tommy found little sympathy at Penrhyn Castle. Edward Douglas-Pennant, resident owner of the magnificent stately castle found it difficult to comprehend why Tommy was so set against his younger brother, a slate cutter at the vast Garddryn Quarry.

He understood why Tommy Standish was afraid of the unions taking hold. Tommy was renowned as a hard task master, a man that took shortcuts, endangering lives to increase the profit of the Garddryn. The same went for Ruby Quarry, the fairly new enterprise, owned solely by Tommy, and acquired through unusual and perhaps not quite legal shenanigans.

Tommy was like the other quarry owners in North Wales, afraid of change, and afraid that they would lose their grip, despotic and financial, if they opened their minds and dealt fairly with the workers and other employees.

Once again he tried to divert Tommy from his madcap idea of not reinstating his brother, when he had given every other man that had defied him their jobs back.

'You're making a mistake,' Edward warned.

They were sitting at the table in the plush dining room, relaxed and content after enjoying an excellent roast beef dinner. The cheese board was between them, and as he spoke Edward was helping himself to a wedge of perfectly matured stilton.

The serving staff had withdrawn. Only the butler remained, and he stood unobtrusively beside the ornate sideboard, waiting for instructions to pass the port decanter.

Sadie Pearson, a housemaid, and Tommy's occasional lover, sat in an agony of impatience in the now empty kitchen. The housekeeper had dismissed the servants more than an hour ago. Sadie remained, waiting for the dining room door to open, anxious that she may not hear the two men withdrawing. Crossing the kitchen she opened the door a crack and peeped out. The hallway was deserted, the wall lamps turned down low.

The dining room door opened and Lord Penrhyn walked out. Sadie pulled her head back quickly, flushing scarlet with embarrassment, certain that the Baron had caught a glimpse of her. If he mentioned it to cook tomorrow, Sadie knew she would be in for a hard time, and have a lot of explaining to do.

Afraid to make a sound, she tiptoed across the slate floor. At the far end of the kitchen was the servants' door; before she went through it, she turned the little wheel on the oil lamp, plunging the kitchen into darkness. An intense panic seized her and she couldn't catch her breath. Her hand went to the lamp, and then the table top, but there was nothing lying there to relight the wick. As her eyes became accustomed to the blackness, the dresser, the long sink, and the cooking range emerged as dark shadows.

With trembling fingers she found the door. The top hinge was dry and always creaked, opening it slowly, she slipped through. The servants' corridor was pitch-black and eerie. Afraid that ghosts lurked in the nooks and crannies, she entered the darkness reluctantly.

The blackness was disorientating and she was trying to guess how close she was to the door at the end of the corridor when the toe of her boot bumped it. She fumbled for the brass knob. It was sticky, and she wondered who the culprit was with greasy hands.

Through the door, the air she breathed was cleaner. The blue haze of fat smoke of the kitchen didn't penetrate this far.

Ignoring the short corridor leading to the aristocrats' part of the house, she went up the narrow stairs to the servants' quarters. Heart racing with fear, she slipped through the darkness.

Standing on the top tread, she looked through the blackness trying to judge how many steps lay between her and the final door, wishing that Matt Taylor, a stable-hand, hadn't taken the trouble to tell her about the ghosts haunting the castle. Whatever lay in wait, she had to run the gauntlet if she wanted to be in Tommy's arms.

Picking up the hem of her skirt, heart pounding, and armpits wet with sweat, she made a dash to the final door. She hadn't realised that she had stopped breathing until she took a noisy gulp of air on finding the door knob and opening the door a crack.

The staircase and upper gallery were bathed in pale lamplight. Glancing left and right, she ran light-footed to Tommy's bedroom. Breathless and afraid she may be seen, she rapped on the door and rushed in.

Tommy was lying on the bed in his shirt sleeves and grey trousers, his head resting on the intricate carved wood of the headboard. He was smoking a cigar, the masculine fragrance scenting the room.

'What kept you, Sadie?'

His smile made him look dapper, a perfect gentleman. Overwhelmed by the love she felt for Tommy Standish, Sadie felt the familiar throb in her vagina.

'Come here, wench,' he said, extinguishing the cigar in the ashtray on the bedside table. 'I have something for you.'

Sadie giggled.

Sometimes Tommy's lovemaking was too rough, but she didn't mind. Being with him, sharing his bed for the night, made up for the bruises and soreness she would suffer tomorrow.

She pulled off her white cap and her dark hair tumbled to her shoulders. Her hands went to the ties on her apron.

Tommy rose from the bed and came to her. Taking the ribbons, he pulled them apart, and the apron slipped to the floor. The uniform frock fell, making a blue puddle at her feet. Her exposed legs were pale and plump, her bare buttocks round and well formed.

Running his hands over her flesh, Tommy sighed, and forgot the row with his father, and the sacking of his brother, entirely.

He enjoyed his times with Sadie, though she wasn't as exciting in bed as Lady Isabelle.

Isabelle had been dangerous to know. She liked her lovemaking brutal. When their affair began he was but a novice to sadism, but soon became an eager devotee of the late Donatien Alphonse Francois, Count de Sade.

During his and Lady Isabelle's time together, it had surprised him that habitual flagellation had not marked her ladyship permanently. Neither Isabelle's ladies-maid nor her husband commented on the cherry red stripes, remaining for several days after an enthusiastic thrashings. But Lord Harvey preferred boys, so perhaps he hadn't felt the necessity to see his wife naked.

Putting memories aside, Tommy turned Sadie around to face him, and squeezed her nipple hard, until she gave a little yelp.

The night passed too quickly and she awoke at dawn to see a chink of light at the edge of the curtains. Rising from the bed she went to the marble fireplace and looked at the face of the French clock on the mantle-piece. It was almost four-thirty. Thankfully she hadn't overslept, and Florence, the new kitchen maid, who shared a room with her, would still be sleeping.

With one eye on Tommy, expecting him to notice her imminent departure, Sadie dressed hurriedly.

Opening the door a crack, checking that the corridor was clear, she gave Tommy a last glance before slipping out of the room.

Walking away, an air of despondency settled on her. From experience she knew that it would take days before she was her normal self again. Today, and maybe tomorrow, she would daydream, dwelling on the time she had spent with him. During the dark hours of the coming nights, lying in her narrow bed, she would see just how hopeless the love affair was. Tommy Standish was not going to marry her, though he was a single man, or take her to his home, Plas Mawr. A house she had never seen, and was unlikely ever to do so.

The small noise of the door clicking closed registered in Tommy's weary brain. The chill of the night air lapped at his exposed shoulder. Pulling the blankets up to cover himself, he slipped back into a dream-state.

Sadie hoped against hope that Cook would order her to take the silver platters into the breakfast room, where the Baron and Tommy were expected at any moment. She tried everything, including getting under the cook's feet, to draw the woman's attention, but to no avail. Matilda was told to do it instead. As the last dish was borne to the table, Sadie knew that she wouldn't see Tommy today, and she must wait until he appeared again at Penrhyn to spend time with him.

She felt like crying, but a whack with a wet cloth, delivered by Cook, brought her attention back to the chores.

The elderly woman's eyes were narrow and menacing. 'There's a stack of copper saucepans to wash and polish,' she said tersely. 'And I'll not be happy until I can see my face in the shine.'

Sadie made a grab for the nearest saucepan. Upending it, she wiped it with a dry cloth.

Cook clicked her tongue in annoyance. 'Take the lot into the scullery and clean them there.'

Sadie was still busy polishing when Matt Taylor came in, dragging muck on his boots.

Sulky, as though he'd lost a precious coin, he frowned. 'The master of the Garddryn has just sent orders for his 'orses to be made ready at once. I swear there isn't a ruder man in Christendom.'

Sadie's cheeks flushed pink. 'Keep your nasty remarks to yourself, Matt Taylor.'

His eyebrows rose in surprise. 'Hark at you, Miss Hoity Toity.'

The flush on Sadie's cheeks deepened. 'Tommy Standish deserves respect from the likes of you.'

Hearing the angry exchange, the cook came from the kitchen to the scullery. She stood in the doorway, her bulk filling the opening.

Sadie's eyes went to the two identical sweat rings at the armpits of the woman's light grey dress. Fearful that cook would notice where she was looking and clout her ears, Sadie looked at the woman's ample chins, and the fat turkey neck spilling over the collar. Cook had grown from fat to immense in less than a year. The sheer size of her was intimidating.

Afraid, Sadie turned her eyes downward and stared at the hem of the enormous skirt, hovering four-inches above the slate tiles. The two booted feet were planted wide, the laces unfastened, the leather tongues lolling, like a pair of thirsty dogs.

'What's going on in here?' she shouted.

With no time to escape, Matt stood with his back pressed up against the stone sink.

Cook flicked a wet cloth at him, cornering the boy between sink and doorway. Then with well-aimed swipes, she shepherded him out like a scabby mongrel. 'I won't have dirty louts littering up my kitchen.'

Matt dashed out.

Sadie tried to get into the main kitchen.

'Come back here, Pearson,' the woman shouted.

Sadie's brown eyes filled with tears.

The wet cloth cut the air viciously. 'You'll not get away from me, Madam.'

Sadie heaved a sob.

'And you can cut that nonsense out,' Cook yelled, spittle flying from her lips. 'You can make a start on the new potatoes. There's a stone of them waiting to be scraped. His Lordship is expecting several guests for luncheon.'

Alone in the scullery, a sack of potatoes beside her feet, Sadie scraped the paper-thin skins off. Dropping them one by one into cold water in the copper pan she had so recently polished.

Tears came easily. She was tired and already missing Tommy. Her privates were tender, and her rump a pale shade of lavender, bruising from Tommy's stinging slaps.

In another part of the house, in the quiet and restful breakfast room, Tommy was enjoying mutton chops, eggs, bacon and grilled kidneys.

After a final cup of coffee, he said his farewells to Edward in the Grand Hall, promising to return in the near future.

Smartly dressed in a dark grey suit, white silk shirt with a black necktie, and highly polished and comfortable shoes, Tommy walked outdoors into the mild morning air. With hardly a backward glance at the castle, he walked across the cobbles at the turning circle to his gleaming black carriage.

Owen Roberts, a Plas Mawr coachman, was standing at the heads of two brown mares, the reins held lightly between his thumb and forefinger.

Boarding the vehicle, Tommy eased himself down onto the leather seat, taking care not to rumple his coat. Leaning back, he relaxed completely. He felt replete, satisfied. Edward's hospitality had been excellent, and the kitchen maid an agreeable bed companion.

The coachman mounted the coach steps rheumatically. Before his knees cramped with familiar pain, he slumped down on the driver's box seat. The body of the coach swayed on the leather springs as he settled himself. The mares were well-trained and obedient and needed nothing but a light flick of the reins to walk on. The wheels turned, rattling on the cobbles.

Tommy wasn't interested in the exotic trees bordering the long avenue or the ornamental bushes growing beneath. His mind was already on the appointment he had in Caernarvon with Madoc his solicitor. Yesterday, Madoc had sent a letter to Plas Mawr suggesting an urgent meeting as something had come up requiring his immediate attention.

The sun was warming the roof of the coach before they reached Caernarvon. On Castle Street the carriage came to a standstill close to the steps leading to the dark green door of

Madoc's offices.

Descending from his perch, the coachman, afraid that the master may notice that he was now too old to do his job properly, tried to put a spring in his step, though pain shot through the worn out bones of his joints.

Whilst waiting for the carriage door to be opened for him, Tommy brushed imaginary bits of lint off his coat.

The door opened and the small foot-step was lowered. Tommy climbed out elegantly. Without acknowledging the driver, he crossed the pavement. Glancing at the castle on his right he saw the stone walls darken as a cloud obscured the sun.

Turning the brass knob, he opened the office door.

A beam of sunlight came through the long windows as he walked into the reception office. The air was dry from the recent glorious weather, and it almost obliterated the underlying scent of damp peculiar to the Georgian house.

A thin, undernourished clerk, sitting on a high stool, slid off. His hair was slicked down with hair oil, a dark strand lying across his brow.

Flashing knowing eyes, hinting at homosexuality, he said, 'Mr Madoc asked that you go into his office immediately on your arrival, Mr Standish.'

He came to the short wooden barrier and opening the waist-high door, he said, 'I'll take you to him.'

Tommy waved him away arrogantly. 'There's no need. I know the way. I'm sure you have enough work to do.' It sounded like a reprimand.

The clerk paused, his eyes following Tommy as he walked down the richly carpeted corridor to Madoc's office. It was a pity that the master of the Garddryn, the most handsome man in the county, with a rumoured dark side, seemed disinterested in the proclivities that were so agreeable to him. But the man had to return this way. He would try to catch his interest then.

Mumbling to himself, he climbed back on his stool, conjuring up images of Tommy Standish in the bedroom of his grand mansion, Plas Mawr.

Tommy entered Madoc's office. It looked the same as always. The décor unchanged for more than a decade. A green carpet covered the old elm floorboards. The windows looking out onto the town square were hung with dark green curtains with an oxblood motif. The seating was brown leather. Madoc worked at a partner's desk, though it had been years since he had in fact had a partner. In the darkest corner stood a cupboard where brandy and whisky were kept. Ceiling to floor bookcases lined two walls, the shelves crammed with leather-bound legal books. The fireplace was of Mona marble, swept clean now, with just a residue of grey ash in the grate.

As Tommy entered, Madoc stood, and shook his hand.

'So what's the urgency? Tommy asked pleasantly.

'I'm afraid an old adversary has come back to haunt you.'

Tommy looked perplexed. 'An adversary, such people have not worried us in the past.'

'This might,' Madoc said, holding out a cigar box to his guest.

Lifting a Havana out, Tommy glanced at it appreciatively.

Madoc came around the desk to light it, and then put the flame to his own.

Satisfied with the quality, he held the fragrant smoke in his mouth then exhaled a grey curl, half-closing an eye against it.

'Lord Harvey's wife, Lady Isabelle, has made an appearance,' he said with a note of concern.

It was hard to hide his surprise, and Tommy's voice was louder than he intended. 'What! Here in Caernarvon?'

Madoc took a speck of tobacco off his bottom lip. 'Yes. I'm afraid so. The blasted woman turned up on the doorstep just as I was leaving last night. She must have waited until the clerks had gone. I was going through the door, when she accosted me.'

An unexplained bang sounded in the corridor. Tommy expected the door to fly open and Isabelle to come thundering in.

Nothing happened, and his eyes came back to Madoc. 'What did she want?'

Madoc's expression was sardonic. 'She wants the money his Lordship lost on Ruby Quarry reimbursed. Someone has put them straight about the profit the quarry is now making. The couple are still living in Ireland, and they are on their uppers. The money you gave them for her jewellery is all gone and they are close to penury.'

'Good,' Tommy said, taking a pull of his cigar.

Madoc's darkly satanic eyebrows lifted a little. 'She meant something to you at one time.'

Just speaking her name made Tommy's hackles rise. 'She betrayed me and caused me to spend a great deal of money on a house in London that I didn't need at that time.'

Madoc was well aware that the relationship had ended badly. But he wasn't curious about the details. 'You get some use out of the house now.'

Tommy was impatient. 'If I do, it's because I don't like to think of the money as a complete waste.'

Madoc knew he was lying.

He checked the clock against his pocket watch. 'She said she would come back at noon. If she doesn't find you here, she proposes to get a ride to Plas Mawr.'

Tommy was ruffled. 'I have no intention of giving her anything. She made her bed and now she must lie in it. Same goes for her husband. If they are destitute they have no one to blame but themselves.'

Madoc wasn't surprised at the harsh line Tommy was taking. He had purposely ruined the Harveys, so he was hardly likely to put his hand in his pocket and see them out of trouble.

Tommy pushed back a strand of dark hair that had fallen across his forehead. 'Noon, you say?'

'I doubt she'll be precise. The woman still gives herself airs.' He had no intention of warning Tommy about Lady Isabelle's appearance. It would be amusing to see the shock on his face when she arrived.

Tommy checked the time. He was considering avoiding her, leaving by the back door and hoping she wouldn't make the journey to the mansion. But at that moment the street door opened and he heard her voice in the foyer.

The clerk knocked on Madoc's door.

'Come in,' the solicitor called.

The skinny clerk entered, his eyes going to Tommy at the window, silhouetted against the sunlight.

'Send her in,' Madoc said before the clerk could announce Lady Harvey's arrival.

The blue taffeta of her gown rustled as she swept in.

It was fortunate that sunlight haloed Tommy's form. Lady Harvey squinted against the bright light but was spared Tommy's shocked expression.

Dear God, he thought, she's aged a hundred years in less than six. The gown he knew of old, but now it hung on her bony frame, the bodice gaping where the flesh of her firm breast had once filled it. As usual she was wearing to much pale face-powder, exaggerating the deep wrinkles on her forehead and around her eyes. Cherry red lip-paint leaked into the puckering lines around her lips. A blue hat covered most of her hair, but what could be seen was dry and lifeless. Lady Isabelle has gone to the dogs, he thought disparagingly.

Standing, Madoc came from behind the desk. 'Lady Isabelle. Please take a seat.'

Tommy ached to send her packing. Embarrassed that Madoc should know that he, master of the Garddryn, had loved and fornicated with this harridan.

'What do you want?' Tommy said rudely, moving from the window.

She saw him plainly now, and took a sharp surprised breath. 'Tommy.'

She was dismayed to see him so virile and handsome, when time and circumstances had been so unkind to her. She shrunk further into the blue gown.

Avoiding his eyes, she said, 'I'll not beat about the bush, I want money. The money I feel is rightfully Lord Harvey's. We sank everything we had into Ruby Quarry and lost it all. Now it's making a handsome profit I think the management should reimburse our losses.'

Tommy laughed. 'Lord Harvey didn't lose his money, he lost the banks. There were several mortgages on the London property held by numerous banks. The Birkbeck alone lost twenty thousand pounds. The money Lord Harvey put into Ruby wasn't his in the first place, it belonged mostly to the Birkbeck, and they lost their financial capital.'

Tears of frustration filmed her eyes. 'But it is unfair.'

'What is?' he asked, nonchalant.

'My husband trusted you, and believed that putting money in Ruby Quarry would solve our financial problems.'

Tommy smiled thinly. 'I always thought he was a fiscal disaster.'

'It didn't stop you getting a great deal of money off him,' she said tearfully.

Tommy sighed. 'Lady Isabelle. I suggest you go back to Ireland and try to make a living in some other way. There's no money here for you.'

'But I demand to be reimbursed. We have nothing. Not even the roof over our heads is ours.'

'Using that tone with me will not help your cause,' he said waspishly.

'But you stole everything from us. You purposely ruined Lord Harvey, tricked him into buying your consortium shares. When he was unable to keep paying the development costs, you took the quarry from him.'

She had guessed it correctly; it was just as he had arranged it. What she didn't know was the reason he did it. He was sorely tempted to explain it to her, but with Madoc in hearing it was impossible.

In his mind he saw her as she was years ago, radiant, beautiful, and sensual. It was then that she betrayed him by taking a new lover. She and her husband had paid a high price for her infidelity.

Seeing her now he reckoned it wouldn't be long before she paid the ultimate price; death did not look so far away. Help her? He would murder her himself before he paid out a farthing.

'If you continue to harangue me, I will have no option but to inform the Birkbeck Bank of your whereabouts. You and Lord Harvey will not survive long in a damp prison cell. Good-day Madam, I do not wish to be in your company again.'

He walked to the door; turning, he spoke to Madoc, 'Usual place for lunch?'

As the door closed, Lady Isabelle covered her face with her hands and wept.

Madoc didn't show sympathy; as far as he was concerned, she and her husband had brought the downfall upon themselves.

Going to the door, he summoned two clerks from the outer office.

The two youths looked perplexed as they crossed the threshold of Madoc's room and saw the weeping woman.

Madoc took control. 'See Lady Isabelle out,' he said unemotionally.

Unused to throwing clients out onto the street, the two stood gawping. Madoc kicked the nearest youth on the ankle bone.

The blow stung; angry, the lad pulled Lady Isabelle clear of the chair.

Watching the pair steer her towards the door, Madoc absentmindedly blew his nose on a white handkerchief.

Thrust unceremoniously onto the street, Lady Isabelle stood on the pavement in a daze. With no thought in her head of what to do, she began walking towards the castle and down the slight incline to the river Seiont.

Never in her wildest dreams had she expected Tommy to treat her so harshly. That he was unwilling to reimburse even a pittance was a bitter blow. It wasn't what she and Lord Harvey had expected. Now she had only the money in her purse, meagre funds by previous standards, to return to Ireland.

Hardly aware that tears were on her face, she reached the river. The tide was on the turn and the river flowing fast. Sailing ships were leaving the quay, running with outgoing surge to cross the Caernarvon bar and head out to sea.

Ireland lay to the west. Tonight, when the tide turned again, she would sail, and by donkey cart journey to the barren land she now called home.

Fresh tears welled in her eyes. She had come to hate Ireland and the penury that Lord Harvey and she were forced to endure.

Tommy had Ruby Quarry, and he was meant to help them rise out of the financial quagmire created when Tommy Standish convinced Lord Harvey to invest in the Ruby enterprise.

All their money was sunk; they were wanted by the police and the directors of many banks. It was hopeless and frightening. She was afraid that in the not too distant future they would be going hungry; starvation and degradation, what a comedown for a woman who was once the belle of London balls.

Lost in dark thoughts, she stepped in a puddle, wetting the hem of her blue taffeta dress and an unsightly ring darkened the delicate material. She sighed inwardly, what did it matter if the entire gown became wet? An image of her wearing the sodden garment came into her mind, and a thought that was to be cataclysmic took root. More calm than she had been for some time, she embraced the inevitable, the solution to penury.

Lady Isabelle slipped into the water quite gracefully. The fast tidal flow pulled at her dress, dragging her down. For the briefest moment she changed her mind and wished she was on the quay, where people were running, shouting, and crying out.

Flailing, she swiftly floated passed spiralling eddies, brown and muddy. Salt water was in her mouth, rank and choking. She was colder than she had ever been, colder than the night spent on the fishing boat that took her and Lord Harvey to their exile in Ireland.

Caught in an eddy, she tumbled, and caught a glimpse of rocks and mud beneath. She put up a struggle to break free; surfacing, her tortured lungs spewed water.

Men fishing on the banks raised the alarm, and running they tried to keep up with her, to keep her in sight, but she was swept into the wide waters of the Menai Strait.

For a fleeting moment, Lady Isabelle saw the blue cloudless sky, and the distant sea, the breaking waves which would embrace her.

Tommy, with a whisky glass in his hand, waited in the hotel dining room for Madoc to show up. Hurrying, Madoc passed the dining room window, and then turned into the hotel foyer. Skirting around the tables laid with silverware, he came to Tommy.

'Everything go all right?' Tommy asked.

'Yes. Two of the clerks got rid of her.'

Tommy let out a breath of satisfaction. 'Good. Do you want a whisky?'

'Yes, with a touch of water.'

Catching Tommy's eye, the waiter came to the table quickly.

'Scotch, the best you have. And we'll have the roast beef,' Tommy said briskly, impatient to hear the details of the ejection.

Madoc and Tommy looked in the direction of the foyer on hearing a noisy commotion coming from there. A moment passed and then one of Madoc's clerks rushed into the dining room. Dishevelled, and obviously upset, he dashed to the table.

Madoc was brusque. 'What are you doing, coming here?'

The boy was close to tears. 'The lady we just saw out of the office. It's horrible.'

'Come on man, spit it out,' Madoc said under his breath.

'She's drowned herself in the river.'

'Are you sure?' Madoc asked, holding onto the youth's coat sleeve.

'Yes sir. A woman saw her come out of the office and followed her down to the quay. She saw her go into the Seiont and be swept away. Fishermen are bringing the body back to the shore at this minute.'

Madoc thought of the recriminations that could quite easily be aimed at him. Throwing the woman out had been poorly judged. To protect his back he must behave calmly and take charge.

With a firm hand he gripped the elbow of the lad's jacket as though to propel him towards the door. 'Go back to the office, and not a word to anyone. Do you hear, Planter?'

'Yes sir. Not a word to anyone.'

Aware that diners were taking an interest, Madoc lowered his voice to a rasp. 'And tell that to the other clerk.'

Rooted to the carpet, the lad nodded. 'Yes sir.'

'Go! We will come along shortly,' Madoc said impatiently.

Staring through the window, Madoc didn't take his eyes off the youth, watching him run along the pavement to the office in the Square. He doubted he could trust the lad not to gossip. But if he caught him out, he would sack him instantly; it was probably a good idea to do so anyway, it was one less witness to the kicking out.

'Bit of a turn-up,' Tommy said, taking a sip from his glass of whisky.

Madoc often wondered if Tommy Standish was human, or just a machine. In the past he had loved Lady Isabelle. But nevertheless he had chosen to ruin her, and her husband, because Isabelle had been unfaithful. She had chosen another man over Tommy Standish.

Extraordinarily arrogant, Tommy couldn't accept that she preferred another, and he struck back brutally, revealing to his cronies that Lady Isabelle's husband preferred boys to his wife.

Soon after the disclosure, Tommy learned that Lord Harvey had massive debts and several mortgages on his London mansion. Seizing the opportunity to land Isabelle in penury, Tommy convinced his Lordship to borrow more money from the banks and invest heavily in the Ruby Quarry enterprise.

Believing that Tommy was offering secure, fast, and immense profits, Lord Harvey re-mortgaged his home once more, and sank everything he owned into Ruby Quarry.

Tommy as landowner of Ruby charged a high rent for the land. It gave him immense pleasure to watch Ruby Quarry take shape, the installation of expensive equipment, the laying of the first tracks for the rail that would carry the slate to the coast for export.

Before the end of the first year, as he had predicted, the investors were overstretched financially and the rent was in arrears. Ignoring their protests and pleas for more time to pay, Tommy reclaimed the land. Ruby Quarry, equipped with the latest machinery, was in Tommy's ownership once more.

Madoc admired Tommy's business acumen, but acknowledged that there was something to fear in the man's ruthlessness. A day never passed, the sun set in the sky, that Madoc wasn't reminded to never double-cross, or anger, the master of the largest quarry in the kingdom.

Lord Harvey didn't blame Tommy for reclaiming the land. The rent had been in arrears, and there had been no money in the pot to complete the project.

Living in Ireland, where he was forced to flee from the threat of prison, he had no knowledge that Ruby Quarry was operational and making vast profits. On hearing that Tommy was again in charge, he persuaded Lady Isabelle to return to North Wales to beg Tommy for the return of the initial investment.

Several days passed without news of Isabelle and he was beginning to fret. The cottage they called home was cold, the pantry practically empty. In the back of his mind he wondered if Isabelle had deserted him. He wouldn't blame her. If she had found a way out of the barren county, best of luck to her. But he'd miss his vixen.

Once again he went to the tiny window and looked out onto the straggly stone path, bordered by neglected grass and decomposed leaves of last year's vegetables, never dug out of the ground.

Though his eyes were dimmer than they had been, he saw a figure approaching the rickety gate, and his heart leaped in his chest.

'Isabelle,' he shouted joyfully, rushing as fast as he was able, to open the door.

He was on the cinder path, the chill wind whipping his white hair, when he saw that it wasn't his wife but a man in a tattered uniform approaching.

For a dreadful moment he thought his hide-away had been discovered by the authorities, and he was about to be arrested.

But it was only the pot-man from the village public house, who delivered the post when there was any to deliver, which was a rarity in the God-forsaken hole.

With little more than a nod of his grizzled head, Jon-Joe, the name now came to him, handed him a small envelope. From habit, Lord Harvey stuck his hand in his coat pocket to offer the man a coin, but his pocket was empty all except an old theatre ticket. God knows how long it had been in there, he thought, giving the man a nod in recompense.

Used to such disappointments, Jon-Joe turned away, the holey sole of his boots clacking on the stones and cinders that made up the untidy path.

Shoulders humped in embarrassment and distress, Lord Harvey retreated into the cold interior of the cottage. Searching for his ancient pince-nez, finding them on the table-top, he sat to read the missive.

It was from Madoc, Tommy's solicitor. Lord Harvey's first thought was that it was a promise of money. Thrilled, his heart did a slightly uncomfortable lurch.

Opening the paper fully, he read of the death of his wife, drowned in the Menai Strait. The funeral had already taken place. Without funds to bury her, Lady Isabelle rested in a pauper's grave in the church of Saint Mary in Caernarvon.

Tears filled his eyes and it was impossible to read the good solicitor's condolences.

Lord Harvey remembered the church, an ancient and pretty building, close enough to the quay to hear the rushing water and tidal flow of the Menai Strait.

'Oh, my poor Issy,' he muttered in deep distress. 'For all eternity she will hear the song of her killer.'

The letter fell to the floor, and he wept with utter sorrow.

Chapter 5

The following week the weather gradually deteriorated, and by Friday a fine drizzle veiled the mountains in grey mist. The lawns at Plas Mawr were sodden, the rose blooms in the deep borders laden with rainwater and drooping. There was a chill in the air, and the level of light hadn't increased since the lacklustre sunrise.

In the dim breakfast room, sitting over a last cup of coffee, Tommy read Madoc's latest letter.

Lady Isabelle's funeral had gone without a hitch, he wrote in his own hand. The clergyman, though reluctant to bury her in consecrated ground, had recapitulated at the last moment on hearing that her ladyship was the victim of an unfortunate accident and not guilty of the crime of suicide.

A handful of mourners had attended: the woman who witnessed Lady Isabelle leaving the office, and a couple of harridans, no doubt expecting a wake and free food and drink.

Naturally, London aristocrats had shunned the church service, which was to be expected. Lord and Lady Harvey were bankrupts, and disgraced by poverty.

Tommy agreed with the sentiment.

A letter had been sent to Lord Harvey explaining his wife's demise and the circumstances, as it was impracticable to send someone to the back-of-beyond to convey the news in person.

Madoc added a postscript. Reading it, Tommy's face flushed with anger.

For Madoc had written that Frank Standish was now employed by the Quarrymen's Union, and was spending his time between the headquarters in Caernarvon, and recruiting quarrymen in the Halfway ale house. Joe Standish's cottage was also being used as an enrolment office.

Anger flushed his face, and he rose from the table.

A footman standing beside the sideboard flinched as the master, looking like the devil himself, passed him.

Without uttering a word, Tommy turned towards the door and flung it open. Once through he released it violently and it swung back banging into the wall. It slammed closed with a crack and the footman jumped sharply, his heart pattering urgently in his chest.

Gingerly, ears pricked for the master's return, he went to inspect the damage and found a four inch gouge in the blue silk wall covering. The white plaster beneath it was crushed and broken, and a sprinkling of white powder had landed on the carpet.

In the kitchen, unaware of the disturbance, the butler, Miles, was brushing the lapels of his uniform jacket. Hearing the master's strident voice summoning, he thrust his arms into the sleeves and ran into the corridor fastening the buttons. Reaching the door which led into the great hall he slowed, but as he passed through, his manner and facial expression went from rushed panic to orderly command.

It was easy to see that something had upset the master; his face was dark with anger, and minions were doing their utmost not to meet his eyes.

Sighing inwardly, Miles strode purposefully toward him.

Hardly glancing his way, Tommy snapped, 'I want the new carriage brought round immediately.'

Miles dipped his head reverentially. 'I will send someone to the coach-house immediately, sir.' Turning his head, he beckoned to an underling.

Annoyed, Tommy frowned. 'Speak to the servant when I have finished giving you instructions.'

Embarrassed to be reprimanded in the hearing of inferior servants, Miles flushed a pale shade of raspberry. 'I beg your pardon, sir.'

Ignoring the apology, Tommy said brusquely, 'Send someone for my grey coat, and hat.' Turning on his heel, he made his way to the library, for no other reason than he couldn't abide waiting in the grand hall with gormless servants gawping at him.

It was annoying to have to wait for the carriage. Normally, if he required the vehicle, he would have sent a message to the coach-house. But Madoc's post-script had thrown his usual routine out of kilter.

Today he had planned to travel to Ruby Quarry to check the progress of the laying of further rail tracks. But he had changed his mind on learning what Frank and his father were up to. His destination was now Garddryn Quarry. Later in the day he would ride to Corn Cottage and have it out with his father once and for all.

He had no doubt that Frank was relishing his new position and bragging to everyone that he had got one over on the master of the Garddryn and Ruby Quarries.

For his entire life, Frank had soaked up the admiration and attention his parents and heaped on him. Sacking him was supposed to send him to Parys Mountain where he would heave copper fumes from his lungs at the finish of every working day. Instead, the bastard still had his feet under the table at Corn Cottage, and was being waited on hand and foot by their jointly owned mother. He'd had more than enough of Frank. There had to be a way to get rid of him once and for all.

An image of George, beaten literally senseless, came into his mind. But common-sense prevailed he wouldn't get away with doing something like that again. There would be a hue and cry from his parents if anything untoward happened to precious Frank. Plas Mawr would be over-run with the constabulary.

Another solution came to him and, grinning, he mouthed, 'Perfect.'

Going to the desk he wrote a hurried message and sealed it. He gave two short tugs on the bell-pull to summon a servant.

A moment later the door opened and an underling stood nervously on the threshold. Tommy was brusque. 'Go to the constabulary office and give this letter to Cameron Chamberlain. If you have to leave it with anyone else, tell them it's urgent. Do you understand?'

The wheels of the coach sounded on the gravel.

With the servant despatched, Tommy came from behind the desk. Opening the mahogany bureau, he replenished his cigar case.

His mind was on Cameron Chamberlain. The man had been useful in the past, mainly because he could be bought. As soon as silver crossed his palm, the men of his constabulary would take care of Frank Standish. Frank would find it impossible to conduct union business from a prison cell. When the young lout's name was dragged through the mud, the union bosses would oust him from his new position.

Smiling thinly, he left the library.

Coming into the great hall, he felt the chill of the vast place on his cheeks. The outside door was ajar, wet air wafting in. There was the sound of rain falling on the stone steps, and a gutter trickling water.

A manservant stood close to the arch of the architrave, holding the grey coat. Tommy slipped his arms into the sleeves. The bristles of a silver backed brush passed across the collar and shoulders. Someone else handed him his hat. Tommy took it without acknowledgment.

The valet slipped outdoors. Standing on the topmost step he unfurled a black umbrella. With the master sheltering beneath it, the pair trotted down the steps to the waiting carriage.

The vehicle gave a jerk as the two mares started out. On the avenue, rain dripped from the drenched trees, falling on the carriage rooftop with tiny splatters. Inside was clammy, smelling of damp leather and old floor boards. Wet weather usually depressed him but with the prospect of retribution for Frank, he hardly noticed the leaden sky and ceaseless rain.

Iwan Rees, the office manager, was in the front office instructing one of the clerks, as the Plas Mawr vehicle came to a standstill at the front door.

Iwan gave a long drawn out sigh. Dreading the discussion he must have with Tommy Standish concerning his brother, Frank. There would be ructions and idiotic decisions would be made. Everyone, quarrymen and office staff, would be faced with uncertainty and possible reprisals.

He sighed again. If the master had not insisted upon sacking his younger brother recently, Frank would still be working in the cutting shed and not recruiting union members every hour God sent. Although it was all Tommy Standish's fault, he wouldn't be the one suffering the consequences.

The main door opened, and Tommy came in bringing damp air and the smell of cigar smoke on his coat.

Tentatively Iwan took a step towards him. 'Good morning, Mr Standish,' he said trying to sound cheerful.

Ignoring the greeting, Tommy snapped, 'Be in my office in five minutes, Rees. We have important things to discuss.'

'Of course, Mr Standish,' Iwan Rees said. But Tommy had already turned towards his office, and the words were spoken to his back.

Iwan Rees sighed again. What he wouldn't give to be back with his former employer. This was the first thought he had every morning on rising, and the last before he closed his eyes at night. Not that sleep came easily. A good night's rest was a thing of the past. Now he always felt as though he was clinging to a cliff-face by his nails. Mentally he counted down the seconds, and then checked his pocket watch. He sighed. Four minutes were up already. With a bend in his neck, he went towards the master's office and knocked on the door.

Tommy hardly glanced up. 'I'm expecting Cameron Chamberlain. I would appreciate it if you made yourself scarce when he arrives,' he said, as Iwan came to the desk.

The manager wondered what Chamberlain and Tommy Standish had in common. But then he had heard rumours that Chamberlain didn't refuse inducements if offered.

It came to him that the master was already familiar with the news of his brother's involvement with the union. It would make his job easier if he wasn't the bearer of such unwelcome news. He waited for Tommy to broach the subject.

Elbows on the desktop, and hands together as though in prayer, Tommy met Iwan Rees's eyes. 'The unions are very active in the quarry. What are you doing about it?'

Iwan's heart lurched. So he wasn't to be spared a difficult

meeting. 'Short of threatening the men, I don't see what can be done.'

'And have you tried?'

'I don't see that it would do much good. These days, the workers are quite at liberty to join a union.'

Tommy rose. He glanced out of the window. 'Liberty and workers are two words that should not go together.'

Sensing he was on shaky ground, Iwan selected his words carefully. 'How do you suggest we solve the problem?'

'I suggest you get the team leaders and quarry steward here and you tell them that if the workers want a union they go elsewhere for employment. If that fails, break a few heads. Get some of the Irish from Ruby Quarry to explain to the Garddryn men what's expected of them.'

Iwan felt bile rise into his throat as indigestion returned. He thought of Joe Standish; he wasn't a man to take this attitude lying down. The men would down tools for the man, although in the past Joe had used his influence to keep them in work, turning the men aside from an inevitable lock-out.

Iwan Rees gave a small nervous cough. 'I'll call a meeting with them for noon-time.'

'Good. No point them losing working time. Send someone to find the steward. He can rouse the team leaders. We'll have the whole lot of them in here at noon and tell them what to expect if they don't comply with quarry rules.'

Iwan hid a sigh. 'I'll do it now.'

Tommy began a litany of the troubles he had endured from ungrateful workers demanding the impossible.

Iwan stood patiently, staring at the pale green wall behind Tommy's head, thoughts of fleeing to foreign climes running through his mind.

Falling silent, Tommy stared at his manager.

When Iwan made no reply, Tommy spoke clearly as though talking to a ten-year-old. 'Do you have a better idea?'

'Your solution is sound.' Iwan flushed pink telling the lie.

Tommy was brusque. 'Then get on with it.'

Deferential, Iwan took a slow step backwards, and then turned to leave the room. Once through the door, he made for the clerk's office. He would send one of the young men to find the steward, Rees Roberts.

Tommy heard the wheels of a vehicle. Craning his neck he got a glimpse of a black Landau, its leather hood up, driving between the stone gateposts.

Thinking aloud, he said, 'Watch out Frank! You're about to get your come-uppance.' He smiled, pleased.

The vehicle came to a standstill at the main entrance.

The drenched driver jumped down, rainwater dripping from the black mackintosh. Opening the door he reached into the cab and brought out a black umbrella; unfurling it, he stood aside for Cameron Chamberlain to alight.

Tommy rose from his chair. Straightening the hem of his long jacket, he went over to the bureau and took out a brandy decanter and two snifters. The cut-glass clinked as he placed it on the corner of the desk. He had left instructions with a clerk to send Chamberlain to the office immediately on his arrival, so he wasn't surprised to hear only one pair of footsteps in the hallway.

The door opened, and Cameron strode in. Hatless, he ran his hand over his damp hair to flatten it. 'Foul day,' he said cheerfully, pushing the door closed.

Cameron's posture was faultless. The immaculate dark blue uniform sat well on his slim frame. Tommy noticed the meticulousness of his closely clipped side-whiskers, and surmised that the police captain had come straight from the barber's shop.

Offering his hand, Tommy smiled.

'It's been a while,' Cameron said, returning the smile.

Going to the desk, Tommy lifted the decanter. 'Not too early for a snifter?'

'Just a small one,' Cameron said, indicated a tiny quantity with his finger and thumb.

Cameron knew the brandy would be delicious, the best. Tommy Standish didn't stint on his pleasures. Envy, he reminded himself, was an unattractive sentiment. Opulent extravagance, he conceded with amusement, brought the worst out in him. He feared that inadvertently he may have smiled, and he checked Tommy's expression, but the man was still relaxed, standing with his arms crossed, resting the brandy balloon in the crook of his elbow.

'I don't think you know my brother, Frank?' Tommy said matter-of-factly.

Cameron had heard the name often enough, and he was aware that there was bad blood between the brothers. He was astute enough to say nothing of this. But his curiosity was aroused.

'No, I haven't had the pleasure,' he said blandly.

Tommy smirked. 'There's no pleasure to be had. The man is a damn nuisance.'

Hitching one trouser leg, Tommy perched on the corner of the desk and motioned Cameron to take the upholstered chair.

Somewhat hampered by the unyielding material of his

uniform, and high collar, Cameron sat uneasily.

Glancing at the man's glass, Tommy saw that Cameron had almost downed the large brandy. Too soon to offer him more; the man would refuse, and ruin the rapport of the moment.

Confident that the police captain was now in the right frame of mind, Tommy launched into an account of recent troubles.

'Last week Frank gave me reason to sack him. It went against my better nature to get rid of a member of my family, but time and time again Frank attended quarrymen's union meetings. I can't tell you how many times I warned him that he was giving me no option but to sack him.' He sighed like a man wronged. 'But he wouldn't listen. In the end I had no choice.'

The debacle at the quarry hadn't escaped Cameron's notice. He knew that the one man to lose his job was Frank Standish, a slate cutter. Tommy's version of events differed drastically to the tale he himself had been told.

Moving off the desk, Tommy stood. The hand at his side was a balled fist, and his face was flushed. 'Now to cap it all, he is working for the union, and actually recruiting workers at the quarry gates.'

Cameron swirled the last drop of brandy around the glass. 'I can understand why you are annoyed.'

Tommy resisted the urge to shout, 'Annoyed!'

Determined to show nothing but a calm façade, he went on, 'Frank has been in my employ since he was a lad. In all of that time not once has he told me how grateful he is, and now this, complete betrayal.'

Although he thought the word betrayal a gross exaggeration, Cameron kept his own counsel. Give a man enough rope and he'll hang himself, being his favourite motto, was the one he lived by.

The calm Tommy was so anxious to achieve began to desert him. 'Quarrymen's union meeting are being held in the Halfway public house. Men are gathering in significant numbers to discuss union membership, and I want it stopped. And I want it stopped quickly. The men should be brought to book for holding meetings in public places.'

Cameron measured his words carefully. 'I'm afraid it is no longer illegal to hold meetings. Gone are the days of unlawful assembly, when men could be stopped from gathering in groups of more than four, either in the street or a public place. Now they have a right of combination, a right to organise themselves.'

Tommy scoffed, 'Right of combination! Rights belong to the people employing the buggers.'

Cameron chose to be placatory. 'The union is in its infancy. There's every chance it will fail.'

Patience deserted Tommy and his true feeling came to the fore. 'Failure will not come fast enough. I want Frank stopped now. Surely you can put him behind bars on some trumped up charge. Caernarvon has at least a dozen unsolved burglaries on the books, put Frank's name to those. I'll guarantee that your financial reward will far exceed the trouble it takes.'

The idea of clearing up the outstanding aggravated burglaries, and getting paid to do it, was tempting. But Cameron was beginning to see that Tommy Standish was dangerous and his thinking askew. If he agreed to arrest Frank, how long would it be before he himself became a Standish victim? There were rumours concerning Tommy Standish's spectacular rise to fortune and the heavy-handed methods he had used.

The man was treacherous, and not to be trusted. It was

essential that he leave Plas Mawr on friendly terms and not as a new enemy.

Rising out of the chair, he closed the gap between them.

Glancing at the closed door, hinting at possible eavesdroppers, Cameron kept his voice low. 'Take care that any accusation you may throw at Frank, doesn't come back to bite you. There are people who will do their utmost to protect him, not just his parents, but the union, and quarrymen. Between them they will dig deep into the past and rake up old allegations. Questions will have to be answered again. No one, however wealthy and influential, is above the law or safe from the gallows. '

A sickness filled Tommy's belly. Had Cameron Chamberlain guessed the true nature of Henrietta's death?

Millie Barker's name and image flew through his mind and for a moment he was back in the old mill, Millie lying beneath him, struggling as he dragged her skirt up to her waist and thrust into her as though his very life depended on a rapid orgasm.

He caught Cameron's eyes and saw that the man was watching him closely, too closely. In attempting to implicate Frank he had drawn attention to himself and was now probably in a dangerous position.

His mind swept back to his youth and the dreadful moment when Twm Tomos, the special constable, came to the old cottage and questioned him about Millie's disappearance and death. That night he had seen doubt of his innocence in his father's eyes, and it remained to this day.

Cameron's voice startled him. 'Some advice, Tommy, the case of the attempted murder of George Bellamy is still not closed. Rumour has it that it may be re-opened in the near future. This may be embarrassing as the callous act happened at Plas

Mawr gateway. It would be foolish to seek new enemies with this hanging over the house.'

The realisation that Cameron knew about George was a shock. Tommy pushed his hands into his trouser pockets to hide the tremor in his fingers.

Standing, Cameron put the empty glass on the desktop. 'Take my advice, Tommy.'

Tommy forced a smile. 'It was good of you to come. I appreciate your help.'

'I'm glad I was able to give it. If I hear anything more about re-opening the case of George Bellamy I'll let you know.'

With the man's footsteps in his ear, Tommy sank into the seat behind his desk.

Glancing though the window, he saw the rain was still falling.

Cameron's Landau was at the front steps, the horse as wet as the driver. Cameron boarded. The vehicle started out immediately. Tommy watched it driving down the avenue. When it was out of sight, he poured another brandy. Cameron's words had left him numb, numb and afraid. It wasn't often that he felt vulnerable, and he didn't like being so.

At noon, after drinking another glass or two of brandy, he called for the brougham to be brought round to the front entrance. He was returning to Plas Mawr. The idea that had come to him earlier, of visiting Corn Cottage to give his father a piece of his mind, was now a burning necessity.

Donning his black hat and outdoor coat, he braved the worsening weather. Heavy rain was slanting down from a leaden sky the colour of a bruise. Making a dash for the open door of the vehicle, he slipped, and just saved himself from a muddy soaking by grabbing at the doorframe, breaking a nail to the quick painfully.

Cursing, he climbed aboard, splattering droplets of water onto the leather seat, leaving marks like small blots of ink.

The vehicle moved forward, and as if on cue, rain hit the roof like hail. The glazed forward window streamed water, the driver's coat was a grey shadow on the pane.

Once through the stone gate-posts, the vehicle picked up speed, either the horse or driver anxious to get the atrocious journey finished with. The body of the brougham swayed drunkenly between the leather springs, the wheels jarring with a crack as it hit potholes. Tommy held onto the edge of the seat; he had no intention of lowering the window to shout to the driver to slow down, and get wet through for his trouble.

It had been his aim to use the travelling time to go over Cameron Chamberlain's words of warning, but the movement was too rough to concentrate on anything but snippets. By the time the vehicle reached the avenue at Plas Mawr, he had come to the conclusion that the Cameron was bluffing. The man had no new evidence to connect him to the attack on George, or Millie Barker's death.

Perhaps it wasn't only Frank that should be removed from the scene. Cameron Chamberlain was too much of a liability to remain in his job as police captain.

The house was ahead; even seen through the rain it had the power to send his blood racing through his veins, just as it had when he was a boy seeing it through a pauper's eyes. Then he had yearned body and soul to make it his. Success had come at a price. Bertram Bellamy, Louise, Henrietta, George, Isabelle, Millie, and others had paid it.

The rain had ceased by six o'clock. Putting aside a brandy

snifter, Tommy called for his favourite mare to be brought to the door. The ride through the lanes to Corn Cottage was uneventful, save for a few quarrymen refusing to salute him as he passed.

Another mile and he saw a light shining in the window of his parents' home; it was probably the glow of a roaring fire, drying out quarry clothes drenched by the ceaseless rain.

His mother would be pleased to see him. It was the only welcome he expected. His father hated him too much for anything but a begrudged word. The old man was another bugger who showed no gratitude.

In truth it was his father's fault that Henrietta had succumbed to the final dose of opium, for on that fateful day he had made her welcome at Corn Cottage. Henrietta had ignored his own orders forbidding her to visit his parents and had gone there with baby Edward. Returning to Plas Mawr in the early evening she had looked relaxed and happy until the moment she was made aware that he had discovered her defiance. The consequent row had been violent. Henrietta had died that same night.

Chapter 6

The day before Frank's and Nora's wedding was muggy with approaching rain; wet grey clouds veiled the mountain peaks. The gentle slopes of the valleys were countless shades of dark green with pewter rivers snaking towards the sea.

Throughout the morning Emily looked to the patch of sky seen though the kitchen window and tut-tutted at the vagaries of the Welsh mountain weather. For weeks the summer heat had been relentless, and almost everyone was lobster pink with sunburn. Now, with the wedding only a day away, rain threatened and the guests and bride were likely to get soaked walking to the village chapel.

The weather was hardly likely to spoil appetites so for several hours she had been baking bread, kneading dough till her hands ached, watching it rise to plump and elastic roundness and ready for the heat of the oven.

Joe was at the quarry, working a usual day. She would have preferred him to be at home helping with the preparations, and running errands. But it wasn't in Joe's nature to take a day off work. Though she thought his keenness today had more to do with escaping domestic chores.

Glancing at the mantel clock, she saw that it was already three o'clock, and she hadn't even cut the garden flowers to make the posy that Nora was to carry to the church. Joe had asked for an identical one to take to Chloe's grave.

She didn't dare dwell on memories of her tiny pansy-eyed daughter buried beneath the soil of a mountainside cemetery and especially today, her thoughts must focus on Frank and the happiness he would enjoy tomorrow. But brushing the past aside was impossible and in her mind's eye she saw Chloe in a pale blue dress walking with Frank towards the chapel to make his vows to Nora. Sniffing back tears, Emily placed three more loaves into the hot bread oven and closed the door quickly.

Again she glanced at the clock and saw it was half past three and started to panic as she hadn't begun making the fancy pastries. Taking a brown mixing bowl from the shelf in the scullery she half-filled it with flour, dropping a chunk of lard and salt into the mix.

At the end of the working day Joe left the quarry to walk home, but he found it impossible to by-pass the Halfway Inn with so many quarrymen, mates, wanting to buy him ale in celebration of his younger son's wedding. Grinning, happy that the marriage was going ahead despite Tommy's interference, Joe strode into the noisy ale house with them.

Emily stirred the cowheel stew simmering on the hob.

The outside door opened and Frank bowled in, his new suit wrapped in paper draped over his arm.

'Where's Nora?' Emily asked, expecting four for supper.

Frank stripped the brown paper from the suit. 'What do you think, Mam?' His eyes lit. 'Smart?'

Wiping her hands on her apron, Emily crossed to him. 'It looks good, Frank. The dark grey will look good with your colouring.'

Frank smoothed his red-brown hair with the flat of his hand. 'There's a silk shirt an' all,' he said, pulling another package from beneath the suit.

'You've been spending,' Emily smiled aware that Frank had been paid a good dividend for the new members he'd signed up for the Quarrymen's Union.

'It's once in a lifetime,' he said eyeing the suit, imagining wearing it to chapel tomorrow.

Emily hugged him. 'I'm so proud of you, our Frank. You've made a real go of the new job.'

'There's a lot more to do yet, Mam. Come Monday I'm going to Bethesda to sign more men up. The union is growing fast. Quarry owners will have to accept the changes, and the unions.'

A frown settled on Emily's brow. 'Our Tommy will never accept a union. He'll fight it and probably lose the Garddryn and Ruby. In the end the men may suffer.'

'If the quarries go under, investors will move in and keep production going. The quarrymen will not lose, Mam. It's the bad managers like Tommy that will fail, and good riddance.'

'Let's not talk about it today, Frank. Hang up your suit. I want to show you what I have cooked for tomorrow.'

'Give me two minutes,' he said, dashing off to his bedroom.

Glancing at the clock, seeing that it was well past Joe's normal time to arrive home from work she guessed he had stopped off at the Halfway Inn. Slightly cross, as she had particularly asked him to come straight home, she moved the pot of stew to the back of the range to keep warm.

Another hour passed before she heard his steps on the garden path. Slightly abashed at being late, he made a show of wiping his feet on the doormat.

'Your dinner's keeping warm under a plate,' Emily said a little crossly. 'Frank and me have had ours.'

He gave his feet another quick wipe before stepping off the doormat. 'Sorry Emily. Time ran away while I was talking to the lads.'

She sniffed. 'That lot haven't been lads for more than thirty years.'

'Still act like it though,' he said, grinning sheepishly.

'Aye, and you do, Joe. Now take off your boots and sit down to table. I'll get you your supper.'

He leaned towards her to plant a kiss on her cheek, and then thought better of it. 'I'll trot out to the privy first. The Halfway ale never stays put for long.' He went out in a rush, undoing the buttons on his trouser flies before he made it to the privy shed.

Hearing the privy door slam closed, Emily gave a thought to the rickety hinge.

He came back in just as she was lifting the plate of food off the pan of simmering water. 'It'll not be as good as it was,' she said, carrying it to the table. 'It never is when it's sat over a pan keeping hot.'

Joe was almost afraid to ask about her day. The house hummed with the smell of baked pastry and new bread and there was a sweet fragrance of fruit jam and spun sugar. Emily was a champion at concocting wondrous creations from a pan of hot sugar and a wooden stick.

The room was silent but for the clink of the fork on the plate, and the embers of the fire collapsing into the hot ashes.

Joe swallowed several more mouthfuls before looking at her. 'Where's our Frank?'

Emily tut-tutted. 'Gone down to see Nora, though he said he wouldn't be late, he's having an early night.'

'Hope he doesn't think he's escaping to his bed on the eve of his wedding before he's had a glass of whisky with his old father.'

'I shouldn't think so, Joe. He'll want a natter with you before tomorrow.'

The cutlery in his hand clattered to the plate. 'What about, not the blooming birds and bees malarkey?'

'I shouldn't think so, Joe. He'll know all about that by now.'

He looked askance. 'Are you saying that he and Nora have been...?'

Emily tut-tutted. 'I'm saying nowt about it, Joe. But the lad is twenty-six, and that's late to be marrying. Anyway it'll make no odds tomorrow, as they'll be a married couple.'

'It will be strange having someone else living in the house,' he said, looking around the familiar room. 'It's been just us three for so long now.'

'Aye and likely there'll be more than four of us soon enough,' Emily said, folding her apron and putting it across the bar on the range with the damp tea-towels.

'You don't think young Nora's expecting?'

'Joe, your imagination is running away with you. Of course I don't think Nora's anything but a good lass. Not two minutes ago you were worrying that Frank didn't know the ins-and-outs of marriage.'

Joe grinned widely and then started to laugh. 'That's funny Emily, the ins-and-outs of marriage.'

She tried to look stern but then began to giggle.

The front door opened and Frank walked in to find both parents laughing uncontrollably.

Looking blankly at them he said, 'What's so funny?'

Clutching each other, Emily and Joe laughed louder.

Moments passed before they released the other's arms.

Still giggling and sighing, Emily wiped her wet eyes on the sleeve of her frock. 'It was just an old joke. We weren't laughing at you, lad.'

Joe nearly relapsed at this, but pulling himself together he too wiped his eyes. 'Excitement got the better of us. That's all.'

'Like a pair of kids sometimes,' Frank said, slipping out of his jacket.

'Well, what about a glass of whisky to celebrate the wedding?' Joe said, going to the dresser and taking a bottle from the small cupboard. 'You'll have one with us, Emily?'

'Aye, that'd be nice. I'll fetch a drop of lemonade from the scullery to mix with it.'

Joe knew immediately that it was lemonade that he'd smelled on entering the house; Emily would have made several jugs of it for the ladies coming to tomorrow's celebrations.

Frank sipped the whisky. 'Do you think the weather will improve overnight? Nora is really worried that everyone will get wet and her new dress will be spoilt.'

Emily caught the end of the conversation as she came back into the room. 'There's never been a bride that didn't worry about the weather on the Big Day. I just looked out the window and it seems to be brightening over the sea.'

Joe didn't mention that she had looked in the wrong direction; the weather was coming from the south, not north.

At Plas Mawr Tommy discontentedly paced the floor of the library. Images of his parents and the bridegroom celebrating at the cottage devilled his thoughts. Up until an hour ago he had half-expected his mother to yield and send someone with an invitation, but with night closing in it became obvious that no such visitor was paying a call. It rankled that he was ignored. That he would have refused to attend, and done so rudely, barely crossed his aggrieved mind.

On a sudden whim he sent a message to the Baron at Penrhyn

Castle inviting him for dinner at the Three Eagles in Bangor on the following evening. When eventually the groom sent to deliver the message returned with the reply, Tommy was delighted to discover an invitation to dine and stay the following night at Penrhyn Castle. An image of Sadie, naked, straddled across a crumpled bed cover came into his mind and his manhood stirred pleasurably against silken undergarments.

He didn't need to search the shelves for his most read book: it was exactly where he'd left it. Taking it down, blowing imaginary dust off the edges of the top papers, he sat at his desk and opening the green leather cover read the first lines of the novel Justine, penned by Marquis de Sade.

Tommy's mind flipped back to Justine as Sadie crept through his bedroom door the following night. The serving wench looked scared, as though she had seen a ghost in the dark corridors she was forced to negotiate to get to the guest room. Reclining on the bed until the door opened, languidly he rose. The neck of his shirt open, and tie draped around the stiff white collar.

Weeks had passed since they had been together, and she saw that the tan on his face had faded and the laughter lines, the tiny crinkles at the corner of his eyes, were no longer very evident.

In a timid way she returned his smile, her eyes filled with tears.

In an almost loving gesture his one arm circled her shoulders pulling her close, and he kissed the soft fullness of her lips lightly.

She was glad to be with him but terrified of the outcome of the encounter, and prayed that she could stay silent until the first light of morning, when she would be forced to rise and creep to the kitchen to stoke the range.

Jiggling the hem of her skirt up, he revealed the nakedness of her abdomen, thighs, and legs. Perhaps that is why, he thought fleetingly, he so liked tupping a servant wench: the poor rarely wore drawers. The once lovely, and now dead, Lady Isabelle had always been so encumbered with petticoats, pantaloons, stays, ties, ribbons, crinolines and whatever else, that it took two women to peel off her shell of haute couture.

Moving his hand from her shoulder, he unbuttoned the back of her dress and let it slip to the floor. Turning her away from him, he gripped her waist firmly. Sadie knew what to expect and bit her lip to stop the wince of pain being heard. It was for Tommy's pleasure that he kept her waiting for long moments; anticipating the inevitable, her entire body was held taut whilst he delayed. It proved impossible for Sadie not to give a little cry as he clouted her buttocks with a stinging slap, a second following swiftly. With each smack she told herself she loved him and would do anything just to see and spend time with him.

A false dawn lit the edges around the heavy curtains, and Sadie awoke from a light troubled sleep. Tommy stirred and she remained still, hardly breathing. If she woke him now he would be cross and not take the news that she was pregnant with his child kindly. Glancing down into his handsome face it was impossible not to trace the line of his lips with her fingertips. Tommy woke with a start and he looked angry, and then his face softened and he reached out to her. Mistaking the expression for love, she found the courage to blurt out her news.

Stunned Tommy jolted up, the bed-sheet falling away from him. 'You can't put the bastard at my door,' he said venomously. 'I haven't been near you for weeks. It could be any one of the stable lads.'

Climbing off the bed he fought his way into his trousers. Keeping his back to her, he flung on the shirt discarded on the floor the previous night.

Scrambling off the feather mattress, Sadie came to him, flinging her arms around his waist. 'Tommy, I swear the child is yours. I'm more than three months gone. I have never been with anyone but you. I love you with all my heart.' Near hysteria, tears streamed down her face.

'A bloody likely tale,' he said, throwing on his coat.

'Tommy, please do not go like this,' she cried. 'The Baron will be angry and guess that there is something amiss.'

Her words cooled him. She was correct. He couldn't leave the castle without a word.

His eyes flashed to her. For the moment he was cornered but at breakfast he would give the Baron a tale about her and ensure that she was sacked.

'Bring me some coffee,' he said churlishly.

'Of course,' she replied with a small curtsy. Going to a chair she picked up her apron.

'No need for that,' he said shortly. 'It is still early there'll be no one around to see you. We can have a little chat when you come back and see what is to be done.'

She tried not to smile, but the relief running through her was heady enough to make her heart beat faster. 'I'll be right back,' she said gleefully.

'Bring a cup for you too. We can sit together and make our plans.'

Bubbling with excitement, the time to see the interior of Plas Mawr growing ever closer, Sadie went down the stairs in a headlong rush, her hand holding her belly where her precious cargo, the child that would grow up in the mansion Plas Mawr, lay oblivious of his shining future.

Tommy swallowed the coffee quickly. Getting up off the chair, going to the window he looked out. Behind him Sadie sat with her hands clasped on her skirt waiting for the announcement she was sure he would make.

'I'll come back tomorrow and collect you,' he said, his breath misting the cold pane of glass. 'Just give notice and be at the main gate at two-thirty. I will be angry if anyone discovers why you are leaving. If it's mentioned when I return I will refuse to take you, do you understand?'

'Yes! I understand, Tommy.'

Turning, he frowned. 'Mind that you do! Now go downstairs and work as normal until tomorrow.'

Standing on tip-toe she kissed his lips and then smiled.

She was gone in a moment. Tommy listened to her tripping down the stairs. Then he turned to wash his hands and face in the hot water she had carried up from the kitchen in a ewer.

Tommy was quiet at breakfast. Several times Edward asked him if there was a problem. But not until the breakfast dishes had been removed and Tommy's horse stood at the main door with a stable lad did he broach the problem.

Eyes downcast, Tommy moderated his voice. 'I don't know how to say this, Edward. But in all the time, the years, I have been visiting Penrhyn there has never been a problem with one of your staff. It pains me now to report an incident that I do not feel I can ignore.'

'Go on,' Edward replied softly.

'Last night one of the servant girls came to my room, flung

herself at me. Of course I got rid of the wench. I have too much respect for you and your home to have it differently.'

Edward shifted uncomfortably in his leather chair.

'This morning, very early, the girl came back with a ewer of hot water. I thought it strange as it wasn't a usual pottery jug reserved for the house but a kitchen variety. She put it down on the washstand and when she had gone, curious I rose from the bed to take a closer look and discovered a ruby cufflink was missing.'

'And which of the girls was it?' Edward asked, embarrassed.

'I have heard you call her Sadie,' Tommy said without a qualm.

Rising, Edward went to the door and walked through it. Tommy heard his steps go in the direction of the kitchen. Muffled words came from that direction and then he returned with Sadie in tow. She looked surprised and a little afraid.

Sitting again, Edward said, 'Sadie, I want you to empty your pockets.'

With her questioning eyes on Tommy, she did as she was bid. Her face changed to one of surprise and incomprehension when her fingers discovered a small object in her apron pocket; pulling it out she held it between her finger and thumb, and then put the glistening red gem on the table.

Snatching it up, Tommy slipped it through his shirt cuff.

Rising from the table, the legs of his chair tugging on the wool carpet, he nodded to Edward. 'I'm sorry I had to raise this unpleasantness. I will contact you in a week or so. Perhaps we can dine together at the club?' Without glancing at Sadie, he turned away.

Her bleak eyes followed his retreating figure.

Edward rose in a hurry. Touching Sadie's arm he said quietly, 'Wait here.'

In a few strides he caught up with Tommy, and then walked with him to the main door. Neither spoke until they were outside and then with a cool farewell Edward turned back to go indoors. Stunned by the sudden and unexpected shattering of her dreams, Sadie stood with head bent and shoulders shaking with her tears.

Edward strode back into the breakfast room. There wasn't a doubt in his mind that Tommy Standish had more to do with the situation than he had revealed. Proud to the point of narcissism, Standish would consider it a matter of honour to take revenge if the girl had refused him.

Anxious to clear one of his servants from the taint of theft, he came to Sadie. 'Sit down and tell me exactly what has happened. I want the truth, Sadie. I will not abide lies or embellishments.'

With her wet eyes on him, Sadie sat cautiously on the edge of the chair that Tommy had vacated only moments before. 'I didn't take it,' she sniffled. 'I don't know how it got into my apron pocket.'

'Did you leave the apron somewhere?' Edward coaxed.

Sadie's eyes flashed to his and she gave an almost imperceptible nod.

'Where was it left?'

In her mind Sadie saw the garment draped over the chair in the guestroom Tommy had used.

'Well,' Edward said. 'Where did you leave it?'

'In Tommy's room,' Sadie whispered, the truth dawning on her.

Tommy's words came back to him. 'Last night one of the servant girls came to my room and flung herself at me. Of course

117

I got rid of the wench. I have too much respect for you and your home to have it differently.'

Edward sighed. 'So you went to his bedroom. If your apron was left there, he must have let you in?'

'Yes,' she answered hollowly.

'Sadie, I want the truth. Has this happened before? Has Mr Standish asked you to stay with him on any other occasion?'

Her face contorted with tears, and she nodded.

He gave a long, drawn out sigh.

It didn't occur to Sadie to lie and words tumbled out unbidden. 'Every time he came here we spent the night together. I thought Tommy loved me. He said he would meet me at the main gate at two o'clock tomorrow and take me away with him.' Dipping her head to her lap she began to cry again.

Her statement baffled Edward; it was not the behaviour he associated with Standish. The man abhorred servants and their cloak of poverty. So why would he say he would take this kitchen maid away?

Thoughtful for a moment, he gave the girl time to blow her nose and compose herself. Then he said softly, 'Are you pregnant, Sadie?'

Fresh tears ran down her face, and she nodded that she was.

She searched his face for condemnation but saw a shadow of kindness and was ashamed. 'I'm so sorry. I never meant to bring trouble here. My father will kill me when he finds out. He'll kick me out as he's always threatened to do if I got in the family way. I might as well be dead.'

He leaned towards her and spoke calmly. 'Sadie there is always a solution to a problem.'

She sniffed. 'Not for mine. Tommy doesn't love me. I'm

having his baby, and me Ma and Pa will kill me if I don't do it first.'

He knew it wasn't logical but he felt partly responsible that this had happened to one of his servants in his employ and in his home. It had also been his guest that had brought the calamity down on this poor girl's head.

'I will help you, Sadie. So stop crying and let us find the solution I promised you. Firstly I want you to take the rest of the day off so you can rest.'

Sadie was about to protest but Edward silenced her with a wave of his hand.

'I will talk to the cook and housekeeper.' He gave her a small smile. 'Remember I'm the boss here. They will both heed my words.'

He took her hand in his. 'Tomorrow I want you to go home and ask both your parents to come and see me. I will break the news to them and ask them to take you home until the baby is born. They will not be out of pocket, I'll see to that. When you are well enough, if they agree to look after the child, you shall go to my house in London and work there.'

He made a mental note to corner Standish and demand a sum of money for the upkeep of the child and the mother.

'I don't know why you are being so kind to me but I thank you from the bottom of my heart,' she said softly.

'It's the least I can do. You have always been a good worker, Sadie.' He smiled. 'Until today, I would have said you were the most cheerful here.'

Shyly, she returned his smile. Then remembering where this had all begun, she said worriedly, 'What about the cufflink? Honestly, I didn't take it. Will you have to mention that to mother and father?'

He patted her hand. 'I do not need to discuss it with anyone. I'm pretty sure I know who the culprit is, and believe me, he will pay for his callousness.'

'Now,' he said, standing, 'I want you to go to your bedroom. I will have a word with the housekeeper and see that you are not disturbed for a few hours.'

Riding back to Plas Mawr, Tommy reflected on his morning's work and decided there was nothing to fear that his duplicity, the planting of the cufflink in the servant's apron, was likely ever to come to light. Edward no doubt went back into the breakfast room, where the wench had been bidden to remain, and sacked her on the spot. Sadie would not be given a chance to put her side of the story, and with luck she would now be trundling down the avenue carrying her meagre possessions in an old carpet bag.

Sure of this, he dismissed the problem from his mind. The day was too glorious to squander time on irrelevances. The sky, a beautiful azure blue, was almost cloudless and a light breeze was blowing off the Menai Strait carrying the scent of salt. The way beneath his grey horse was dry, making easy riding. Within an hour he would be trotting along the avenue at Plas Mawr in the dappled sunlight filtering through the rustling leaves of the lime trees.

Sadie should count her blessings; at least she isn't getting wet walking to wherever she's putting up for the night. He grinned. Sometime in the near future he would probably meet her plying the oldest trade on the streets of Bangor. If she was still comely, and not ruined by the pregnancy, he would give her a turn and put a few pennies in her purse, if she charged that much.

The idea made him laugh out loud. The horse's ears twitched nervously at the unfamiliar sound.

A fortnight passed before Edward and Tommy met up again at a music night held in a local dignitary's house on the outskirts of Bangor.

During an interval, when champagne was being served to the ladies and the gentlemen were enjoying brandies, Edward suggested going into the garden to Tommy.

The terrace windows were open and he and Tommy walked out side by side. There was a distinctive tang of coal smoke in the air and Edward glanced up into the twilight, but there was no haze from the numerous chimney stacks at the apex of the steep roof. A few bright stars were visible but they were obliterated for a moment by the flight of a large sea-bird, its luminous white wing span ghostly in the inky sky.

During the evening Tommy had noticed Edward's coolness; the Baron's attention had been easily drawn away to less well known acquaintances, and it seemed that at the slightest reason to withdraw from him the Baron had done so. This aloofness was disturbing for he considered the Baron to be a close friend, and he was aware that it added to his standing in the business community to be a frequent visitor at Penrhyn Castle and something of a favourite of Edward's.

Unease made Tommy brash. 'I hope you got rid of the wench that stole my cufflink without too much bother.'

Before he answered Edward took a cigar out of a leather humidor, and without offering one to Tommy lit it with a match. A trail of smoke escaped his mouth. 'I was rather disturbed when I listened to Sadie's side of the story.'

Though he sensed he was on shaky ground, Tommy couldn't

resist maligning the girl. 'I'm surprised you listened to a thief's tale of woe. After all, she's only a servant and they're ten a penny.'

'In my home,' Edward responded gravely, 'servants are respected for the work they contribute to the running of the house. I do not regard them as commodities to be thrust aside and left to starve when convenient to my mood.'

'Are you accusing me of such behaviour?' Tommy responded hotly.

'Accusing? No, I don't think so. I am just stating a fact,' Edward said calmly. 'It is common knowledge how badly you treat your quarry workers and household servants. Even your brother has suffered at your hand.'

Tommy was unaware that several people were glancing out of the terrace doors to witness the disagreement.

Forgetting himself entirely he sneered, 'That is rich coming from a man whose estates were founded on sugar plantations and the slaves that toiled there for nowt but the lash.'

Edward's jaw was tight with aggravation but his speech was calm. 'Yes, I too abhor the old practice, and am thankful that slavery is a thing of the past. I believe everyone deserves to be treated properly and with courtesy. That is why I offered a solution to Sadie and her family. Sadie has returned home where she will bear your child.'

Tommy spluttered with indignation.

'Please let me finish before you interrupt with questions,' Edward said coldly. 'When the child is weaned, Sadie is to go to my house in London to work there. Her parents will bring up the child until Sadie can manage without their help.'

Tommy's face was pink with rage. 'I don't expect they are

doing all this for nowt.'

It surprised Edward to hear Tommy slip into the dialect of his childhood. He thought that he was too schooled, too well practiced to allow his tongue to make the faux pas.

Edward took a pull of the cigar and then inspected the glowing tip. 'You are quite correct; they are not doing it for nowt.'

Tommy blushed scarlet with embarrassment.

Edward tapped the halo of ash off the tobacco. 'I have made an offer to them on your behalf. My solicitor will be in touch with you with the details. Default on a payment and the entire county will hear of your tupping with a servant, which is quite surprising when you profess to hate the lower classes.'

His eyes glittered menacingly. 'Every man that knows you, and many of those do not hold you in high esteem, will joke about your progeny going back to the Standish family roots. So beware of me, Standish. I do not like straw men that name a girl a thief to get rid of her and his own obligations with an outrageous lie.'

Throwing the cigar aside, he strode alone to the house, the small audience standing aside to let him pass.

Furious, afraid a blood vessel would burst in his head, Tommy walked swiftly to the stables to claim his carriage.

Chapter 7

Picking tiny weeds out of the gravel of his little daughter's grave, Joe was ruminating on the rumour circulating Garddryn Quarry. It hadn't surprise him to hear that a girl working at Penrhyn Castle was pregnant with Tommy's offspring. The mischief between Tommy and Sadie Pearson had begun when Tommy was married to poor Henrietta.

The other wench that had fallen into Tommy's clutches during his marriage, Lady Isabelle, had drowned in the Seiont River in Caernarvon; he couldn't put that death at Tommy's door but he'd had a hand in her demise and her husband's bankruptcy, which led to the suicide.

Tugging a blade of deep rooted grass out of the turf, he added it to the tiny pile of greenery that he would take to the compost heap at the back of the church.

Absentmindedly he looked across to the mountain tops but his mind stayed focused on Tommy. Death and destruction followed his son like a pair of friendly companions.

Long ago, Millie Barker had been murdered at the old mill. Tommy, a youth at the time, had acted strangely following the calamity. His behaviour had raised suspicions that Tommy had something to do with the lass's death.

George Bellamy, heir to the Bellamy fortune, had been struck on the head with a lump of rock at the gates of Plas Mawr. He'd sustained a horrendous injury and it left him an idiot, his mind and memory gone. Tommy had left Plas Mawr in a hurry and had kept to his lodging in the early part of the investigation. In his bones he knew the lad had something to do with it.

It grieved him to think that a son he had raised was capable of such violence. Too often disaster courted those that became involved with Tommy.

Once, during a lockout at the quarry, when men and their families were threatened with starvation and worse, he'd told Tommy to his face that he wished he had left him in the gutter in Manchester the day he and his mother had upped sticks and come to Garddryn village. It probably wasn't true, the lad had been three years old with the face of an angel, but even then he'd had the temper and nature of the devil incarnate.

Even little Chloe had been touched by Tommy's meanness, and the child was only three when she died in the cholera outbreak that decimated the county.

Tears filmed his eyes. Twenty-eight years had passed since he held his daughter. Grief for his pansy-eyed child had walked with him every day, and at night she came into his dreams and he was blessed with her babyish laughter. For more than two decades he had climbed the slope to the small graveyard on the mountain-side where he could sit a while and talk to Chloe of his days, heartbreaks and celebrations.

Sniffing, he wiped the tears away with the back of his hand. 'There's going to be another change in Corn Cottage,' he said softly. 'Our Frank and Nora are expecting. Your mother swears its twins.' He smiled. 'Maybe she's right, Emily usually is. Anyway she's knitting for two. If there's only the one it'll have plenty of matinee jackets and leggings to its name.'

The wind blowing from the south, rolling down the mountainside into the valley, penetrated his old coat. Joe glanced at the sky; it would begin to rain before he reached Corn Cottage, even if he got a move on.

Emily was sitting at the fireside as Joe came in. Putting aside the blue bonnet she was knitting, she put the kettle to the hob. Noting that the shoulders of his coat were wet through, and he had been missing for more than two hours, she didn't need to ask where he had been, but she wondered what disquiet had taken him up to Chloe's graveside on a Saturday afternoon when he normally went there on Sunday after his dinner.

'Take your coat off, Joe, and put it on the fireguard to dry,' she said, heaping two teaspoons of tea into the old pot.

'Nora's having a lie down. The poor lass tires easily with the weight she's carrying. Mark my words Joe, she's carrying a pair of lads.'

'If you're wrong, and it's a girl, the poor thing will have a drawer full of blue clothes to wear,' he said, shrugging out of his coat and draping it over the brass guard.

Emily tut-tutted. 'It'll not be a girl, Joe. Nora's not carrying right for a girl.'

'Women and their old wives tales,' he said, plumping up a cushion on the fireside chair and sitting down.

Glancing at her as she poured the tea, he said 'What's for supper?'

She handed him a steaming mug. 'I was wondering how long it would take you to get around to that. Its rabbit pie, taters and carrots. Nora made the pastry.'

She gave him a stern look, a warning that he wasn't to mention that Nora's pastry wasn't as light as her own.

His one eyebrow rose questioningly. 'Apple pie?'

'No, Joe. There's no apple pie.'

His face fell.

'I've made apple dumplings instead.'

'Good,' he smiled, opening last Saturday's newspaper.

Supper was almost ready, and as Nora had not risen, Emily went to the bedroom to rouse her and found the young woman curled up on the bed clutching her belly.

'Joe!' Emily shouted.

He was in the bedroom in three strides. 'I'll go and get the doctor and our Frank,' he said, taking in the situation at a glance.

'Take the pie out of the oven and put it on the table. Turn down the pan of dumplings,' Emily shouted to him as he passed through into the parlour-cum-kitchen.

'Ever practical, my Emily,' he said, opening the oven door and slipping the pie out. The simmering pan he put to the back of the range, and grabbing his damp coat off the fireguard, he slung it over his shoulder.

Outdoors it was still raining. Opening the garden gate, letting it clack shut behind him, Joe went towards the doctor's house at a trot. His stomach rumbled and he wondered how late it would be before he got to eat the rabbit pie.

The clock struck two before the cries of a baby sounded in the bedroom. In an instant Frank leapt up off the chair where he had sat like a coiled spring for several hours.

Joe caught hold of his sleeve. 'You'll have to wait until the doctor says you can go in. It's the rules of the game, lad,' he said sympathetically, looking into his son's wan face.

'What rules?'

'Women's rules. This is their time. You'll only get in the way and probably embarrass Nora.'

Frank looked askance. 'It's a bit late to be shy.'

'Couldn't agree more, son, but wait you must.'

The baby hadn't stopped wailing and then its cries were joined by another.

'Well, I'll be darned,' Joe said. 'Emily was right all along.'

Frank fell into the chair by the fireside in a near swoon.

'If it's two lads we'll never hear the last of it,' Joe said, grinning from ear to ear.

The bedroom door opened and Emily poked out her head. Her eyes wet with tears, she said, 'You had better come and say hello to your two sons, our Frank.'

Joe helped him up from the chair. 'Go on, lad. Then I can go and see.'

Emily expression was easy to read. 'Told you so,' she whispered in Joe's direction.

He wondered if he would ever stop grinning.

'Caleb and Abel,' Frank announced, coming back into the parlour.

'Are you sure lad?' Joe said, astounded.

'It's what Nora wants.'

'Aye, I see. And as the lass can do no wrong today, it'll be the twins' names for a lifetime.'

Frank looked surprised by his father's perception.

Joe smiled. 'It's the way of the world, Frank lad, the way of the world.'

The first glimmer of dawn was on the horizon before stillness and quiet descended on the cottage. Joe reckoned that it probably lasted two hours before the household rang with the cries of two damp and hungry babies.

Frank was making tea as Emily came into the kitchen.

'Did you get any sleep, Mam?' he said, looking slightly guilty.

'Aye a little, but your father probably fared better. He's got his head under the pillow. He's likely to stay there until midday as it is Sunday.'

'It'll do him good,' Frank said in male solidarity.

Raising her eyes to the ceiling beams, Emily tut-tutted.

With no routine established, the day was chaotic. It was early evening before Frank had a chance to sit down. As soon as the babies were settled he fell into bed beside Nora, praying that there would be peace for a while.

Sitting beside a small fire resting, Emily watched steam rising from the new tiny clothes draped over the fireguard. There's something very satisfying about having young ones in the house, she thought, yawning with tiredness.

Glancing at Joe engrossed in yesterday's newspaper, she said, 'With all the excitement yesterday, I forgot to ask what took you up to visit Chloe.'

'It was nowt,' he said, casting a side-long glance at her.

'It was something, Joe.'

He remained silent and she poked him in the ribs.

'That hurt,' he said, looking pained.

'So tell me.'

He looked shifty. 'I don't think it's an appropriate time.'

'I'll decide on that, Joe Standish. So tell me before I get cross.'

'You haven't the energy for cross, Emily.'

'Try me.'

He gave a sigh of long suffering. 'It's our Tommy.'

'Not him again,' she said crossly. 'What's he done this time?'

'See, I told you it wasn't an appropriate time.'

'Joe,' she said giving him a stern look.

'He's got a wench in the family way.'

Her eyes opened wide. 'My God, have we not got enough babies to last us a lifetime?'

'See, I told you.'

'Stop saying that, Joe, before I clout you. Now tell me which lass.'

Sniffing he rubbed the tip of his nose with the back of his hand. 'It's a young woman at Penrhyn Castle.'

'Not a Pennant?' Emily said, aghast.

'No, she's a servant. But he's left her high-and-dry and disowned her and the baby.'

'Typical.'

'We don't have to do anything about this, Emily. As you said yourself, we have enough babes to last us a lifetime.' He grinned. 'It tickles me to say that.'

Emily looked serious. 'But this is our grandchild too. We can't ignore that. What if the mother is in dire trouble? We couldn't stand by and not offer to help.'

He gave a long sigh. 'What do you want me to do, Emily?'

'I want you to go to Penrhyn Castle and if the girl's not there I want you to find out where she is.'

Seeing more trouble ahead, Joe frowned. 'Tommy will not like that.'

Emily said sadly, 'It's been a while since we worried what Tommy thought.'

'Aye you're right there, ever since we started picking up the pieces.'

'Are we going to bed, Emily? I'm worn out.'

'Not till you tell me when you're going to the castle.'

He sighed. 'Sunday suit you?'

'Aye, that'll do fine.'

Chapter 8

The morning was grey, a gale force wind blowing from the west roughing the tidal water of the Menai Strait, forcing herring-gulls, redshanks and oystercatchers to the sky, wheeling over the roofs of Plas Mawr with their distinct cries.

The tall lime trees on the avenue thrashed, yielding to the fiercest gusts, tearing away leaves and small branches, the green debris littering the carriage way.

Inside the mansion fires were smouldering, refusing to draw, and a cold dampness lingered. The constant rattle of sharp needles of driving rain struck the windowpanes, obliterating everything but the keening of the wind.

With a sense of being hemmed-in and held captive by the weather, Tommy sat at his desk in the library listlessly rifling through yesterday afternoon's post. A cream coloured envelope marked Private and Confidential caught his eye and he slit it open with a silver paper knife that was close to hand. The handwriting of the enclosed letter was small and neat, perfectly parallel. A printed heading revealed that it was sent from Morrison's, solicitors in Bangor. As he had no previous dealing with the firm his curiosity was aroused and he read it with interest. A moment later he was blustering with indignation and he flung the letter to the carpet without reading it entirely; he had the gist of it, Edward Pennant had interfered and set up a quarterly payment to go to Sadie Pearson.

Furious and unable to contain his temper, he moved from the desk and went to the fireplace where he gave the feeble excuse of a fire a forceful kick with the sole of his shoe. The coals fell into the grey ash and were more or less extinguished. He was tempted to kick it again to blast the burning embers to papery dust.

Hot ash had spilled out of the grate and onto the marble hearth, and coal dust off his shoe had marked the Turkey carpet with a streak of ebony. Turning away, he crossed to the window and looked through the veil of water streaming down the pane.

A black carriage was approaching. The two dapple greys in the traces matched stride perfectly. Tommy didn't recognise the vehicle; it was too old to belong to one of his landowner acquaintances. It came to a standstill at the foot of the entrance steps.

Curious, he lingered, the cold air leaching through the glass chilling his face. The door of the cab swung open and a woman in a black hat and long green coat climbed out. Tommy thought her vaguely familiar.

His eye was caught by a rotund footman trotting down the entrance steps, ineffectually trying to hang onto a black umbrella buffeting in the wind. Before he reached the last step the brolly blew inside out and with a ridiculous pirouette he turned into the wind so that it would right itself, but the brolly flew out of his grip and went soaring over the lawns and was lost to view.

Tommy swore and then said, 'The idiot.'

Forgetting the visitors, the footman looked towards the clipped yew trees.

The woman helped a frail man down the carriage step. On level ground he hung onto the woman's arm for support. Tommy couldn't make out who he was as the collar of his black coat was turned up, hiding his face.

For the briefest moment the rain lightened and the man looked back to the avenue and to the whipped up water of the Strait. The wet wind tore at his limp grey hair and the hem of his coat, but he stood quite still, looking towards the terrace and the Italianate gardens stepped down to the sandy shore. Turning very slowly he looked at the house, and his glance came to the figure standing at the library window.

Tommy saw the man's features clearly. 'George Bellamy!'

A surge of terror, the like he had never experienced before, ran through his vitals. A sudden blackness filled his head and suddenly he was lying on the carpet with the smell of dust in his nostrils, and sharp grit against his cheek. His breath was beating out of him, rapid and shallow. He'd fallen into the vortex of a nightmare and all around him the furniture had taken on a life of its own and was rolling and heaving. In the distance there was the sound of keening, the cries widows make at graves, and then he realised that the noise was coming from deep within him. At all costs he had to stop the noise, and gain control, make an immense effort to pull himself together, but it was like climbing through treacle and it took a moment for him to come to his knees and then push himself up. Balanced against the windowsill, he took a deep breath and exhaled slowly through his mouth. Slowly the room came back into focus, and he thought he was strong enough to make it to the desk. Forcing himself to stand upright, to square his shoulders, he started across the room, and catching his reflection in the glass of a painting he brushed his ruffled hair, smoothing it with palms slick with perspiration.

Hollow, echoing footfalls came from the Grand Hall.

Safe behind his desk, the leather chair supporting his weakened body, he listened to the approach. He could deal with this, he told himself. George is mad, an idiot, incapable of pointing a finger of blame at anyone. Bellamy has been imprisoned in Denbigh asylum for years. To get him in there it took the word of two people, himself and a doctor he had paid handsomely to swear that George was a lunatic and should be incarcerated for life. So who ever has let the bastard out has broken the law. Just one word from himself, and George would be locked up again in an instant.

An immense sense of relief sluiced through his mind, and the adrenalin pulsing made him alert and ready to squash any accusation hurled his way.

The door opened and two constables came in, closely followed by the woman and George.

The uniformed men were unexpected but Tommy hid the shock well.

Raising his voice, he said, 'I don't expect anyone to come in here without being announced by one of my servants.'

The taller of the two constables made a noise in the back of his throat like a short cough. 'It's not a social call, Mr Standish. Mr George Bellamy has made an allegation and signed a document to state that you attacked and left him for dead at the gates of this house several years ago.'

Tommy's eyes narrowed spitefully. 'Are you aware that Bellamy has spent many years housed in Denbigh asylum for lunacy?'

The constable cleared his throat again. 'Mr Bellamy was released from Denbigh two years ago when his memory improved. A doctor signed him out, certifying that he had a clean bill of health.'

Though he appeared calm, Tommy's mind raced frantically. If

George truly had regained his memory then monumental dangers lay ahead. Plas Mawr, Ruby and Garddryn Quarry, the London mansion, everything he treasured was at risk. In the time it took to flutter an eyelid, he could be destitute and facing a prison sentence, or worse. He had no idea what the penalty was for attempting to murder a man. Not so very long ago it was execution. Millie Barker's young face flashed into his mind, blue and engorged as he throttled the last breath out of the girl.

Suddenly he was hot, and a film of perspiration was on the back of his neck.

The woman stepped forward. There was anger, resentment, and loathing in her expression. 'Perhaps you remember me,' she said coldly. 'I was George's nurse at his mother's house in Chester. His mother, Louise Bellamy, employed me. When the lady died you came and evicted me and the others servants and snatched George from his bed, and pushed him into a carriage, with no words to where he had been taken to. It took me a while to locate George and I haven't deserted him since that day.'

Tommy found it impossible not to glance at the man. There was nothing left of the handsome young rake he had once been. In his place was a prematurely aged man with strands of grey in his dark hair. There was no mistaking the malevolence in his expression as his eyes met Tommy's. In an instant Tommy was aware that intelligence, memory, and hatred had resurfaced in George's mind. A good lawyer would convince a jury to believe his story.

The dress the woman wore beneath the green coat swished as she came to stand at the desk.

'I am now George's wife and under his direction I have come here to reclaim his home and inheritance, including Garddryn

Quarry and all the other business assets that belong to the Bellamy family. You, Tommy Standish, will rot in gaol and then in hell for the grievous harm you inflicted upon my husband.'

'So you were his nurse,' Tommy said maliciously. 'Then perhaps I too have a complaint to make: jewellery that had belonged to Louise Bellamy went missing on the day George was carted off to live as a lunatic in Denbigh asylum.'

George's eyes glittered with hatred. 'Jewellery that belonged to my mother was used to keep me in essentials during the years I was held in the asylum. Mary, my wife, stole nothing for herself but sold the sapphire necklace and diamond brooch to pay for basic necessities and to go towards a small home for us. You, Tommy Standish, the malevolent usurper, stole my mother's jewels for your own end. The crime will be added to the other offences the police are investigating against you.'

Tommy had no time to enquire what other offences George was referring to before one of the constables came alongside him.

'Mr Tommy Standish, I'm arresting you for attempting to murder George Bellamy,' the man said, grabbing Tommy by the upper arm and hauling him out of the leather seat.

Catching George's troubled expression; Tommy wanted to blurt out, 'I wish I had made bloody sure you were dead. Hit you again and again with the fucking rock.'

The cold metal of manacles clamped around his wrists.

With a constable walking on either side, he was shepherded to the door.

George and Mary Bellamy were silent as Tommy walked passed but there was no mistaking the triumph in Mary's eyes. Neither made a move to follow. The door closed softly.

As Tommy passed into the long hallway he thought he heard the chink of glass on glass coming from the drawing room. He had never been more in need of a drink, desperate for the taste and the fire of brandy on his tongue, and its warmth in his belly,

The butler appeared, wringing his hands, and asked if there was anything he could do for the master.

'Get out of my way,' Tommy shouted, turning his head so that the servant should not see his tears.

At the main door two astonished footmen stepped aside to let the entourage pass.

At the bottom of the steps the carriage that had arrived earlier was waiting to drive him away. The driver sitting on the box, his coat collar turned up against the worsening weather, looking agog at the sight of Tommy Standish manacled.

His legs failed him and he faltered. He felt a hand at his back and he was shoved forward, barking his shins on the small metal step at the open door. Two steps and made it inside, hard to balance with his hands tied, and he fell down heavily onto the worn leather seat, the old fashioned manacles biting into his wrists.

On the opposite seats his gaolers sat shoulder to shoulder, both staring intently at him. It passed through his mind that either one may have relatives or friends working at the Garddryn and would just as likely to molest him before they reached their destination.

The driver whistled to the two horses, and the vehicle moved forward, the wheels scrunching on the newly laid gravel.

He was going away from Plas Mawr. This would be the last time he saw the lime trees in the avenue, or looked out over the parkland.

'Going away from Plas Mawr, going away from Plas Mawr,' the words went through his mind like a mantra reminding him of the first time he had run towards the mansion, the excitement bubbling inside him hard to contain, and for the entire length of the avenue he had chanted Plas Mawr, Plas Mawr, Plas Mawr.

He wept.

The butler had followed them out and now he stood on the top step watching the carriage until it was lost to view, heedless of the wind whipping his grey hair and the torrential rain drenching his uniform. Floundering, wondering what to do, he sent for the groom and dispatched him to Caernarvon to fetch Madoc, the solicitor. He vehemently hoped that the horse and rider would overtake the police vehicle and the master would realise the groom's destination. Satisfied that he had done the right thing, he returned into the house to change his coat before entering the library to enquire of the wishes of the two visitors.

The news of Tommy's arrest swept through the village and beyond faster than a wild fire in summer heat. It reached Frank within half an hour of the calamity, and he ran the entire length of the village heading towards the quarry to search for his father. Several men stopped him and asked, 'Where's the fire?' but Frank ran on without saying a word to anyone.

Joe was sheltering through the worst of the rain in the caban on Jerusalem terrace. Alone, he was brewing an urn of tea for the men that would come there at noon. Brewing always began early as the tea they preferred to drink was tar brown.

Frank stumbled in, startling Joe.

'Look at the state of you, our Frank. You're wet through,' Joe said, beginning to panic.

There was a painful stitch in Frank's side, and he bent over, his hand covering the sore spot. Short of breath, he wheezed. 'Aye, I know. But there's summat more important than the state of me.'

Joe's fear grew: perhaps something had befallen Emily, or the two babies. 'Out with it then lad, don't keep me in suspense,' he said sharply.

'Sorry Da, I was only trying to get me breath back. I ran all the way from the top end of the village.'

'Aye, well!'

Frank came upright slowly. 'It's our Tommy, Da.'

Joe gave a long drawn out sigh. 'What's the bugger done this time?'

'He's got himself arrested.'

'Arrested for what?' Joe shouted in astonishment.

The stitch clipped Frank's side again, and he leaned forward, his hand automatically going to the tender place. 'You're not going to believe this, Da,' he said catching his breath. 'Tommy's been taken into custody for trying to murder George Bellamy.'

'I bloody knew it,' Joe yelled out. 'I always thought the bugger was involved. As a lad our Tommy was as jealous as hell of George.'

Frank couldn't hide his amazement. 'So you're not surprised?'

'Am I buggery. It was only a matter of time before someone put a stop to him.'

Frank sat down on an old wooden chair, the legs scraping on the uneven floor. 'So what are you going to do, Da?'

Joe stirred the tealeaves with a long wooden spoon. 'Going to do? I'm doing nothing, lad, besides brewing this tea and then sitting down to drink a mug or two.'

A look of bewilderment crossed Frank's face. 'What about

Mam? She'll be really upset when she hears what's happened.'

Joe sighed again. 'Aye, you're reeght. I'd best get home and prepare the poor lass for more trouble.'

As he spoke he turned the flame under the urn down low, and put a shovel of coal on the burning embers in the grate. Absorbed in thought he shuffled into his damp coat, and then only one step behind Frank he followed his son out.

The door of the stone cabin slammed closed behind them, separating them from the warmth of the fire. It was raining hard, pellets of icy water slanting horizontally in the wind. With a sidelong glance at the grey sky they pulled up the collars of their coats. Shoulder to shoulder, they walked in virtual silence.

There were plenty of questions Frank wanted to ask, but out of deference to his father he left him with his thoughts.

With his eyes on the saturated mud of the track Frank concentrated on keeping his already soaked boots out of the deepest puddles. Several times he stepped on a tile of waste slate and the muddy water beneath spurted up, drenching the hem of his trousers.

However harsh it is out here, he thought stepping over a large dislodged stone, it was preferable to where Tommy was, languishing in Caernarvon County gaol. It was an old bleak building, not a place anyone would like to wake in tomorrow morning.

The rain eased, turning to drizzle. Frank looked across to Snowdon, to the twin summits rising above a swirl of ethereal white mist. The view, the distance, the immense grey sky gave him a great sense of freedom and he breathed deeply on the damp clean air.

'It's brightening,' he said, giving his father a sidelong glance.

'Aye, maybe for some,' Joe replied despondently.

Frank's mood evaporated, replaced by guilt for his moment of pleasure.

Branwen, a wizened shrew of a man in a damp and dirty fustian coat, walked into their path. 'Is it true?' he said in a tone bordering on reproach.

Hardly breaking stride, Joe said, 'Is what true?'

The man was much shorter than either Frank or Joe and he had to trot to keep pace with them. 'That your son was arrested today?'

'My son walks beside me.'

'Aye but you've another,' Branwen answered with a cackle, amused by his own wit.

'I have one son, and he walks beside me. His mother may have two sons. Now go your own way and don't heed my path,' Joe replied, waving the man away with his arm.

Lacking courage to follow, Branwen came to a standstill. 'Not a good day to be a Standish,' he shouted. 'Oh how the mighty fall.'

'Do you want me to go back and duff him?' Frank said his chin near his wet coat collar.

'No, lad, he's not worth the trouble.'

Frank tut-tutted. 'I don't know where you get your patience from, Da.'

A smile passed over Joe's face. 'Raising Tommy, I reckon.'

They both laughed.

Then serious once more, Frank said, 'What'll become of the Garddryn without a master?'

They were walking past the Halfway Inn. Noise spilled out through the open door. Earlier many quarrymen were drawn away from the wet and dangerous galleries by the atrocious weather. It was easier to fall into the ale house and pour ale down their necks than it was to return home to irritable women and questions about loss of pay. The men that lagged behind the general exodus had heard the rumours of the master's arrest and dashed from work to discuss it in the comfort of the saloon bar.

Joe didn't glance in. The last thing he needed was someone to heckle them as they went by. Instead he concentrated on Frank, knowing that the lad was worried, and what man wouldn't be with a wife and two little lads depending on him?

'The Garddryn will carry on as usual either with a new master or new owner,' he said, swiping at a long stem of grass growing out of the stones of the Halfway's garden wall. 'Business will not cease because Tommy's not there. It's a lucrative enterprise and I don't expect it'll lose a day's production. The manager, old Iwan Rees, will run the quarry.'

'It's a worry though, Da.'

'Aye a lot of things are. But your Ma's me biggest concern at this moment.'

'I know that, Da. But do you really expect the Garddryn to carry on as though nothing has happened? Our Tommy has run it for so long.'

Joe stopped at the garden gate. 'The graveyards are full of indispensable men, Frank. Quarrymen will be breaking slate tomorrow, just like always.'

The day was brightening, a glimmer of sunlight glistening on the wet stone walls of the castle as the Plas Mawr groom, Pierce Price, reigned in his mare at the stable-yard close to the quay wall. Dismounting he walked the animal into the yard.

A boy came out of the tack room and taking the reins, looked up into the horse's long face; smiling, he patted the mare's neck. 'Hallo my beauty. We haven't seen you here for a week or two.'

'Good morning, Master Jones,' he said, trying to sound cheerful as though nothing was amiss at Plas Mawr. 'I want you to take care of Dolly for me for an hour or two.'

Smiling, the boy patted the mare's neck again. 'Well, Dolly, we can have a right good natter in that time. You can tell me all the news from Plas Mawr and the Garddryn.'

The horse snorted, shaking its head.

Thank god that the animal's mute, Pierce Price thought, an image of the master being carted away earlier this morning springing into mind.

Climbing the short incline from the quay wall, he walked in the shade of the castle walls, and turning right at the corner he came to the Georgian building housing the solicitor's offices. The door was unlocked and he walked in.

A young clerk without an ounce of spare flesh on his frame looked up from the document he was copying. Sitting at a high desk, on a wooden stool, his shoulder were slumped, chin almost resting on his hollow chest. Uncoiling slowly, as though his body was as stiff as the stool, he came upright, and with an expression of complete disinterest wiped his ink stained fingers on a dirty cloth, before taking the few steps to the reception desk.

'I wish to see Mr Madoc,' Pierce Price said brusquely, not taking kindly to the lad's attitude.

A lock of greased hair slipped onto the clerk's forehead and he pushed it back carefully with his fingertips. His chin rose and he gave a little sniff. 'I'm afraid he's busy this morning. Can you make an appointment?'

'Is he here?'

'Yes, but he will not thank you for disturbing him,' the lad said airily.

'You tell him I have urgent business to do with the master of the Garddryn, and I have ridden at all speed from Plas Mawr.'

The clerk sniffed. 'I'll tell him, but he may not see you. Who shall I say is calling,' he said, coming around the desk.

'Pierce Price, head groom at Plas Mawr.'

The boy headed down the short hallway.

He returned a moment later looking slightly aggravated. 'I'll show you to Mr Madoc's office.'

Madoc was sitting behind a large cluttered desk. As the groom entered he stood. 'What brings you here on urgent business? Has there been an accident?'

'Not an accident exactly but a calamity all the same,' Price said. 'The master was arrested this morning and has been taken into custody.' Price looked out of the window in the direction of the County Gaol.

'Are we speaking of Mr Standish?' Madoc said coolly, though his mind was jigging at what the law may have uncovered. If Tommy had been charged with fraud, selling consortium shares to Lord Harvey, bankrupting the man, and then reclaiming the shares as his own, it would not only be Tommy in dire straits, he himself could be implicated. There were many instances of flying close to the wind and most had the stench of corruption.

He was almost afraid to ask when he said, 'What's the charge?'

The groom coughed nervously. 'I only have information from the butler, sir. He believes that it's attempted murder.'

Madoc, though relieved that he wasn't implicated, was shocked to the core. 'Attempted murder? When, where, and who?'

'I know nothing of this, sir. But Mr George Bellamy came to the mansion this morning and he had two constables with him. It was those men that carted him off. I apologise sir, I meant to say, took the master away with them.'

Madoc came around the desk. 'And you say that they brought him to the police station here, in Caernarvon?'

A knock on the door interrupted the groom's reply.

'Enter,' Madoc shouted.

The door opened and the skinny clerk inched around the door. 'Mr Iwan Rees, the manager of Garddryn Quarry, wants to see you, sir. He says it's very urgent.'

'Tell him to come in,' Madoc said, hopeful that Iwan Rees would shed more light on the subject. The clerk was about to retreat but Madoc called him back. 'Take Mr Price to the waiting room. Get him some coffee or tea.

'Please wait for further instructions. I'll need you to take a message back to Plas Mawr,' Madoc said as the groom walked towards the door, his footfall silenced by the plush green carpet.

Iwan Rees, looking flushed, strode in. 'Have you heard the news, Madoc?'

'In part, yes, but I do not have the details.'

'I too have very few details, save that Tommy Standish was arrested this morning and taken into custody. A message came to the office from the Plas Mawr butler. I rode over there immediately and came face to face with George Bellamy. He told me the few details I do have, that it to say that Tommy Standish was arrested for attempting to murder Bellamy.

There's also a mention of theft. Don't know anything more than that.'

Iwan Rees glanced out of the window, looking in the direction of the police station. 'I'll get over there and try to see him.'

'No, don't do that,' Madoc said hastily. 'I'll go. I can see Cameron Chamberlain, the police captain, and discover exactly what the situation is.'

'Do you think Standish will get bail?' Iwan said, pulling a handkerchief out of his pocket to clean the lenses of his spectacles.

'Doubtful,' Madoc said. 'But I will try to talk Cameron into saying a good word for him. His name will carry some weight. In the meantime, will you go to Edward's school and bring him back to Plas Mawr? The boy will be hounded if we don't get him out of there before the story breaks.'

'Yes, of course. Thoughtful of you to consider the boy,' Iwan said, trying to remember the times of the trains.

A moment later, Iwan was outdoors. He was grateful that he didn't have to go to the station and see Standish. Travelling to Cheltenham to pick up young Edward was much more preferable. He glanced in the direction of the prison and then at the greying sky. He shivered as though a ghost had passed by.

After despatching the groom to the mansion, with a message that he would arrive there later, Madoc left the building and headed for the police station.

The entire journey to Caernarvon, knives twisted in Tommy's gut turning his bowels to water, which the swaying and bouncing of the coach made dire.

The two constables eyed him like they would a rabid dog,

ready to strike with their brutal wooden truncheons if he made the slightest move.

The heavy rain ceased, and then there was only the chime of iron rimmed wheels, the clopping of hooves, and occasional birdsong until the vehicle drew near the town. Then there were carriages passing by, men on horseback, and pedestrians thronging the pavements and the roadway. Terrified someone would recognise him, Tommy turned his face away from the window.

Once inside the castle walls, the wheels rumbled over cobble-stones and he knew they were nearly at the end of the journey; road's end for him. For if his gaolers discovered he had murdered Millie Barker and Henrietta he would swing on a short rope over a long drop in the execution tower or the County Gaol.

The vehicle came to a standstill and the door opened and through the crack he saw they were outside Castle Ditch police station. The two constables jumped down. Tommy's mind froze and he remained rigid on the seat. Ducking back in, the two men grabbed him and hauled him out roughly. Losing his footing on the carriage step, he nearly fell to the cobblestones. People passing by stared and Tommy cringed with mortification. One of the constables shoved him in the back, and he went forwards towards the station's open door, closing his eyes as he walked in the shadow of the door lintel.

Descending a stone step the manacles on his wrist clinked, and though humiliated beyond endurance he stiffened and straightened his shoulder. He would not give the bastards the satisfaction of seeing the master of the Garddryn brought low.

The entrance door slammed shut snuffing out the daylight, and the anteroom became truly dismal and the formidable grey walls closed in on him.

Shoved in the back again, he was propelled towards a desk where a mousey haired man of about thirty, with weary eyes and sallow complexion, stood waiting.

The constable shoving him said with a jeer, 'We've brought gentry to you today, Constable Hoskins. The man here is the master of Garddryn and Ruby quarries, wealthy landowner and resident of Plas Mawr, the grand mansion situated on the outskirts of Garddryn village.'

He gave Tommy another poke between his shoulder blades. 'Step up to the desk, your Lordship.'

Tommy was caught off balance and the toecaps of his shoes thumped on the wood.

It amused the constable and he gave another weak smile. 'Hoskins, would you kindly remove the esteemed gentleman's bracelets?'

Sighing, Hoskins indicated to Tommy to raise his hands and Tommy put his wrists on the top of the desk. Withdrawing a small key from his pocket, Hoskins released him.

Tommy rubbed his bruised wrists and then seeing that he was watched, dropped his hands to his side.

'Empty your pockets,' Hoskins ordered.

There was no escaping the command, and delving into his coat Tommy withdrew a few personal possessions, not expecting to see the gold fob watch, cigar case, silver hip flask, and wallet again.

Hoskins raked everything together, and then his glance went to a male subordinate leaning against the wall. The man's arms were folded, and he had a look of contempt on his pockmarked face.

'Don't just stand there,' Hoskins shouted, 'Escort the prisoner to cell three.'

Sullen, the young man pushed his buttocks off the wall and came forward. Grabbing Tommy by the upper arm he shoved him towards a corridor. The man's grip was like a vice; Tommy tried to pull away but the man increased the pressure.

The moment he was taken prisoner Tommy's thought processes had shut down; now the pain brought a moment of rationality and he shouted over his shoulder to Hoskins, 'I want to see Cameron Chamberlain. He will sort out this misunderstanding immediately.'

A smile spread across Hoskins face. 'I'll ask the police captain to step by.'

'He's a good friend of mine,' Tommy shouted, anxious to be heard.

Still smiling, Hoskins picked up Tommy's costly possessions and put them into a safe. Locking it, he wondered at the value of the items. The gold watch alone would settle the crippling debt plaguing him.

The door of cell three was open and the station warder flung Tommy inside the small room. The heavy door clanged closed and the key was turned.

Tommy was alone and unaware that he had stopped breathing. Taking two short steps backward, he slumped on the bare board that doubled as a seat and bed. The room was bare but for a bucket and a bowl for washing. The dirty window was too high to be seen out of. There was no way to escape. All was lost: wealth, Garddryn, Ruby, Plas Mawr, weekends at Penrhyn Castle, the mansion in London, the opulent life he had become accustomed to and richly deserved was gone, and in its place was prison, humiliation, disgrace and probably a public execution. Dry eyed, he began to rock back and forth. He wanted to die. His manic eyes scanned the room for a means of killing himself. There was glass in the window but the casement was out of reach. The ceiling was smooth and without a beam to hang from. He had little choice but to choke on a sock or suffocate within his jacket. Both options were an unpleasant way to die but still preferable to facing imprisonment, a humiliating trial, and the awful possibility of a public execution. He rocked faster, the room swaying as he pitched back and forth.

There was a commotion in the corridor and the clack of two men's footsteps ceased at the door of the cell, but Tommy was too far into a nervous collapse to notice. A metal key turned in the lock and the door swung open. Madoc stood on the threshold. He came in and the door clanked closed behind him. Seeing the state of Tommy, it was impossible to hide his shock.

Sitting beside him on the plank of wood, he took hold of Tommy's hand. 'We must talk,' he said earnestly.

Tommy didn't appear to hear him and he repeated the words. 'Tommy, we really must talk if I am to help you.'

The mention of help registered in Tommy's foggy brain and he stopped rocking.

Madoc gripped his hand more firmly. 'It is imperative that we get the best legal brain to get you off this charge.'

'Can't you get me off?' Tommy said weakly, like a child.

'We need expertise in criminal law to present the case at the assizes.'

'When is the next assizes?'

'Soon,' Madoc urged to hold Tommy's attention. 'We have but a short time to formulate a case against your accuser. At all costs we have to show that George Bellamy is still a lunatic. That these charges are trumped up by his wife to get her hands on Plas Mawr and all that goes with it.'

Tommy's reason returned and a myriad of ideas to thwart Mary Bellamy came to him. Euphoria, ten times more potent following the desperate and suicidal thoughts of only moments ago, swept through his veins.

'Madoc, you are a genius. I don't mind admitting to you that I had given up all hope of getting out of here. I want you to find me the best legal brain in England and get him to work at once, whatever the cost.'

Though he kept his expression hopeful, Madoc saw the problems ahead. Given the situation, Tommy could not touch the assets of the Garddryn or the Bellamy estate. That left him with funds from Ruby, unless there was a legal charge slapped on the quarry and associated business interests. There was a Secret Fund. This was money Tommy had filched from the Garddryn quarry and Bellamy fortune for his own ends. It amounted to several thousand. But it was well known that legal expertise was ruinously expensive, and the best man would run through such a sum in no time at all.

And there was another problem facing Tommy, one the man had yet to consider, but penned up in a cell it would probably come to him pretty soon that Madoc would be implicated in the embezzlement if it came to light that money that could not be accounted for was being spent on Tommy's defence.

Though his face remained pleasant and friendly, Madoc's brain ticked at a fast pace as he considered the appropriate moment to abandon Tommy to the wolves. Only he and Tommy knew of the Secret Fund and had access to it, a dangerous position for Tommy to be in considering the circumstances.

Oblivious to Madoc's train of thought, Tommy said optimistically, 'So what happens next?'

Somewhat uncomfortable with the traitorous line of thought, Madoc stood. 'I expect you will be questioned soon. Tell the constables nothing. Wait until I have a barrister in place. Let the man speak for you. Whatever bully tactics the police try on, do not succumb. I will be back tomorrow with news. On my way out of the station I will inform the constable on the desk that a barrister is being employed.'

The words 'on my way out' smarted and Tommy wondered how he was to endure the day and long night ahead.

Madoc knocked briskly on the door and a warden could be heard walking along the corridor; a key turned and the door opened. Madoc raised his hand in farewell and the door clanked closed behind him.

Tommy listened to Madoc's footstep, and tracking his steps he imagined the solicitor walking out of the door and into the fresh air. In his mind's eye, Tommy followed Madoc to the local hostelry where he would eat lunch and enjoy a glass or two of brandy.

Tommy sat on the edge of the plank and although he tried to keep his spirits up with thoughts of the barrister and the reprieve that lay ahead, he was as low as he had been before Madoc's arrival.

The entire day he waited for something to happen, and at every sound he came up off the plank and then sat down again when the slight disturbance passed. Expecting to be interviewed he remained on tender-hooks, turning over in his mind how to respond, what information to give and which to hold back.

Eventually twilight dimmed the room. A meal of sorts was brought to him, the slops reminding him of his mother's interminable stews dished up to table in his youth. Changing the direction of his thoughts, he set his mind to the time of his boyhood in Plas Mawr and the idolisation he had for the mansion. Those years were happy enough, ambition growing, as was his hatred of George. His future looked bright with Bertram Bellamy backing him, until the fateful day when old Bellamy told him his services would no longer be required as George was going away to school so had no need of 'a bit of competition' to get him through his lessons.

Bile like poison rose to Tommy's mouth, as he recalled the old man's words delivered without sympathy.

When Henrietta Bellamy fell in love with him he grasped the opportunity, and once again his star ascended when he made the wench pregnant, forcing her parents to accept him as a son-in-law.

Skirting over the problems with Henrietta, he turned his mind to George. As a young man he had been a rake, pilfering from the Bellamy fortune at a great rate of knots, his doting parents constantly handing him money to pay off creditors and gambling debts. They had Tommy Standish to thank for saving their aristocratic hides, for left to their own devices they would have handed everything to George, and true to type, he would have frittered it away until the coffers were laid bare.

It was his courage that saved the family fortune, his courage to lie in wait for George and clobber him over the head with a large stone. The only pity was that he hadn't stayed around to make sure his life had been entirely snuffed out, and how he cursed himself for that fateful omission.

A cold watcher within him relived the attack, and once again he was walking the two miles from his lodging to the gates of Plas Mawr in the darkness.

Close by the gate there was a hedge of rhododendrons. Hunkering down amongst the small branches he'd settled to wait for George to appear. To this day he couldn't stand the sickening fragrance of rhododendron bushes.

The ground had been damp with a musty smell of fungus. Time crawled and he had begun to wonder if George would appear. There was always the chance that he would be too drunk to walk home and would doss down at the inn.

Eventually a whispered sound in the stillness announced his arrival. Drawing back into the blacker refuge of the leaves, heart hammering with the torture of suspense, he had waited until George was close.

He remembered every detail of that night, even the night noises shifting, and the few notes that birds called ceasing; a small animal tripped over his shoe as it ran for cover.

The waiting had been interminable, prolonged by George stopping every few steps to lift a bottle to his mouth and drink. Slowly if somewhat unsurely he came on, and when he was only a few yards distant it had been necessary to leave his cover and crouch in the shadows.

When George was only feet away, he had jumped out of the shadows and clubbed him just above the ear. For the briefest moment George remained upright, with a look of disbelief on his face, and then he had crumpled, blood spurting from a raw wound.

Each time he recalled this scenario, Tommy edited out the disturbing moments when his brain imploded and a dark mist rained down, and falling to his knees he had howled like an animal.

When he had recovered sufficiently, he checked George's pulse and was sure he was dead; how he cursed himself now for this mistake. He had run to the bushes and retrieved a canvas bag.

Sprinting over a five-bar gate he ran to the fast flowing stream and washed off the sticky blood in the icy water.

He had planned the attack well, and with fresh clothes to hand he stripped out of his garments and changed into fresh ones from the bag.

Timing was the essence of the job, and he worked quickly; making a fire he burned the bloodied clothes and scattered the hot ashes with his boots.

There was nothing to link him to the attack. Madoc was correct: all they needed to do was prove that George was a lunatic. Not so difficult when the man had spent years in an asylum.

Suddenly he felt weary, and lying down on the bare board he pulled the meagre covering given to him earlier over his clothes. Though he didn't expect to sleep, and it wasn't the noise in the corridor, nor the man banging on the door of the adjacent cell, but the terrible images of his capture whirling endlessly though his mind.

He woke to sunlight streaming through the high window. For a moment he lay still, confused by the unfamiliar surroundings, and then realisation came to him, and frightened, he scanned the dismal cell.

Chapter 9

Mary stood at the library window watching the carriage taking Tommy Standish to gaol disappear from view.

George stood in the centre of the room, drained and hesitant. Coming face to face with Tommy had disturbed his equilibrium. For two long years, since he began to recover his memory, he had done his utmost not to think of Tommy Standish and the night of the attack.

It was Mary's stout heart that had carried him back to Plas Mawr, his family home. Coming into the house, bearding the lion in his den, terrified him. Though Mary and the two constables were there to protect him, he was still afraid of Tommy, scared that a sudden rage would take possession of the man and he would rush at him and attack his fragile head.

Mary turned from the window and helped George into the leather chair beside the fireplace.

'Try to keep calm, dear,' she said affectionately, stooping to him and taking hold of his chilled hands. 'Tommy has gone, and can no longer harm you.'

What she said was true. But still his stomach fluttered dreadfully and the nausea he'd suffered since Mary had suggested that they visit the police had refused to settle down. His cold hands began to tremble and he felt the exquisite pressure of Mary's hands cocooning his own.

The little sign of affection gave him courage and he gave her a wan smile. 'Thank you, Mary,' he said softly.

'Is there anything I can get you, George?' she said, straightening.

'It is so strange being here at Plas Mawr,' he said, eyes

scanning the room. 'This library is virtually unchanged. The desk, chairs, even the old bureau in the corner where my father kept his favourite malt is the same.'

Though she hardly expected the bureau to hold a decanter of whisky, she went to it and opened the centre cupboard. She gave a little laugh. 'Someone has kept up the tradition, George.'

She took two glasses and put both on the desk-top. 'A snifter will steady our nerves,' she said, pouring generous measures.

His hands steadied as he took a glass from her. Putting it to his lips, he sighed with pleasure and took a decent swallow; the warm amber hit the spot in his belly that so ached when he got flustered and unsure.

Perching on the arm of his chair, Mary ran her fingers through his prematurely greying hair. 'The visit to the police station and the arrest went better than I expected.'

George swirled the whisky around the glass. 'Yes, without a hitch. Once Cameron Chamberlain got involved it was dealt with quickly. He was very helpful.'

Her mouth pursed. 'And so he should be. You are the rightful heir of the estate.'

George smiled. 'I sensed that he didn't actually like Standish.'

'I don't suppose many people do, the man's arrogant, and an insufferable tyrant. But you know that better than anyone, George. '

Even the most indirect reference of the attack unsettled him, and he hurried to change the subject. 'What time did Chamberlain say he was arriving?'

Mary glanced at the clock on the mantle-piece. 'About twelve o'clock. Do you think we should invite him to stay for luncheon?'

George was uneasy.

Mary gently pinched his ear. 'George, it's important that you remember this is your home. You have every right to be here and to order the staff to do your bidding. If we wish Cameron to stay for luncheon we just tell a footman, or the butler, or whoever.'

George frowned. 'I understand, but I feel very uncomfortable, as though we have walked into someone else's home.'

Her hand brushed the folds on his brow. 'It is your home, George. The same home you shared with your parents and sister, Henrietta. God rest her soul.'

He started to rise from the chair and Mary put her hand on his shoulder, pushing him back down gently. 'Tell me what you want, George, and I will get it.'

'The bell-rope is the other side of the fireplace. I was going to give it a tug to summon a servant.'

'I can do that for you,' she said standing.

A servant appeared almost immediately and she wondered if the man had been eavesdropping at the door.

The suspicion made her sound sterner than was usual and without a trace of a smile she said, 'Please ask the butler to come to the library.'

The footman bobbed his head but gave no reply, as he hadn't an idea of how to address the woman.

George rose a little shakily and stood in the centre of the Turkey carpet but before he could speak the footman made his escape through the door.

The footman didn't have far to go to find Miles the butler: the man was waiting anxiously in the hall for instructions. In the back of his mind was the thought that Tommy Standish would be released from custody and would come charging back to Plas

Mawr to throw George Bellamy out of the house. But of course George had every right to be here, he was the true heir to the estate. It was so confusing and worrying, for if Tommy Standish did come back there would be the mother and father of a row. Thank goodness he had sent the groom to fetch Mr Madoc. He was the best man to deal with the catastrophe.

The library door opened and the first footman came out and beckoned to Miles.

On soft slippers the butler crossed the marble floor. 'What do they want?'

'You,' the footman said ordinarily.

Miles pulled the hem of his jacket down and straightened his shoulders. With a little 'Hmmm' to clear his throat, he knocked on the library door.

'Enter,' George said, just loud enough to be heard.

Miles nodded once to acknowledge Mary and then crossed to the edge of the Turkey carpet to greet George. 'It is a great pleasure to see you home at last, Mr George.'

He shook the butler's hand. 'It's been a long time, Miles. I never thought to see the house again.'

'No sir. It has been a long time.'

Mary cut in gently. 'We would like to have luncheon. The police captain will be here soon and we would like to invite him too.'

George noticed the deferential tone in her voice and stepped in immediately. 'I would ask you to gather all the staff together, Miles, so that I can introduce them to Mrs Bellamy, my wife.'

Miles bowed from the waist. 'Welcome to Plas Mawr, Mrs Bellamy.'

He turned his attention back to George. 'The servants will

await you in the grand hall, Mr George.'

Privately Miles wondered what the house was coming to. The master carted off by police at breakfast time, a new master in charge before luncheon, and to cap it all a new mistress, a woman without breeding to be the lady of such a grand house as Plas Mawr.

Taking two steps back he dipped his head to Mary. 'Luncheon will be served at any time you wish.'

Mary was about to say, 'That will be inconvenient to cook,' but stopped herself in time. Instead she nodded and said, 'Thank you, Miles.'

As the door closed, George smiled. 'I told you that you could do it, Mary dear. A charming demonstration of upper-crust breeding, you'll have the servants adoring you in no time at all.'

She looked slightly wan. 'It'll take a bit more than a please and thank you to get them to like me.'

His face clouded. 'Henrietta was kind, very much like you are, Mary. Mother could be a right old Tartar at times.'

He took her hand. 'I'm quite sure the servants will appreciate your style. Now let's go and introduce you to everyone. They'll make you feel at home in no time.'

The formalities over, they went back to the library, a tour of the house postponed until their expected visitor had departed.

George was pointing out an oil painting of the Bellamy sugar plantation in Jamaica when a servant came in to announce that Mr Cameron was waiting in the hall.

'Show him in at once,' George said with a noticeable shake in his voice.

As the door closed on the footman, Mary came to George's side. 'There's nothing to worry about.'

The door reopened and before she could finish the sentence, Cameron Chamberlain walked in. Though he was of medium height and build he was impressive in his uniform, with his straight brown hair brushed back from his brow, and clean shaven face revealing a strong jawline and chin.

'Thank you for coming, Mr Chamberlain,' George said, extending his hand.

Cameron nodded to Mary. 'Mrs Bellamy, it's good to see you again.'

'Let me get you a drink,' George said. 'There's a whisky or I can ask the butler to bring you whatever you wish.'

'Whisky's fine.' If it was the same malt that Tommy Standish offered his guests in the library, Cameron knew from experience that it would be exceptional.

Mary declined George's offer. Perching on the arm of George's chair to give him moral support, she waited for George to speak of his suspicions.

'What is on your mind, Mr Bellamy?' Cameron asked, settling into the chair on the other side of the fireplace.

George looked into his drink. 'Did you know my sister, Henrietta?'

'I knew of her,' Cameron answered noncommittally.

'She was a fine woman,' George said looking back into the past. 'Until she met Tommy Standish she was carefree and loved life.'

Mary put her hand on George's shoulder. 'Try not to get upset,' she said softly.

Cameron saw that George was a great deal more fragile than he had first thought. He waited for the man to go on, to explain what was on his mind.

'She was very young when she started seeing Standish and she soon became besotted with him. Of course they married and had a son. Even as a boy Standish was pure evil. I dread to think what sort of life poor Hen had with him.' He turned his eyes to Mary. 'Mary met her at Denbigh asylum when I was an inmate there. Sadly I don't remember Henrietta's visit, but Mary does and she knows that Hen was very unhappy. We didn't know then, we discovered it later, that Henrietta died very soon after the visit.'

'She killed herself,' Cameron said sympathetically.

George's eyes met Cameron's. 'No. Tommy Standish killed her.'

The revelation sparked Cameron's interest and he saw the chance of getting rid of Tommy Standish. The man was arrogant, telling tales of money paid in exchange for information. Though he hadn't yet named the police captain as the recipient, it was only a matter of time before he did so. If it reached the chief's ears there would be hell to pay. Personally he would be looking at a long stretch in prison. Dead, Standish posed no threat. In gaol he may talk. To save his own neck he had to convince Tommy that he would be rescued from the hangman's gallows.

Suddenly he realised the silence had lasted too long. Looking intently into George's eyes, putting emphasis on his words, he said, 'Do you know this for a fact?'

George didn't reply immediately, and then without faltering in his usual way, he said, 'The Plas Mawr staff may be able to shed light on the last hours of my sister's life. Personally I do not doubt that he wanted me out of the way so he could marry Henrietta. Murdering her enabled him to gain everything, the quarry, the plantations in Jamaica, substantial finance, and this house. Everything is his until Edward, his son, reaches the age of twenty-one. I just pray to God that the bastard doesn't get the chance to injure Edward and render him incapable of running the business. If that happened Standish would have a free run of the Bellamy fortune for the rest of his natural.'

He looked earnestly at Cameron. 'You must convict the swine and save Edward's inheritance and his life.'

Unconsciously Cameron picked at a chipped fingernail. 'If you can provide new evidence the police are obliged to re-open the case.'

George began to feel hopeful of getting somewhere at last. 'Miles the butler, the cook, and Henrietta's maid who is now the housekeeper were here at the time of Henrietta's death. No doubt they can shed light on her last hours.'

Cameron's right eyebrow rose quizzically. 'Henrietta Standish's maid would have been questioned very carefully at the time.'

Anxious to get his point across, George spoke quickly. 'Yes, but the woman would have been afraid to say anything whilst Tommy Standish was in residence. She may be more forthcoming now that he's locked up.'

'Well, you may be right.' Cameron was determined to have a word with the woman before he left Plas Mawr and ferret out all he could about the domestic situation between Henrietta and Tommy. Questioned in the right way the woman could reveal scraps of useful information that could nail Tommy to the proverbial cross. Considering Standish already done for, he smiled, asking, 'Is there anything else that could shed light on the death?'

Remembering the conversation she had with Henrietta at Denbigh asylum, Mary said, 'I recall Henrietta saying she was friendly with Tommy's parents, Joe and Emily Standish. Though Tommy disapproved wholeheartedly, and banned her from visiting their cottage. It had something to do with him disliking being reminded of his humble background. Though I can't imagine Henrietta rubbing his nose in it, she was just too nice to do something like that.'

Cameron brought a small black notebook out of his pocket and a pencil. Prepared to make notes, he looked across to George. 'I'll ask Mr and Mrs Standish about it. As I recall they live in Garddryn village.'

'Can't help you there,' George said. 'Being away so long my local knowledge is rusty. But I do know that Joe Standish was a quarryman at the Garddryn. '

Cameron snickered. 'That would cause friction in the family, the father being a quarryman and the son the master of the quarry.'

George remembered the boyhood fights and name calling, some of the unpleasantness instigated by him. The village boys were no better, envious of Tommy visiting Plas Mawr and taking his lessons with the heir of the Bellamy fortune. Perhaps Tommy hadn't weathered the bullying, and forced to fight his corner too often it had turned him into the monster he now was.

'Awful situation for them all,' Mary added.

A light knock sounded on the library door. It opened and the elderly footman entered. 'Sorry to disturb you, sir, but Mr Madoc the solicitor is asking for a moment of your time.'

George vaguely remembered Madoc as Tommy's sidekick. Like Tommy the man had risen from the lower echelon and climbed up the muddy slopes to the top of the pile. 'How the deuce does he know that I'm here?'

'Beg your pardon, sir. I didn't ask him that,' the footman said solemnly. 'Shall I request he waits, sir?'

George looked towards Cameron. 'Do you mind the interruption?'

Cameron stowed the notebook into his pocket. 'No, not at all. Perhaps Mr Standish's solicitor has visited him in the County Gaol and been made aware of your presence at Plas Mawr.'

George mouth pursed. 'Yes, it's probably so.'

Anticipating that George would be alone, and familiar with the layout of the house, Madoc came striding into the library. Smart in a light grey suit, cream silk shirt, and dark blue cravat, his straight dark hair brushed back of his brow, he looked the professional and affluent legal man.

Madoc, shocked to see the police captain in conference with George Bellamy, stopped short, a look of confusion flitting across his face. Obviously the presence of the police captain in Plas Mawr had implications for Tommy.

'I am so sorry to interrupt this meeting,' he said curtly.

George rose out of the chair a little unsteadily. 'Please do not worry about it, Mr Madoc. As it is close to noon may I offer you a drink? The malt whisky in truth belongs to your client but I'm sure he will not begrudge you a tipple.'

Listening to George, Cameron hid a smirk. He was surprised at George's spark of humour, for the man had appeared docile and even feeble. Perhaps there was some truth in the tales he had heard about George Bellamy being something of a rake and a raconteur during his misspent youth.

Madoc shed his light grey leather gloves. 'A small one would be welcome.'

Rising off the arm of the chair where she was perching, Mary went to the desk to pour the drink.

Taking a nearby seat, Madoc crossed his legs at the knees. 'The purpose of this visit isn't to discuss my client but to inform the family that I have arranged for Edward Bellamy to be collected from his boarding school and brought back to Plas Mawr. It would have been most unfair to expect a boy to endure the ridicule of his fellow scholars on learning that his father stands accused of attempted murder.'

Mary brought a glass of whisky to him. Thanking her politely, Madoc took it from her hand.

Mary couldn't resist saying 'Theft too. Tommy Standish also stole Louise's gems from the house in Chester. '

Madoc gave an almost imperceptible nod of his head. 'Perhaps he was taking them for safe keeping.'

His condescension riled Mary, but catching George's eye she remained silent.

Glancing towards Cameron Chamberlain, Madoc hoped the police captain would explain his presence at Plas Mawr. The man looked too comfortable to be here on police business, his demeanour was more like a family friend.

Cameron caught Madoc's eye. 'Another serious accusation has been directed towards your client, Tommy Standish. At my instigation the case will be reopened.'

Madoc remained composed, showing neither shock nor surprise. 'What is the accusation?'

'Murder,' Cameron said calmly.

Madoc believed that this had something to do with the drowning of Lady Isabelle.

'What murder?' he asked, with an image in his mind of Lady Isabelle being thrown physically out of his office building.

Cameron noticed that Madoc's face had blanched. Curious, he delayed answering and took a slow drink from his glass before explaining, 'The police are reopening the case of Henrietta Standish's death.'

With relief that it had nothing to do with him or his office, Madoc almost shouted, 'But she killed herself!'

Cameron remained calm. 'Not according to her brother.'

'But George Bellamy wasn't even around at that time.'

Cameron gave a wry smile. 'No, indeed he was not. George Bellamy was suffering from injuries caused by Tommy Standish when he tried to murder him.'

Putting the glass aside, Madoc stood. 'The purpose of this visit was to let you know that Edward will be returning from school at the latest by tomorrow. It would be very unprofessional of me to get into discussions about my client. I await a formal notice that this case is being reopened.'

Politely he bowed his head to Mary.

Turning to George, he said, 'Thank you for the whisky.'

Without glancing back he crossed to the door and went through into the long hall. The footman was waiting and they spoke but Madoc's words were indistinct in the library, blurred by the heavy door.

Out in the fresh air, the house at his back, Madoc cursed himself for not dealing with the news of the reopening of the case more calmly. If it was established that Tommy killed Henrietta, Tommy was hangman's fodder. Even if he hadn't touched Henrietta, and the case for attempted murder went against him, the jury would believe that he had also killed his wife and the outcome would be the same. Tommy's future looked bleak. But his was far from rosy. Tommy's incarceration would have a negative impact on the legal practice. Tommy was the main client, a major financial asset. But there were benefits to be had out of his imprisonment or death; he would be the beneficiary of Tommy's Secret Fund. Besides that, he would be in an excellent position to erase his name on recriminating correspondence and account entries. The fraudulent business to scupper Lord Harvey would be dead and buried and he would be entirely in the clear.

Perhaps there were more pluses to be had by getting rid of Tommy than seeing him walk free. Satisfied that everything would turn out in his favour, Madoc breathed deeply on the damp air, savouring the fragrance of wet trees and plants.

The hired cab with two chestnut mares in the traces came to a standstill beside him, and Madoc climbed in.

Chapter 10

Emily lay awake in the near darkness, looking up at the grey ceiling without actually seeing it. Her entire thoughts were of Tommy, and images of him in a dreary prison cell, sleepless, alone, afraid, and friendless circled in her tired mind.

The moment she heard the news of his imprisonment her heart began to break. She was sure the beat in her chest was less strong and there was a nagging pain, a tightness that had not been there before today. She wondered if she was slowly dying. It was a known fact that people died of a broken heart, and hers was broken and never likely to recover from this terrible day.

She tried to remember when the pain had begun to nag, perhaps when Joe sat her down on the old kitchen chair, his caring manner a sure sign that great trouble lay ahead. Holding her hand, Joe explained that Tommy had been carted away in a police cab and was now in the County Gaol accused of trying to murder poor George Bellamy, a lad that had been a boyhood companion.

The charge was nonsense of course, and she explained this to Joe, but he just looked at her as though she had gone completely barmy.

No sooner had she finished having a good cry than the front door was flung open and Mrs Barker stood on the doormat shouting the odds and saying that Tommy had killed her girl, Millie.

Joe had done his best to calm the raving woman, but she was having none of it, and the result was smashed plates and teapot when she overturned the shelf on the dresser.

For years she had asked Joe to nail the shelf down, not because she feared that someone would grab it in such a way as Mrs Barker had, but she worried it may overbalance and come crashing down on the slate floor. In the end it was all the same: the shelves were smashed, and she didn't have enough plates to put the supper on, and no teapot to make a brew.

What a day!

Emily wiped her eyes on the corner of the old sheet.

Now Tommy was locked up. Not in a proper gaol, she had been telling herself throughout the long day, but somewhere he may remain until the assizes.

She sniffed, wiping her eyes again.

What shame for poor Tommy to be up before the assizes. It'd he hard for a man such as Tommy to prove his innocence; as the master of the Garddryn people were likely to be envious of his job and big house. But with the help of Mr Madoc he could pull through it. She had to pray that he did for all their sakes, Tommy's in particular.

What of Mrs Barker? The raving woman said she was going straight to the police station in Caernarvon and telling them that poor Millie had been walking out with Tommy Standish and the lass had expected him to marry her.

Well that was true. Tommy and Millie had been courting until his eyes fell on Henrietta Bellamy.

Emily's tired brain tried to unravel the dates between Millie Barker's murder and the beginning of Tommy's romance with Henrietta.

The quandary brought her to the day Millie was raped. The terrible deed had happened at the mill. Two boys were accused, and they both fled the county before they were charged. There was no stain on Tommy's character. So that proved that he had nothing to do with Millie's murder. Mrs Barker was mad; everyone in the village knew that her mind was turned by her daughter's death.

Emily's eyelids fluttered with impending sleep. Closing her eyes, she drifted into the darkness.

Without a teapot, Joe brewed the morning tea in a small saucepan.

Emily had lain awake almost the entire night, and several times he had woken and heard her tears. Stirring the leaves, he cursed Tommy for bringing more heartache to his mother.

The lass still believed her son was innocent. Innocent! The lad hadn't had an innocent thought in his head since infancy.

There were instances of Tommy's malevolence that still had the power to tear at his soul. The worst, the awful day of little Chloe's funeral, Tommy had buried the child's dolly saying she had no need of it any longer. How he hated his son that day.

Tight lipped, Joe threw the teaspoon onto the tabletop, and poured the tea into two mugs.

Leaving the kitchen-cum-parlour he went into the bedroom.

Emily was awake and sitting up in bed.

Sitting on the chair that doubled as a side-table, he took a sip of tea.

'Joe, I have decided to go into Caernarvon to see Tommy.'

Joe gave a long drawn out sigh.

Emily started to lose patience. 'It's no good taking that attitude, Joe. I mean to go and I will. I would prefer it if you would come with me.'

'Well, I won't,' he said vehemently.

'He's our son,' she pleaded.

Joe sighed again. 'Emily, he's no longer a son of mine.'

171

'But Joe…'

He stood and the bed creaked with the change of weight. Clutching the warm mug to his chest he went to the window and drew back the curtain and looked out. 'Emily, me mind is made up. I'll not give the bastard the time of day.'

'Well, I'm going,' she said belligerently.

He turned to face her. 'Emily, I'll take you to Caernarvon but I'll not step inside the police station or the County Gaol if that's where he's being held. Tommy can rot in there for all I care. When I think what misery he's brought to so many people it makes me blood boil.'

'But surely you don't believe that he's capable of trying to murder George Bellamy?'

'Yes I do, Emily. I think he's capable of anything to get his own way and get his hands on money.'

Her eyes filled with tears. 'You can't mean that you believe what Mrs Barker said. The woman was raving.'

'Aye and I'd be bloody raving if I thought some bastard had murdered one of mine.'

'But Joe…'

'There'll be no more discussion, Emily. I've told you what I will do, I'll take you to Caernarvon but I'll do no more than that. That's me final word on it.'

Emily's lips pursed in annoyance. 'That'll have to do then, won't it?'

Throwing the sheet and blankets aside she got out of bed. Shuffling her feet into a pair of worn slippers, she threw an old coat over her nightgown and went to the outdoor privy.

Frank was up and making a brew for Nora when Emily came back into the kitchen. Joe was polishing his boots energetically, trying to raise a decent shine on the cracked and crazed leather.

Brushing past him, Emily said, 'I'll be ready to leave in twenty minutes.'

Joe gave the boots a final swipe of the brush, and glanced at the clock on the mantel. 'We'll catch the nine-thirty ride.'

The wagon, an ancient vehicle that had once done service as a shop delivery cart, now carried passengers between Garddryn village and Caernarvon twice a day, four times a week.

Following a quick wash in the scullery, and a vigorous brush of her long hair which she caught up in a bun, Emily donned a green cotton frock, and throwing a lightweight shawl around her shoulders she was ready with five minutes to spare, which gave her enough time to swallow half a mug of lukewarm tea.

Joe was standing at the garden gate, looking in the direction of Plas Mawr, when Emily came out of the cottage.

Shouting a goodbye to Frank and Nora, she closed the front door and joined him.

Walking in virtual silence they went towards Maisy's shop, the starting point of Eric Donnington's passenger service. Emily prayed that Mrs Barker would not be travelling to Caernarvon this morning as she had threatened yesterday. The small group of people waiting for Mr Donnington to finalise the trappings on his two mares did not include Mrs Barker.

Joe helped Emily up onto the wagon and then swung up to sit beside her. The stained hessian seats felt damp to the hands; the barn where the wagon is stored must leak, Joe thought, taking off his coat for Emily to sit on.

With everyone aboard Eric Donnington cracked a whip above the heads of the animals and the pair plodded forward in near unison, the old wagon creaking and swaying on its ancient

173

suspension, and wheels rumbling over the uneven surface of the roadway.

Everyone's eyes but Donnington's were on Emily and Joe. Hot with embarrassment Emily looked away, staring across the valley to the mountains beyond.

Though he was annoyed, and had not wanted her to make this journey, Joe felt immense sympathy and picking up her hand where it lay on her lap, he drew it to his side. Her eyes came back to him and she gave him a small smile.

Not wishing to begin a conversation, Joe looked out over the countryside wondering why his elder son sought riches above all else and had not seen the beauty that surrounded him: the mountains, the summits touching the endless sky, the glittering tidal water of the strait, the infinite sea, green woodland and exquisite shore. Even the Garddryn quarry, from a distance, looked monumental and astounding, but Tommy had to own it, not appreciate its man-made beauty, the stepped terraces glistening in the infrequent sunshine.

Eventually arriving at Slate Quay, close to the harbour office, the driver slowed the horses, the wheels crushing the shards of slate covering the ground to grainy dust. A train hooted and the rumble of wheels on tracks was almost lost in the general bedlam around the quays, where hundreds of men were loading slate onto sailing ships moored bow to stern along the stone walls.

The journey from Garddryn village wasn't without embarrassment, initially being ignored and stared at, and then being whispered about by the other passengers behind the shelter of their hands.

As parents of Tommy Standish, the convict, it was something

they would have to live with, Joe thought with resignation.

Harrumphing, he climbed down and then assisted Emily, less agile on her feet now.

Stowing his pipe and baccy, Joe took her arm and they walked away from the wagon and the other passengers.

Avoiding the water's edge, both were aware that recently Tommy's former lover, Lady Isabelle had jumped off the quayside and drowned, carried away by the fierce tidal water. It was just more fodder for local gossips.

Until Tommy is cleared, Emily thought worriedly, the Standish family couldn't avoid being the nub of tittle-tattle. Despondent and tired, she leaned on Joe, letting his strength take her up the hill past the castle walls.

Walking in silence, Joe mentally added Lady Isabelle to the list of folks that had perished at Tommy's hand.

The steep slope took them towards the police station and County Gaol. Joe's eyes strayed to the execution tower close by, unable to comprehend that a son of his may take the short walk there in the near future.

The police station stood between the castle and the sea wall and caught the breeze sweeping off the Menai Strait.

The verdant isle of Anglesey on the opposite banks looked peaceful, serene to Joe's troubled mind and he had a sudden urge to distance himself from the mess and stand on the soil of the ancient isle Ynys Mon, and walk between megalithic standing stones that had survived millennia, and were familiar to Boudicca and her warriors. Roman invaders had slain and were slain in the shadows of the stones. How small Tommy's troubles looked by comparison.

Come Sunday he would go there and touch the stones, and

175

draw strength from the history bound up in the land.

Turning his face into the breeze, raising his hand to his forehead to shade his eyes from the clear sunlight, he looked out over the far-away sand bar, gateway to the sea. Sailing ships, white sails blooming from tall masts, were navigating a passage over the fierce churning water, heading for America, China, Australia; he knew not, but he would give a year's wages to be sailing away with one of them with Emily by his side.

Emily stopped at the open door of the police station. 'Are you coming in with me to see our Tommy?' she asked, her face still pinched with annoyance.

Joe curbed the desire to sigh. 'I'll take you in, but I'll not visit Tommy,' he said determinedly.

Emily tut-tutted. 'Reeght, I'll go on me own,' she said, lifting the hem of her skirt off the pavement and climbing the steps to the entrance.

Silently, Joe followed her.

Inside was dim, the daylight blocked by the castle's high walls.

Her stomach fluttering with nervousness, Emily went straight to the desk manned by a special. 'I would like to see my son, Tommy Standish,' she said, voice splintering.

The man was as officious as his position allowed. 'The police captain is with Standish. When he has finished with the prisoner I'll ask him if Standish is allowed visitors. If not, you must leave the premises.'

Joe stepped in before Emily started a row with the young special. 'We would be grateful if you would ask the captain,' he said politely.

Emily glanced sideways at Joe; it wasn't like him to be

appeasing to a man who thought himself superior to other mortals.

Footsteps came briskly down the long passage.

'That's the captain coming now,' the special said, straightening his back and pulling down the hem of his tunic.

Coming into the entrance hall, Cameron Chamberlain threw a ring of keys onto the desk top, and placed the hat he was carrying onto his straight brown hair.

'If anyone needs me,' he said to the special curtly as he headed for the doorway, 'I'll be back here at four o'clock.'

Though he was afraid to disrupt the captain's arrangements the special said quickly, 'Excuse me for just one moment, Captain. These people are relatives of Tommy Standish and are asking to see him.'

Cameron Chamberlain turned back into the room. Meeting the parents of Tommy Standish was more fascinating than a gathering of Caernarvon's top brass at the Royal Welsh Yacht Club. Standish had paraded himself often enough in the club toadying up to Llewellyn Turner, ingratiating himself amongst famous and wealthy aristocrats. Some members may be amused to hear of the quarry master's father, a humble quarryman. The circumstances of the meeting would certainly be of interest. Tales of murder and attempted murder had a fascination for everyone whatever walk of life.

Taking off his hat, he placed it on the desk and addressed Joe. 'So you want to see your son?'

Joe answered briskly. 'My wife wishes to visit Tommy.'

'Not you?' Cameron said, showing surprise.

'No, I have no need to see him.'

Cameron glanced at Emily and their eyes met. There was a

look of determination and intelligence in the woman's face.

It would upset Standish to have his humble beginnings paraded in the station and the goal. Perhaps the prisoner would be more cooperative and less arrogant after a visit from his mother. As the prisoner was particularly obnoxious this morning and making veiled threats about the compensation he'd paid out, Cameron decided to send the mother in.

He smiled thinly at Emily. 'I see no harm in you going in for half an hour. Someone will show you the way to the cell.'

The special came from around the desk. Emily got a whiff of his body odour. His side-whiskers were untidy and his hair unkempt.

'Follow me,' he said, and Emily caught the reek of his breath.

The corridor to the cells was dim and dreary with the hollow sound of an unfurnished room. The air was dry and dusty without a hint of the outdoors. Very unlike what Tommy is used to, Emily thought, adding another thread to her worries.

A constable came out of a small room, a thin undernourished man with sparse hair and grey featureless eyes.

'What's your errand, Blake?' he barked at the special.

The younger man stopped in his tracks. 'I'm escorting this woman to the prisoner Standish's cell.'

'Who gave you permission?'

'The police captain said I was to take her there.'

'Give me the keys.' The constable put out his hand and snatched the ring from the special.

Emily noticed the crescent of dirt beneath his fingernails.

'Get back to your desk. I'll take her,' he said, putting a hand on Emily's upper arm and directing her down the corridor.

Passing the first grey door, cell one, Emily heard a man crying despairingly.

Her questioning eyes met the gaoler's, and he put pressure on her arm to hurry her along.

At the door of cell three the constable put a key into the lock and it turned with a metallic clank.

The door opened inwards and Emily was pushed into the small square room. The door clanged closed behind her.

Tommy was standing at the high window, looking out at the sky. He turned quickly on hearing the door open and was speechless at seeing his mother standing there. Outdoors a clock struck twelve o'clock with a tinny note, the last strike quivering on the air.

Fists clenched at his side, Tommy strode towards her, standing close he loomed above her. He didn't try to hide his anger. 'What the devil do you think you are doing coming here?'

Emily was shocked at his appearance; his self-control had fled and he looked unkempt, his hair uncombed and a dark shadow on his unshaven face. Her natural instinct was to hold him close to comfort him, but the anger boiling within him was too raw and uncontrolled and a part of her was afraid to close the small gap between them. 'I came to help, even if it's only moral support,' she said calmly.

'Too late for all that now,' he shouted rudely.

Tentatively she touched his sleeve. 'Tommy, please be patient. Soon the police will see that they have made a mistake and they will let you go. You're innocent.'

Tommy gave a snort of derision. 'Innocent. Innocent,' he said twisting towards the bed where he slumped down, the boards cracking with his weight.

Emily rushed to his side and put her hand on his shoulder.

'Hush Tommy, you'll be out of here soon. '

'You can be sure of that. Are you a fortune teller now?' he ridiculed.

'Of course not Tommy, but the police will not lock up an innocent man.'

His anger frayed Emily's nerves and she thought that if she screamed now no one would come to her aid. Beyond the cell was complete silence. The cell was a cocoon trapping Tommy's desperation and anger within.

She didn't know if to retaliate and meet like with like, and scream her frustrations and fears, or cloak his anger with motherly love and hope to comfort and rekindle the original bond.

In a hopeless gesture she tried to hold him, to pull him close as though he were a small boy, but Tommy jumped from her and stood a yard away.

In complete disarray, hair falling wildly onto his brow, he spat words. 'If I'm innocent, why has the police captain just given me the news that they are reopening the case of Henrietta's death?'

Pausing, he waited for her to comment but Emily remained silent, standing close by.

'Are you too shocked to reply, Mother Dear?'

Emily didn't move.

He could not abide her stoicism and went all out to rock her self-control. 'Oh, but that's not the worst of it. I am now accused of murdering Mille Barker. Do you remember her, Mother? Millie was the whore that lived in the village.'

An image of Millie Barker's mother pulling the shelf down off the dresser came to Emily and she heard the crash of crockery again. The demented wailing of the poor woman crying for her murdered child would remain with her for all time.

Emily's eyes remained on him. 'Millie was no whore, Tommy. She was a sweet girl. You liked her a lot. I thought that you would marry her.'

He gave a snap of derisory laughter. 'Marry that trollop. She went with all the boys.'

Emily was tight lipped. 'I don't believe you. Tommy you liked her, and she liked you.'

The smile came off his face and he flushed red with anger. 'Millie threatened to tell Bellamy about my affair with Henrietta if I finished our courtship.'

In an instant Emily knew what was coming next and her face paled.

Tommy snorted. 'The whore was bellowing like a drunk, it's a wonder the entire village didn't hear her.'

'So you shut her up?' Emily whispered.

'Yes, I closed her blasted mouth forever. If I hadn't done that what would have happened to me? I'll tell you what! A life of bloody drudgery, married to a simpleton, babies every year. Instead I have Plas Mawr, the Garddryn, and Ruby, a fair swap.'

'But you no longer have those things,' Emily said, feeling the strength leave her legs.

The words wormed into his anger and he saw that he had said far too much. 'I'll get it all back.'

'No, Tommy, you will not. They have cost too many people too much for you to be in that position again. George and poor Millie had their lives snatched from them. After what you have told me today I must consider that Henrietta also got in the way of your crooked thinking. Men at the Garddryn died because of you, there are orphans in the village that can name their fathers killer: you Tommy, you. The little boy that I loved with all my heart and soul, God forgive me if I made you into the monster you became.'

It shocked him that she should turn against him, but he found the vitriol to send her away impotent to name him a murderer. 'Yes, old woman, I killed Henrietta and Millie, also maimed George but there is nothing you can say that can send me to the gallows where you think I belong. The jury will believe that you are jealous of my success and wish to see me brought down. So don't think of running to the authorities with your mad claims. A clever barrister will knock your story to hell.'

Turning away from him, Emily banged on the door for the constable.

The door creaked open, and she looked over her shoulder to her son. 'God forgive you Tommy. For your mother never will.'

The door clanged closed behind her. 'Good riddance,' she heard him call. 'You and you alone are to blame for all of this.'

Joe was waiting on the outdoor step smoking his pipe when she appeared. Seeing him, Emily burst into tears. His arm circled her shoulders and he drew her close.

When her tears dried and she had blown her nose, he said, 'They are moving Tommy to Chester. It's feared he may not get a fair trial here with him being the master of the Garddryn.'

He sighed. 'Whatever is it all coming to, Emily?'

'Just take me home, Joe,' she said calmly.

'I'll take thee to the Black Boy and buy thee a sherry first,' he said, slipping into the dialect of his childhood, as was usual when he was worried.

They caught the late afternoon wagon back to Garddryn,

receiving similar treatment from the other passengers as was meted out earlier. Emily no longer cared, she had much bigger worries, and she wasn't even sure she could tell them to Joe.

They arrived home in the early evening, when the sun had begun to dip behind the mountains, and a new freshness was in the air after a warm afternoon.

Their spirits low, they came along the lane arm in arm, their shoes dusty, and with hardly enough energy to finish the last yards of the journey.

It was with a sense of relief that Joe opened the gate and let Emily pass through. Turning to close it behind him, he jumped when Emily gave a shout of pleasure.

Edward was sitting on the doorstep. Getting up he rushed to hold Emily. Joe arms circled them both and tears came to his eyes.

'Welcome, lad,' Joe said sniffing back tears.

Releasing the boy, Emily drew the front door key out of her bag. Turning it in the lock she was reminded of the clank of Tommy's cell door.

Indoors she quickly busied herself with putting the kettle to the warm hob, thankful that for once Nora had remembered to keep the fire in low. Parched for a cuppa, she reached for the caddy off the mantelpiece.

'There's some ginger beer in the scullery,' she said to Edward. 'Fetch a couple of bottles for you and your grandpa, there's a good lad.'

Edward leapt up and was back in a few moments holding two fizzing bottles.

Sitting at the wooden table, Edward grinned. 'I really love coming here. It's like home is supposed to be.'

'Oh Edward,' Emily said catching a tear with a sniff. 'That's the nicest thing anyone has said to me for a while.' Blanking out the cruel words she had heard from the mouth of her son, she repeated, 'The nicest in quite a while.'

Edward's grin widened. I'm glad you are pleased to see me, because I am back at Plas Mawr for good.'

Joe opened the bottles, froth spurting onto the scrubbed pine. 'That's great news, Ed.'

The boy took a sip and then his face clouded. 'There's something wrong, papa is not home, an aunt and uncle I have never met have moved into the house and no one will tell me anything.'

Joe pulled a chair from under the table and patted the wooden seat. 'You come and sit here, Edward. I will tell you all I know.'

Emily sat in the comfortable chair beside the dying fire listening as Joe explained as kindly as he could to the young boy.

There were no tears but the bubble went out of the lad for a little while and then he said, 'So I'm not going back to school because I did wrong, but because it would be too shaming to go there.'

Joe met the boy's eyes. 'If there's any shame to be apportioned we'll place it slap bang where it belongs, with the person that has done wrong. That is not you, Edward.'

Emily rose stiffly. 'I'm going to make some ham butties, who wants one?'

Edward brightened. 'Can I have two, Nan? I'm starving.'

'Course you can, lad.'

The scullery was cold but Emily cut the ham and the bread there to give herself time to calm down, and get the tears that threatened under control.

Coming back into the kitchen-cum-parlour with a stacked plate she put it onto the end of the table; the far end was taken up with a chess board. Edward appeared to be beating Joe, but a wink from Joe told her that everything was under control.

Swallowing a mouthful of bread and ham, Edward said, 'As I'll be here all the time, and papa will be away, do you think it would be a good idea to have a dog? I really loved Nick when he was here.'

Chewing, Joe nodded. 'Aye, it sounds like a really good idea. I liked having Nick around too. He was a funny old dog.'

Edward broke a piece of bread off the sandwich. 'Do you think we could find another just like Nick?'

Joe took a swig of ginger beer. 'Hard to find exactly the same, but we may find a close enough match.'

Edward's eyes sparkled. 'Can I come with you to look for him?'

Joe pretended to think about this for a moment and then he said slowly, 'Aye, that a good idea.'

'Can we go on Sunday, Grandpa?'

'Aye, we could do that and at the same time we could walk up to the Macphersons, I heard that they have a bunch of puppies they are trying to find homes for.'

Edward leapt off the chair and into Joe's arms.

Circling the boy, feeling the warmth of his narrow body through his light shirt, Joe remembered his idea of going to Anglesey on Sunday to stand amongst the megalithic stones and touch history. He wouldn't go now as he had a puppy to find for a boy. Sometime in the near future he would cross the Strait to Anglesey with Edward and they would climb the green hills to see standing stones; Ynys Mon had an abundance of them. There he would teach the boy the history of Boudicca, the Romans, and Owain Glyndwr, the last native Welshman to hold the title of the Prince of Wales.

'What time shall I come on Sunday?' Edward asked earnestly.

Joe grinned. 'Whatever time you wish, Edward. Just pop over whenever you feel like it.'

Edward's eyes shone. 'Really?'

'Really!' Joe matched his grin.

Chapter 11

Leaving his office just before noon, Madoc walked beneath the looming walls of Caernarvon Castle, and passing the entrance to the arch in the town wall he walked down the short slope to the medieval palace.

The sun was high in a clear sky, and the town baked in the heat trapped by the castle walls and the flanking buildings; the pavement radiated heat and it penetrated the soles of his handmade shoes.

Wearing a suit and a stiff collared shirt with a silk tie, he was uncomfortable, the sun scorching the nape of his neck.

His errand didn't please him, but he saw no way out of taking the heavy portmanteau he was carrying to the police station and attempting to deliver it into Tommy's cell. The whole plan was preposterous, dreamed up by Tommy who had now reached desperation point.

Nearing the police station he slowed his pace, glancing at the pedestrians, looking for the dark uniforms of specials or constables. There were several dark coated men and he had to look twice before deciding that they were no immediate threat.

At the police station he crossed the narrow street, just avoiding a horse and cart, and stood with his back to the castle walls eyeing the open door. Nobody was shifting inside. To make sure, he re-crossed the street and shielding his eyes with his hand, squinted through the window of the reception office, but saw little more than his own reflection staring back in the darkened glass.

Glancing from left to right to make sure no uniforms were approaching, he took three light steps and stole a nervous glance into the entrance room.

The lanky and rather dirty constable was manning the desk, just as Tommy said he would be at this time of day. Gathering his courage, telling himself that this had to be done to save his own neck, as well as Tommy's, he walked in.

It was obvious that the constable was waiting for him, for the man came around the desk and with the slightest nod of his head escorted Madoc immediately to Tommy's cell.

Cooped up, sweltering in the heat trapped in the small and virtually windowless cell, Tommy had no way of knowing if everything was going according to plan in the reception area. Though he had promised Constable Lloyd money to help smuggle in the bag, there was always a possibility that a special or another constable would turn up with a prisoner and the plan would go awry.

Though the temptation to pace was strong, he denied himself the pleasure, and stood with his ear to the cold metal door listening intently for the sound of footsteps in the corridor.

With no pocket watch he had to rely on the town clock striking the hour and half hour to judge the quarter and minutes, and his guess could be wrong, which would mean that Madoc wasn't yet in the station. Then to his absolute relief the first peal marking noon rang out, the long and loud dong quivering on the hot dry air.

He let out a heavy breath and it rasped against the cold metal. A frisson of excitement and nervousness made him feel wide awake; any moment, if everything was in order, he would hear Madoc's footsteps approaching. His ear and the flat of his hand was against the cold metal to catch the merest vibration of moved air; holding his breath, he listened.

Footsteps approached, and he kept his position, listening intently for the sound of a voice raised in alarm.

The tread ceased outside cell three. Tommy stepped back quickly.

The door opened inwards and for the briefest moment Madoc stood beneath the lintel. Tommy's eyes lit on the portmanteau and then his glance went to the constable standing behind Madoc. The thin rake of a man winked and a grin passed over his weasel face.

Madoc stepped into the cell.

The door shut with a bang and the key turned in the lock.

Madoc breathed a loud sigh of relief.

Almost throwing the bag onto the bed, he slumped down beside it. Pulling a clean white handkerchief from his pocket, he wiped his sweating face.

Tommy's eyes glinted with excitement as he passed his hand over the leather. 'Well done, Madoc.'

Madoc sighed. 'I can't say it was easy. Every moment I expected to be apprehended and the bag searched.'

The release of tension made Tommy slightly light headed. He chortled. 'You've an honest face, Madoc.'

'Honest!' Madoc grimaced. He drew the handkerchief once more over his face, and wiped the back of his neck.

Tommy undid the leather straps and drew the two sides of the bag apart. A jacket, neatly folded, lay on the top and pulling it out, he threw it down on the bunk. Two pairs of trousers and shirts followed it as did a stack of small clothes and toiletries.

Stuffing the handkerchief back in his trouser pocket, Madoc slipped out of his frock coat and threw it down on the foot of the bunk.

Glancing at the open bag, he said, 'All the money that was in you private account is there. Why did you need it all today?'

Pulling out the last garment, Tommy came to the notes and gold coins that half-filled the portmanteau. The sight of it made his escape bid more real, and now he felt he had a chance to throw off the shackles and the threat hanging over him like the sword of Damocles. Extracting a wad of cash he weighed it in his hand.

Though he hated his decisions to be questioned, Tommy answered Madoc calmly. 'I need it all today to pay the bribe to the constable that kindly let you in here with it. And as the authorities have seen fit to move me to Chester gaol, I need a hefty amount to bribe my way out of custody. Who knows how much I will need, it's better to be safe than sorry, especially when trying to keep one's neck out of a noose.'

Madoc's brow furrowed. 'I suppose it is necessary,' he said, sorry to see the money leave his own control. There was no doubt in his mind that had he refused to bring it, and Tommy's life was about to be cut short, Tommy would have wreaked revenge and spoken out about their joint nefarious financial deals and the fraudulent contracts that he, Madoc, had instigated to regain Ruby quarry from Lord Harvey and his cohorts. Such a disclosure would ruin him and he would also serve a long gaol term. Tommy was a dangerous man and it was better to help than hinder him in his break for freedom.

Both men jumped at a sound outside the door. Stuffing the clothes back into the bag, Madoc pushed it under the narrow bed and sat down quickly.

When silence returned, Madoc said, 'So what is the plan?'

'They are moving me to Chester gaol on Wednesday. I'm to

be driven in a police carriage to Bangor railway station and then by train to Chester. A second carriage will drive to the gaol. I believe that there will be two guards throughout the journey.'

'And what's the likelihood of them both turning a blind eye for the right amount of cash?'

Tommy sighed. 'I'm in the hands of our trusty constable, but he seems to think that it's a possibility. We have to wait to see which two guards will be chosen to escort me. The constable is going to volunteer. He'll tell a tale about his aged mother being very ill in Chester and wanting to go and see her for the last time.'

Madoc looked serious. 'It's all a bit vague.'

'Yes, I know. Don't think I'm not worried. Relying on a person such as Constable Lloyd is far from ideal but it's the only option.'

'I can see that,' Madoc said thoughtfully, imagining Tommy Standish a fugitive. 'Are you planning to escape from the train or the carriage?'

'Depending on the cooperation of the guards, I shall take the first opportunity that presents itself. If they can't be bribed, I'll fake an illness and take my chances then.'

In truth Tommy already had his plans in place, but he wasn't going to divulge them to Madoc; he didn't trust the solicitor entirely, there had been occasions when Madoc had double-crossed witnesses in court.

Madoc moved his backside on the hard bed. 'If you could make a break for it at Bangor station, a cab could be waiting close by to carry you to a safe house in the town.'

Tommy ran his hand over the short growth of a recent beard. 'It's a good idea, Madoc. Can you make arrangements for that?'

Another hour passed before Madoc departed.

As soon as his footsteps receded down the corridor, Tommy pulled the bag from under the bed, and flinging the clothes onto the thin blanket he grabbed wads of notes and counted them roughly. A quick calculation confirmed that the amount was probably correct.

Reluctantly he placed the money back in the bag and folded the clothes neatly on top. Closing it, he hid it once again beneath the bed.

With nothing to do but stand looking at the afternoon sky through the high window, or lie on the plank bed, he did the latter and waited for the day to come to an eventual close.

Idleness throughout the day made it impossible to sleep at night, and Tommy tossed and turned eventually awaking from a light doze as daylight slipped into the sky.

The flesh on his hip was sore, bruised by the hard bed, and there was a pain in his shoulder. Getting up, sitting on the edge of the bunk, he made slow circles in the air to relieve the pain at the top of his arm.

There was a chill in the cell which he was grateful for; yesterday had been a blisteringly hot day and the airlessness remained until well into the night.

Standing, he looked through the high window to the sky, still grey with false dawn. It told him nothing of the predicted weather for the day.

With nothing else to do before a meagre breakfast was brought to him, a piece of bread thinly spread with dripping and a cup of weak tea, he sat with his head in his hands remembering the breakfast brought to him by servants at Plas Mawr. Kidneys, bacon, lamb chops, fried eggs and excellent coffee and plenty of it. It was torture to recall the rich aromas, and it made his mouth water and stomach clench with hunger.

Imprisonment was terrible, and perhaps the hardest thing to bear was the loss of ordinary coming and going that a free man takes for granted. The simple things like mounting a horse and riding away from the office or the mansion, or driving to Penrhyn Castle, Caernarvon, Bangor or anywhere else in a smart carriage, new enough to attract the attention.

Good food, properly cooked came high up on the list of deprivation; day and night he caught the fragrance of new bread, meat roasting, or bacon cooking in a pan.

At the beginning of his incarceration food had been the last thing on his mind. Most of those dreadful hours were filled with a sickness in his belly so severe that his limbs shivered and his fingers trembled every time he moved his hands.

Now after several days in the cell, hunger was getting the better of him, and he thought of food a good part of the time, the taste of it, texture, aroma, and even the heat of it.

A good brandy, malt whisky, a shimmering glass of cold white wine was a denial too far. What he wouldn't give to feel the fire of a Napoleon trickling down his throat and warming his belly. Madoc had lost an opportunity when he brought in the bag and forgot to hide a bottle in there. But then he may very well have drunk the entire contents of the bottle and been found incapable and that would have given the game away. Madoc may very well have considered that and kept to the side of caution, though a small flask wouldn't have gone amiss.

He wondered if he could survive another day of imprisonment, another hour of this interminable boredom, the silence, the waiting.

George and Mary Bellamy were to blame for it all, the dispossession, imprisonment, dreadful tedium, and the fear of hanging that gnawed into his very being. When he gained his freedom he was going to kill them both, place his hands around their scrawny necks and strangle the life out of them, squeeze until the last breath leached out.

A clanking in the corridor brought his attention back to the moment. The cell door opened and a special came in with an old tray balanced precariously; on it, sliding back and forth, was a plate of bread and a mug of tea.

'Can I have hot water to wash myself?' Tommy said, taking hold of the tray. 'Please,' he added when a look of denial crossed the man face.

When the hot water was brought he considered shaving but decided against it. A beard was a good disguise and besides, he liked the silky feel of it against his fingertips.

The morning dragged by and was only relieved by a visit from two policemen intent upon getting a confession out of him for Millie Barker's murder. As much as they questioned him, bullied and harassed, Tommy remained calm, answering that he was a very young man when Millie died, not much more than a boy. Two men had raped her only days before the murder, those two fled the country; surely it was these fugitives that the officers should be searching for and making enquiries in Ireland, where it was rumoured the men had fled.

After the men departed, Tommy thought of his mother and the pressure she was under to keep the secret of the murders of Millie and Henrietta, impossible for her to confide in her husband; if Joe Standish learned the truth he would go immediately to the police and tell all.

As long as she lived his mother was forced to keep the secret, if she weakened her son would hang. Now she would suffer for all the times she had shown more love to Chloe and Frank and left him out in the cold.

At noontime he endured another dismal bowl of soup for the midday meal which reminded him so much of his mother's interminable stews and vegetable mush that he almost pushed it away; only the biting hunger in his belly urged it passed his lips.

Late in the afternoon, expecting Cole, a barrister from London, Tommy changed into clean small clothes and a fresh shirt.

The barrister was punctual and for more than an hour he sat on a hard chair, brought in by a special, and began to prepare a defence. Eventually the afternoon came to a close and the light began to fail in the cell; the man suggested that he would come back the following morning to finish the meeting. Tommy was glad to see him leave.

Alone, Tommy sat for a while on the edge of the bed, occasionally moving to the chair that the special had forgotten to remove.

The evening meal was brought in, broth reeking of old bones and vegetables boiled in water. Swallowing it soaked up moments of absolute boredom.

Eventually the empty dish was removed. The cell door closed on the last person he expected to see for many hours. The cell grew dim and when he could no longer see the walls clearly, he slipped out of his clothes and climbed under the thin blanket and tried to sleep.

Images of George sleeping between freshly ironed sheets brought a hot flush of temper. Throwing off the threadbare blanket he sat on the edge of the bunk with his head in his hands, his mind plunging into the abyss of regret. If he had hit the bastard harder, and for another time, he would not now be locked in a cell sweating his guts out. He cursed that he had been too feeble to check that the bugger had perished; it was crass stupidity to be put off by the blood and gore. Better to have got his hands dirty that night than be here, and blasted George sleeping comfortably in Plas Mawr.

Thoughts of the house brought the festering anger, building up for days, to the surface and unable to remain still he flung himself away from the bed and paced the floor. The urge to let out a solitary scream, to pit a raw sound at the silence was so great that he bit down on his fisted knuckle to contain it.

Tasting a trace of blood, he licked the small wound, and stuck both hands in his trouser pockets.

He sat back down, breathless and heart pounding, shaken by the torrent of anger that had spewed out. The font was far from empty, and there would be no peace in his mind until George Bellamy lay dead. It was unfinished business and he meant to remedy the failure at the first opportunity. But first, he would physically tear the bastard from the house and make him wish he had never set foot in it.

Mary would take the same path as her weak husband. The whore had ingratiated herself with the lunatic George to ultimately possess Plas Mawr, the quarries, the overseas businesses and all the trappings that went with wealthy landowners' privileges.

In a million years she wouldn't belong, she was nothing but a jumped up servant. By witchery she was now living at Plas Mawr, and eating at his table and sleeping in one of his beds.

Rough stock like Mary could never appreciate fine food and good wine, each bottle in the cellar worth more than a quarryman earned for a month's labour.

Mary would rue the day she saw fit to dispossess Tommy Standish. Her moment of glory in the library, accusing him of stealing his mother-in-law's gems and trying to murder George, would cost her dear.

Wrapped in a shroud of self-importance, she must have thought herself very clever.

How he had itched to wipe the supercilious sneer from her mouth. To blurt out that George was too feeble a character to put up a fight, and that he had swooned like a woman at the first clout of the stone.

Cowardice ran in the family. Henrietta was weak like her brother, weak and obstinate. She too thought she was above her husband, even better than him, when in reality she hadn't a day's work in her.

Defiant, she deserved what came her way. Quite plainly he had strictly forbidden her to go to Corn Cottage to visit his poverty gloating parents, but the moment his back was turned, she walked out of Plas Mawr and headed there, taking young Edward.

When she returned home there had been a row and he clouted her so hard she fell against the corner of the desk. Even then she still tried to escape him, but he was faster, and catching her by the hair he hauled her back and clouted her again.

Escaping the room she had run upstairs; he had followed, but Edward's nurse was standing on the landing. Turning away, he retreated to the library. But later, he crept into Henrietta's bedroom. By then she had taken a dose of heroin, the doctor's cure for the opium addition that lay claim to her. She was drowsy, and he lifted her head and dribbled another dose into her mouth.

She had fallen back almost instantly. Minutes later he had roused her again. Befuddled, the stupid wench drank down another dose.

Leaving her to her slumber, he went downstairs and sat in the library with a glass of brandy.

Chapter 12

Though Mary loved walking through the parkland and picnicking with George on the hottest days at the lakeside, she found it hard to live in Plas Mawr with its plethora of servants; there was no privacy or solitude.

George hadn't been himself since they arrived at the mansion, his temper was less certain and he worried about trivia. She wondered if the house held other bad memories for him beside the time he spent here initially recuperating after the attack.

Not to love the house was ridiculous; anyone else would be delighted to have servants waiting on hand and foot, and wonderful meals conjured up as though by magic, with no preparation or dishes to wash. In the cottage she and George shared in Chester, laundry days were the bane of her life, but in Plas Mawr quite miraculously clothes went from her dressing room and appeared a little while later washed, ironed and generally spruced up.

Perhaps it was George's change of mood affecting her, or the constant police presence in the grounds or the house, as uniformed men searched for evidence of Tommy's involvement in Millie Barker's murder amongst his personal possessions.

Impossible to wander into Garddryn village, people were naturally curious and would ask questions. Every spare room in the quarry cottages was taken by newspaper men intent on feeding the masses with salacious stories. She had no intention of becoming part of the circus; it was bad enough that reporters banged on the front door and had the temerity to stare into the ground floor windows until chased away by the outdoor staff.

The staff were agog at the change of circumstances and

around every corner they were caught gossiping behind their hands.

It was wearing, and she wondered if she and George had done the correct thing in coming to stay here.

They had been sitting on the terrace for some time, watching a pair of blackbirds in the elm tree, when George unexpectedly stood and, taking her arm, he said, 'Let's wander over to the kitchen garden. I bet you would love to see vegetables growing in straight lines, so unlike my attempts in our small patch in Chester.'

Falling into step, arms linked, they crossed to the stable yard and then beyond to the arched gate in the redbrick wall surrounding the garden.

'I used to love coming here when I was a small boy. The gardener in charge was kind to me, and unbeknownst to my parents I would play with his children, two boys and three girls.' He gave a genuine smile, the like she hadn't seen for days. 'They were a raggedy lot those children, and spent more time in the trees that on the ground.'

'Did you climb with them?' she asked, taken with the tale.

George pulled his tight trouser leg up to his knee and said, 'This scar is an emblem of my success as a forester.'

Laughter lines at the corners of her eyes crinkled into tight folds. 'A forester?'

He kicked a stone off the path and into the dormant carrot bed. 'It's what we called our gang, the foresters. They were happy days.'

She put pressure on his arm and turned him to face her. 'Are you unhappy now, George?'

'No, just a bit unsettled, that's all. I wish all this business was over and we could get back to some sort of normality.'

'We can go back home if you wish to.'

'Yes, I know that. But I feel I'd be letting the side down to go now, before Tommy Standish has his day in court.'

'What side, George?'

A film of tears came to his eyes. 'The side is my father, mother, and poor Henrietta.'

'I understand, George,' Mary said softly patting his arm.

Sniffing back tears, he said, 'Now look at that spinach, Mary. Did you ever see such orderly vegetables?'

Mary laughed. 'No George, I didn't, and certainly not in our patch of garden.'

'Tomorrow I will ask the gardener for tips on straightening up the garden. There'll be no frolicking peas and certainly no haphazard runner beans ever again.'

'George, you are a love,' she said, standing on tiptoe and kissing his mouth.

It was the last time that George and Mary would walk in the beautiful gardens of Plas Mawr.

For a second night, sleep refused to come to Emily and she lay dwelling on what Tommy had revealed to her about Henrietta's and Millie Barker's deaths.

Tommy, once the little boy she loved so dearly, had murdered two people and tried to kill another. How could it be that her son had become such a monster that he could snuff out a life on little more than a whim?

Not daring to think of the quarrymen that had died at the quarry gates, she turned her mind to the people that had at one time been part of Tommy's life. Lady Isabelle had died, though perhaps not at Tommy's hand. But she had been driven to suicide, by whom if not Tommy? Louis Bellamy had died in the garden at Plas Mawr. Where was Tommy then? He swore he was at Penrhyn Castle but had anyone checked his whereabouts. And whatever happened to the two youths that disappeared from the village after the rape of Millie Barker? The rascals vanished into thin air overnight. Did Tommy have something to do with their exodus? Were their bodies hidden in graves in the woods?

It was doing her no good thinking along these lines and she called a halt to it.

She glanced at Joe, lying on his back sleeping soundly, the blanket up to his chin, as though he hadn't a care in the world.

During all the years they had been together there had been no secrets between them, until now. By confessing, Tommy succeeded in ruining a special part of the marriage. It was a betrayal not to tell Joe. But if she revealed the truth, which she longed to do, he would feel a responsibility to the dead women and go to the police, and Tommy would hang.

As quietly as she could she turned onto her side, away from Joe, and burying her face in the pillow she cried secretly.

Waking, Joe listened to her tears. He felt like crying too. Since Tommy's arrest he had swallowed back so many tears that there was a permanent lump in his throat.

Turning to Emily, he slipped an arm around her waist and tried to comfort her.

The moment the news of Tommy Standish's arrest reached Garddryn and Ruby quarries, work had slowed down. On the terraces and in the cabans where the men met to eat the midday meal and drink tea little else was talked about; the standard debates on prose and music took a back seat as entertainment as the lives of the Standish family was dissected and examined.

Everyone expected the quarry manager to hold a meeting on the quadrangle and explain what the new circumstances meant for the workers. Mr Iwan Rees kept his own counsel and no information was forthcoming. Everyone, including the clerks, was tight lipped and unhelpful.

So the questions went on with no one offering an answer to the one most frequently asked: would there still be work after Tommy Standish's trial?

Some men left the village to find work in the copper mines at Parys Mountain. Afraid if they stayed too long at the Garddryn or Ruby, the few jobs that were available at Amlwch would have been snapped up.

In the kitchens of the quarry cottages, wives began rationing food, saving pennies for the hard times that may be ahead. Fruit from the hedgerows disappeared overnight as children gathered everything that was edible for the pickling and jam pans. Wooden makeshift shelters for pigs and hens began to appear again in back gardens, and the manager of the local livestock market saw an increase in sales of animals.

The leafy growth of turnips, swedes, parsnips and winter spinach sprang out of the ground where summer flowering plants had recently flourished as families turned their hands again to growing vegetables.

For many it was turning the clock back to the time when uncertainty ruled quarrymen's lives, and the threat of strikes and lock-outs was a permanent worry. With the growth of the new union, deprivation and injustice was to be a thing of the past. Quarry masters would be forced to treat workers fairly and honestly, and pay them a proper wage for their labour. No longer would a quarryman have to work the extra hours a master demanded. The union promised quarry hospitals for the sick, the injured and dying.

These great transformations were coming, and it would break hearts if the Garddryn and Ruby were shut and the workers that had strived for so long under terrible hardships were not to benefit from the great upheaval.

Quarrymen were stoics and whatever came to pass the union would benefit them all, thanks to men like Joe and Frank Standish.

Chapter 13

The day that would be momentous for Tommy Standish began drearily, the sky a flat uninteresting grey and the air humid.

The weather was unimportant to him, and the clammy atmosphere he could try to ignore.

He rose early, unable to stand another moment beneath the blanket. The wooden plank of a bed had made the joints of his hips and elbows sore, and it was near agony to lie for more than a short while.

The cell door opened and a special brought in a bowl of lukewarm porridge. Tommy ate it standing, shovelling it down before it became cold.

Later, perhaps in an hour or two, the barrister would return and he would be subjected to another mountain of questions by the man. It was all very tedious, especially when none of the information he imparted was to be used in a court of law.

He dressed a little more carefully, brushed his dark hair neatly and even ran the bristles over his emerging glossy black beard. Going to the door, he listened but heard no one approaching. Toying with the idea of repacking the portmanteau still secreted beneath the bed, he decided against it, as the breakfast dish had not yet been collected.

The door opened, startling him a little.

Coming into the cell the special said cheerfully, 'I'd say you'd be glad to be getting out of here come Wednesday. Locked up these past days you must be going barmy. I know I would.'

Tommy put the friendliness down to youth and naivety and he answered equally pleasantly, 'I will not be sorry to see the last of these walls, I seem to have done nothing but stare at them for days.'

'I'll bring you yesterday's newspaper,' the lad said, going out with the dish.

The door clanged closed and Tommy stared at it for a moment, bemused by the special's cheerful banter. It worried him that Constable Lloyd may have spoken out of turn and made the lad aware that the prisoner could be relied on for a bribe.

The key turned in the lock and the door opened again. Tommy looked closely at the lad's face, trying to detect the reason for the special's kindness.

He handed Tommy a rolled up newspaper. Grinning, he went out and the door clanged closed behind him.

Unsuspecting, Tommy opened the paper and a picture of his face stared back at him. The headline above the picture read Wealthy Landowner Murder Charge.

Shocked, he flung the newspaper at the wall. The headline was an outright lie. He was not charged with murder. The charge against him was attempted murder, and he'd tear the scrotum off the man that wrote it.

Gathering the strewn pages he checked the front page for the name of the correspondent. 'James Black,' Tommy sneered, sorry that he had fed the man stories and helped him step up the pecking order of the newspaper.

Angry, he wondered how long it would be before the toe-rag that carried the paper in would appear again. He'd like to kick the lout's arse for him, but there was too much at stake to give vent to his anger. One swipe at the youth and he'd find himself carted off to the Chester gaol and his plans would topple and he would fail to get clear.

For once he would have to be tight lipped, and sit on his hands smiling at the imbecile, as though he had enjoyed the joke.

Hearing a clatter in the corridor, Tommy took a step back and sat on the edge of the bed, hands beneath his rump, and a smile fixed to his mouth.

The door opened and the youth came in.

The smile didn't leave Tommy's face. 'You're a brave young man,' he said jovially. 'A lesser person would be afraid that a so-called murderer may get off and come searching the alleyway of the town for him, a quick swish of a knife along the throat and whoosh, gone.'

The rosy glow of amusement vanished from the youth's face.

Though stiff from lack of exercise, Tommy came to his feet quickly and crossed the small space.

To avoid him, the special took a step back, colliding with the metal door.

Tommy smiled thinly. 'Thank you for the newspaper, it passed a few dreary moments. Trust me, I shall not forget your kind thought.'

Stepping sideways, the special opened the door and went through quickly.

Tommy's laugh was loud.

The look of trepidation on the special's face as he departed kept Tommy amused throughout the long morning.

The midday meal was another distraction, and though it looked unwholesome, a thin broth of overcooked vegetables, pearl barley and fibrous morsels of scrag of lamb, Tommy swallowed it down and drank the mug of weak tepid tea.

Two hours of the afternoon were taken up by the barrister, intent upon discovering a flaw in the charge against him, but it was obvious by the look of tedium in the man's expression that he saw little chance of actually winning the case. The man droned on until shadows dimmed the cell and he took his leave, promising to be at Chester gaol the following week.

A sudden heavy shower of rain pebbled the high window with drops of water. Gazing at it, Tommy caught the shifting colours of the day outside. Women hurrying by were the blues and greens, the black and grey numerous umbrellas. The horses drudging past painted the glass with shades of dull brown.

How he yearned to be walking along the pavement, water splattering beneath his feet, and the castle walls dark and damp with rain looming above him. He'd go briskly down the slope to the quay, and climb down the stone steps of the landing stage and look out to the sandbar, gateway to the sea. Overhead circling seabirds were calling, and all around was the sound of water flowing in runnels, rinsing the long tendrils of bright green slimy weed on the quay's stone walls. Though he would be drenched, hair flattened to his head, he would take long moments to look out over the Strait and watch raindrops splashing into the pewter grey water, patterning it with ever-increasing haloes.

The town clock struck six, the long peals falling flat on the wet air.

Tommy started.

A heavy door slammed closed. There was a blare of masculine laughter. Then a door slammed again. He was becoming familiar with the noise heralding a change of shift. If everything went to plan, two constables would be in charge of the station from now until twelve o'clock tonight. Lloyd had swapped his shift with Constable Hanrahan, and he would bear the longer stint lasting until six o'clock tomorrow morning.

Going to the door, Tommy put his ear against the metal trying to pick up the sound of Constable Lloyd's voice. If the arrangement went awry now he would be crushed with frustration and tomorrow he would be carted off to Chester gaol. If an opportunity to evade the guards on the journey didn't materialise, he would land in the gaol without a hope of escaping and he would be dead meat following the next assizes.

The door opened and Constable Lloyd walked in, rubbing his hands together. 'I can't do anything until the old fellow on the desk has gone at twelve o'clock. At that time I'll bring in some old clothes for you to change into.' He grinned broadly. 'Five minutes after that, God willing, we will be out of here. Hope you've got the money because I'm not risking me own neck for nowt.'

Now that the time for going drew close, Tommy's nerves tingled with anticipation and excitement.

'The money is counted and ready for you,' he said, keeping his voice moderate.

'Good. You can give it me now.'

Sensing a double cross, Tommy's eyes flashed with suspicion. 'Time enough for that when we are out of here.'

Lloyd grinned. 'Don't fret. It'll work out. Now I must to get back to the desk or I'll be missed, and old Hanrahan gets narked if he thinks he's been left with all the chores.'

Minutes later, Hanrahan came in with a bowl of broth and a lump of bread. Departing without a word, he closed the door.

Tommy flinched hearing the key turn in the heavy lock and he wondered how long his nerves would last out if he was incarcerated beyond tonight.

The broth was pale yellow and he tried to guess the

ingredients. Though tempted not to eat it, he was afraid that if he veered from the norm it would arouse questions and he may very well be watched more closely that he had been of late. Guardedly he sipped from the edge of the cheap spoon, but failed to name what the thin liquid was made from. Hoping that it was an old boiling fowl, he dipped a hunk of bread into the bowl and then ate the soggy piece. There was no knowing when he would next eat.

The town clock struck the half hour.

Putting the empty bowl aside, Tommy paced the small space. There were five and a half hours to kill and nothing but the fear of failure to keep him company.

For an hour he listened intently for the slightest change coming from within the station, but there was nothing out of the ordinary going on. Occasionally a clatter from the street, a drunk passing by, would block the indoor sounds and, vexed, Tommy pressed his ear flat against the cell door to check that he had missed no change.

Daylight began to fail and the cell dimmed to grey.

At ten o'clock he was roused from the bed, where he perched uncomfortably, by the raucous noise of an inebriated fool being hauled into the station. Coming to his feet, Tommy stood in the centre of the small space, heart pounding and a sickness in his belly, seeing his plans fall asunder two hours before being accomplished.

The complaining drunk was hauled down the corridor. The adjacent cell door was opened and the man was thrown in, shouting his innocence. A thump followed and Tommy guessed that Lloyd or Hanrahan, or the constable that had brought the drunk in, had seen fit to hit him. He was still shouting when the cell door banged closed.

Tommy felt no sympathy; given the opportunity he would have walloped the bugger a great deal harder.

The man vomited noisily. Queasy with anxiety, Tommy's stomach turned.

The new prisoner fell silent and Tommy felt his way in the pitch dark to the cell door to listen for voices in the entrance office, trying to pick up a third, fearing that the constable that had come in off the street with the drunk may stay in the station and ruin his escape.

It seemed such a long while since the town clock had struck, he wondered if he had missed its now familiar peal. Losing track of time was torture, and though he would have preferred to pace back and forth, he perched on the edge of the bunk, his entire being centred on the clock.

The key to the cell door turned and the door opened; a light from the corridor briefly lighting the cell, Lloyd stuck his head in and gave him the thumbs up. The cell door closed quietly and once again the key turned and he was in the dark.

The intrusion took Tommy's attention away from the clock but before he could begin to get anxious it struck eleven and he breathed a sigh of relief. With only one hour to go, he began to count the seconds adding them into minutes, unaware that he was breathing irregularly, waiting for the clock to strike the half hour. Time slowed torturously, passing on iron shod shoes. Then he remembered that the clock never struck after eleven at night. It could be almost time for Lloyd to come back.

Now he wanted to don his coat and be ready, but it would look strange if Hanrahan came into the cell.

Without knowing how much longer he must wait, he lay on his

back on the floor, without energy to stand or sit.

Eventually the key turned and Lloyd threw a bundle of clothes in. 'Put these on and be ready to go. Don't waste time. The bugger patrolling the streets could be back at any moment, so hurry.'

Tommy needed no second telling. Throwing off his clothes, he drew on a pair of thick woollen trousers and fisherman's jumper and donned the black cape and hat.

Pushing his own clothes into the portmanteau, he fastened it. Carrying it to the door, he tapped gently on the metal. Keeping watch, Lloyd opened it and Tommy slipped through. Relocking it, Lloyd pushed the ring of keys into his pocket.

Heart pounding, Tommy followed him down the corridor to a back entrance, a lamp burning in the office throwing a dim light their way.

The door creaked on opening, and Tommy nervously glanced back, checking that the corridor was still empty. Following Lloyd out, Tommy breathed fresh air, the first for days. Both were silent. Crossing the narrow road, they walked in the deep shadows of the castle towards the quay. So far it was going according to plan, but Tommy wasn't rejoicing just yet. There was a long way to go, and there were too many things that could go wrong.

The tide was high, the water lapping at the quay wall and the wooden hull of the fishing boat, *Mary Ellen*, moored alongside.

Clambering on board, Lloyd whispered furtively to the two men standing close to the tiller.   Tommy caught part of what he said about needing to hurry if the night was to be a success. Tommy glanced behind him, making sure that no one was following, and then clumsily negotiated the slippery steps; in the dark he misjudged the distance from the gunwale to the bottom boards and landed heavily. The starboard side dipped to the water and he nearly lost his balance. Lloyd stuck out his hand and grabbed him before he fell.

John, a young man wearing rubber wellingtons, a fisherman's dirty smock, and baggy trousers, was obviously not impressed with Tommy's performance, and he elbowed him out of the way as he went past to go up the steps to the quayside bollards to let go of the mooring lines. Without showing much care, he threw the heavy wet lines down onto the bottom boards. To impress the inept landlubbers, he trotted down the slimy steps and placing one foot on the gunwale he stepped back on board smoothly.

Charlie at the tiller smirked. He didn't care for landlubbers either, but he cared even less for youths that thought they knew it all.

The light breeze pushed the *Mary Ellen* away from the wall. Charlie steered her into the river and towards the fast flowing water of the strait.

The sound of hurrying footsteps came along the quay. Expecting constables and prison guards to come running and the alarm to go up, Tommy's heart started racing. A lone man ran past, keeping to the shadows of the castle walls, his flapping coat tails illuminated by the intermittent moonlight. Held breath oozed from Tommy's lips, and he glanced at Lloyd, and even in the darkness he read the fear in the glint of the man's eyes.

A glance passed between Charlie and John, and Tommy wondered if the two men were already regretting accepting the job of sailing clandestinely to Liverpool dock. It was a risky undertaking, helping a prisoner escape, but they were being paid more money than they would see in a year catching fish and working on the dock loading slate.

Lloyd wanted out of a bad marriage and the job he hated and to do that he needed money, enough to see him settled in America. Tommy's predicament was the answer to Lloyd's problems. But the risk he was taking was great: if caught assisting an escape he would face a long gaol sentence. Other prisoners would make the life of a former constable miserable, and there would be violence too.

Tommy was aware of the precariousness of his own position; if he was recaptured he would most likely be charged with the murder of Millie Barker and hanged. Following the assizes he would have perhaps two weeks of life left. He would be dead by the middle of next month. It was a sobering thought.

The *Mary Ellen* turned to port coming into the strait, and then straightening, she headed for the sea. Tommy glanced over to the far banks of Anglesey. The trees growing near the shore were towering sloe-black shadows in the darkness; there was something sinister about them and the tiny hairs on the back of his neck tingled.

Drawing his eyes away, he looked across the stern to the ancient castle emerging out of the blackness, the high turrets stark against the translucency of moonlit clouds. He had never seen King Edward's palace from this perspective. This was his first experience on the water; it slipped his memory that he had arrived in Caernarvon as a three-year-old with Joe and Emily, his parents. On a freezing cold night the three of them had left the sailing ship the *Hardwick Lady* and made for lodgings in the town.

The night air, tainted with the scent of fish and the sea,

brushed his face. Caernarvon gaol was behind him, the sea ahead. The sense of relief he felt was immense and he breathed deeply on the chill night. Tipping his head back, he glanced at the inky sky; a crescent moon glinted on the seams of heaped cumulus cloud.

Whilst in the cell he had forgotten there was a world just beyond the prison walls. His mind flashed to Plas Mawr, George and Mary sleeping comfortably there. His blood boiled at the thought of the undeserving pair living in his house, ordering his servants to do their bidding. No doubt depleting the wine cellar when he had so carefully replenished the racks with fine wines and brandies. The biggest regret in his life was not finishing George off properly when had the chance. It was impossible to get this thought out of his head, and it went round and round, tormenting him day and night.

A sudden gust of wind filled the sail and it cracked with a startling boom. The *Mary Ellen's* speed increased another couple of knots and a trail of phosphorescent water was left in her wake. The bow bit deep into a spume topped wave, and rising, casting off water, it threw spindrift sparkling with moonlight into the air.

'It'll rain before dawn,' Charlie at the tiller said plainly.

'Aye, if not sooner,' John said even less cheerfully.

Lloyd moved from the gunwale on the starboard side and went to Tommy, hanging onto a halyard for support.

His eyes were on the portmanteau tucked between Tommy's feet. 'That should go in a sack,' he said. 'On Liverpool quay it'll stand out like a sore thumb with you rigged out as a fisherman.'

'I'll see to it,' Tommy said a little too sharply.

Picking his front teeth with a dirty fingernail, Lloyd made a

215

sucking noise. 'Pay out will be when?'

'The moment we dock.'

Tommy understood that men were ruthless. It had crossed his mind that Lloyd and the two strangers could throw him overboard for the contents of the bag and he was braced for a fight, to kill or be killed. Lord knew how he would get the boat to shore if the worst should happen.

Dipping into his pocket, Lloyd brought out a small bottle of brandy and taking out the cork, he offered the bottle to Tommy.

Wary, unsure if the gesture was friendly or a sign of something sinister, Tommy took it and held it to his lips; the brandy was cheap and rough, but longing for a drink for almost a week he drank it with true relish. Handing it back to Lloyd, he thanked him. Lloyd took a long swig and then held the bottle to his chest like a comforter.

Legs braced against the movement of the vessel, Tommy looked to the point of land where a stone fort stood sentinel. Ahead, the turbulent waters of the sandbar, and beyond that, the sea. They would sail to Holyhead at the tip of Anglesey and then into waters that would carry them to Liverpool Bay. It would be a long night and most probably wet too, but anything was preferable to the confinement he had endured in the cell.

The vessel was running with the tide, dipping her nose into the water and rising with the rhythm of the waves.

'When we cross the sandbar,' Charlie shouted above the clatter of halyards and wind drumming in the sails, 'Best you both sit down and brace yoursens.'

The water was already choppy, the vessel running less smoothly. Glimpsing the sea ahead, the maelstrom of confused water, Tommy inched down to the slickly wet planks and hung onto a heavy coil of rope. Lloyd sat with legs outstretched, finding comfort swigging from the bottle of brandy.

Sailing into the turbulence, the two fishermen took the wetting and battering in their stride. The wooden planks creaked and groaned, and the halyards rasped and scraped against the wooden mast in protest. The bow rose to the dark sky, slamming back with a thump into the inky water, and rose again on the next chaotic wave. Once through the maelstrom, the sea was relatively calm and running with the tide the *Mary Ellen* recovered speed quite quickly.

Charlie still gripping the tiller hard, shouted, 'The sea will be flattish until we arrive at South Stack, then we may get a bit of a mauling as we sail past the rocks and the old lighthouse.'

Lloyd, resting his chin on his chest, said, 'Charlie, what would you call what we just went through?'

Charlie grinned. 'Oh that was nowt, just a bit of a cuddle.'

Lloyd took another suck from the neck of the bottle.

The night seemed endless, the sloe black sea stretching to the hidden horizon, and the land of Anglesey a dark shadow. The Snowdonia mountain range on the mainland had vanished into the night.

Chilled, Tommy half dozed, sitting on the portmanteau, back against the ropes, head nodding with the rhythm of the vessel.

Charlie watched the beam of light from South Stack lighthouse; from experience he knew there was treacherous water there, but he had judged the tide and now at ebb the sea was fairly calm, so with luck they would make way without too much fuss.

Almost asleep, Tommy was vaguely aware that the vessel was moving quite violently, but was too tired to do anything but sink against the ropes propping him up. Behind him Charlie fought the tiller, weaving the fishing boat through the waves, putting her nose into them instead of taking them broadside on dangerously.

Lloyd came awake suddenly; still clutching the bottle he raised his head to peer over the side. Threatening grey water brushed against the gunwale, and he wondered if they were sinking.

Wide-eyed and terrified he looked to the high rugged cliffs looming out of the sea, swept by the moving beam of light from South Stack lighthouse. Brighter than the brightest moonlight, the beam kept to its designated path illuminating the ominous steep seas following the *Mary Ellen*. Sweeping on, the radiance stretched to the far horizon and painted the dark line where sea meets sky with an unnatural luminosity. The following sea terrified him, dark and forbidding; the waves, higher than the stern of the *Mary Ellen*, rushed toward her and just as he thought they were sure to get swamped, the wave hit the stern and Mary Ellen lifted her rump and the wave disappeared beneath her, the dreadful processes repeated and repeated till he thought he would surely cry out with terror, and he shrank beneath the gunwale head bent to his knees and gently rocked.

'Nearly through,' Charlie shouted cheerfully to his mate John eating a lump of bread and cheese, his back against the bow planks.

'Aye, sooner the better,' John called back. 'I'll take a spell at the tiller and give you a break.'

Charlie nodded and then went back to fighting the next spume topped wave.

The light began to change, night giving way to day, and

Holyhead was visible, and then they passed the coastal town on the starboard side and then struck out for deep water.

The backs of dolphins, shiny grey, popped out of the water and two swam alongside the hull, an eye out of the water to inspect the boat.

Now standing at the tiller, John shouted, 'They're doing an early morning run to check their patch.'

Unimpressed, sitting with his back against the bow, Charlie began to chew a hunk of cheese.

Waking, Tommy peed over the side. His mouth was dry and tasted like a camel's hoof. Buttoning his trousers, he stood near the stern looking back the way they had come.

'Want a drink?' Charlie shouted.

Tommy nodded. 'I'm parched.'

Charlie climbed to his feet. 'I'll make a brew.'

A small stove was lit on the bottom boards, and soon a kettle whistled with steam.

Though the tea was tainted with an unrecognisable flavour, and was not the best Tommy had tasted, it was certainly the most welcome.

Lloyd grunted awake. Taking a steaming mug from Charlie, he tipped the dregs from the bottle of brandy into it and took a sip, smacking his lips.

The day crept by and at noontime Tommy's stomach clenched with hunger, rumbling audibly.

John heated a small cauldron of broth over the stove and produced another loaf of bread from a flour sack. Four mugs were balanced on an ancient wooden tray, and hot broth poured into each. Tommy sipped his, thankful that it was recognisably chicken.

'This is good,' Lloyd said, his appetite returning after his fright. 'Who is the cook?'

Charlie shouted cheerfully, 'John's a regular housewife and makes all manner of meals in his kitchen to bring onboard.'

'It's nowt but a bit of boiling and baking,' John said modestly.

'Aye he makes the bread too,' Charlie chipped in. 'And bloody good it is an' all. I haven't convinced him to turn his hand to cheese making, though we practically live on it.'

'We eat eggs too but I don't lay the buggers,' John shouted back crossly.

Charlie laughed. 'I wouldn't eat 'em if you did, John lad.'

The sun was high in the sky, drying the bottom boards until the wood was hot to touch. Tommy dozed in the baking heat, his shirt sleeves rolled up to his elbows. His mind centred on the end of the journey and he wondered what awaited them on the quayside. It had already been decided that if police were on the docks, the vessel would carry on up river and dock at Runcorn. When the dust settled he would make his way back to Liverpool and from there, who knew where a ship would take him?

The afternoon was long and tedious, with nothing to view but the endless sea. Then suddenly, John pointed to the far distance and shouted, 'Liverpool.'

The city rose out of the sea like a grey whale basking on the surface.

'It's been a long night and day,' Charlie said. 'But I suggest we stand off, and wait until dark before we moor up and go ashore.'

'It's a better idea than just going in and hoping for the best,' John agreed.

Charlie nodded. 'When we get closer, we'll make it look like were doing a bit of fishing and bide our time till nightfall.'

With hours still to kill, Lloyd lay on the bottom boards with his hat over his face and slept.

Tommy sat silently, the events of the last week circling in his mind. The loss of Plas Mawr was hard to bear, as was the affluent state he was used to. The future was uncertain and he wondered if the authorities would immediately guess that Liverpool was his initial destination. It was a possibility, though no one but the random man running along Caernarvon quay last night had witnessed the fishing boat pulling away from the quay wall.

Tired, he made himself as comfortable as he could and tried to sleep, but raucous common gulls circled overhead, sweeping and diving to the water, and perching atop the mast, and the best he could do was a light disturbed doze.

The sun descended, the red orb appearing to sink into the sea on the western horizon. The water changed from pale blue to grey, and then to dark pewter as daylight dimmed.

For hours the boat had rocked at anchor, the movement tiring to both Lloyd and Tommy. The cloudy sky darkened to pitch black without a trace of moonlight. A light rain drizzled down, soaking the boards, and the men were forced to stand. Going to the bow, John dragged the anchor up from deep water; hauling it aboard, he tied it down securely.

Charlie unfurled the sails, and going back to the tiller he turned the boat and she headed towards the city docks, still at least another two hours away.

Lloyd produced another small bottle of brandy from a recess in his clothes and took a large swig.

Tommy stared at him with cold eyes. 'You'll need to keep

your wits about you when we dock, only a fool would risk getting picked up by the police.'

Lloyd took another swallow before putting the stopper back in the neck of the bottle. He was rattled that Tommy Standish, his former prisoner, should dictate to him. He'd come away from Caernarvon to stop the aggravation at home where his wife told him what to do every moment of the day, work had been the same, order upon order with never a please or thank you. Grudgingly he stuffed the bottle back in his pocket.

Words he had often spoken to his wife he now addressed to Tommy. 'You can't watch me every moment of the day.'

'I do not intend to,' Tommy said seemingly unruffled. 'All I ask is that you keep a cool and sober head. We'll need a great deal more than good fortune if we are to evade the law when we walk along the dockside and into the city.'

The man consumed too much alcohol and he could be a dangerous liability, Tommy thought darkly, Once ashore he would dodge him and make his way to a whore house and hide there until a ship was due to sail to America or Australia.

Lloyd was easily bought, that had been proved the moment he opened the cell door and set him free, and if the man knew of his whereabouts he may quite readily sell the information to the highest bidder.

Dangerous days lay ahead and were likely to be even riskier if Lloyd roamed the streets inebriated and careless. Many a slip was made by a man walking along the banks of the Mersey. Drunk, he was likely to fall under the waves in an instant.

Darkness fell early. Heavy clouds and drizzling rain obscuring what remained of daylight.

Sheltering in the lee of the sails, ducking the showers of spray breaking over the bow, Tommy kept his eyes to the fore watching the city emerge: pin pricks of light from homes, grog shops, masts of tall ships, and gas lamps on the docks shimmering through a watery veil of falling rain.

Entering the Mersey, the bow steadied on calmer water. Ships lined the dock walls; tethered dark shadows, mastheads lights bright beads dancing in the night sky.

Charlie on the tiller called out, 'When we get close I'll sail along the waterfront and take a gander, keep your eyes peeled for trouble. We're making for Albert Dock, tide's right for us to enter. We'll tie up there and then you two can scarper. When we get close, be mindful that sound carries over the water and what you say on board will be heard by many ashore.'

Tommy reached for the portmanteau secreted in an old sack, and opening it carefully he took out a brown cotton bag, closing the leather bag quickly before the breeze took away any of his few and now precious possessions.

With the bag planted firmly between his feet, he stretched over to Charlie and handed the brown package to him.

'It's all there,' he said, trying to sound cheerful, though in truth he was unhappy to part with the wad of money. What remained in the bag, barring Lloyd's share, was all he now had to his name.

Holding the bag in his hand, Charlie called to John, 'Take this, count it, and then put it safe in your pocket until we are moored up.'

Pushing the worn wooden tiller to starboard, he closed the gap between boat and shore and the *Mary Ellen* skimmed close to the ships moored alongside the granite walls.

On shore a clock struck ten o'clock, and the peals rang out like an alarm. Tommy, looking out, froze but Lloyd had supped from the brandy bottle and his nerves were slow to react. Glancing at him, hearing the solitary hiccup, Tommy decided that the sooner he dumped the man the better.

There were very few people roaming about, besides those that looked as though they had business on the dockside; the night was too wet and the breeze getting up was too chill for a recreational saunter. With his hands placed firmly on the wet and cold gunwale, Tommy kept vigil, eyes peeled for the dark uniforms of constables.

'I see nowt,' John said, coming alongside him. 'It all looks routine to me.'

'Good,' Tommy whispered. 'The sooner we are away from here the happier I will be.'

John glanced at Lloyd balancing precariously against the gunwale. 'He'll hold you up, the man's pissed.'

'Yes, I realise that. I'll chivvy him along, and we will look like two mates, one helping the drunk along.'

John snorted. 'Good camouflage. If he doesn't sing or make too much noise the police will turn the other cheek. They're used to drunks down here on the docks.'

Charlie peered beneath the bottom of the sail. 'We're almost there. Get ready to turn into the dock.'

'Right, Charlie,' he said, stepping up to the mast ready to bring the sails down the moment the hull kissed the dock wall.

'Hold tight, and mind your heads on the boom,' Charlie shouted as the boat gybed and turned into Albert Dock.

Drawn down from the masts the wet sails covered the bottom boards, water slewing into the bilge drains.

'I'll go up top and take a gander,' John said, climbing off.

Tommy's eyes followed him. Lloyd lifted the bottle to his mouth and poured brandy in. Charlie manhandled him off the boat and rolled him onto the stone dockside, shuffling to his knees; Lloyd hiccupped several times.

Charlie grinned. 'Best of luck with him,' he said, turning away, glad to see the dangerous venture completed and the two passengers wanted by the law cleared off from his *Mary Ellen*.

John came back. Whispering, he said, 'It's all clear.'

Lloyd lurched against him and John fended him off.

Tommy climbed off and turning to Charlie, he said, 'Thank you, and to you John.'

Grabbing Lloyd by the elbow, he shoved him forward, and linked together they staggered passed the red brick warehouses enclosing Albert Dock. Overhead gantries, like hangman's scaffolds, jutted out of the buildings, the thick beams of wood stark and black against the night sky. Gas lamps cast a feeble light, too ghostly and thin to penetrate the deep shadows of the colonnades.

Once out of earshot of Charlie and John, Tommy changed course and instead of heading for the pedestrian and vehicle entrance which would take them into the streets, he drew Lloyd towards the Mersey.

Shaking Tommy off, Lloyd raised the bottle to his lips again and took a swig, sighing with pleasure as the brandy hit his throat. He stumbled and Tommy caught his arm and held on, steering him towards the water's edge.

Glancing over his shoulder, Tommy scanned the shadows for movement, listening intently for the tread of footsteps, but the only sound was the soles of their own wellington boots squelching on the wet stone slabs.

'Where we going?' Lloyd said drunkenly, trying to shrug Tommy off so he could raise the bottle to his lips again.

Tommy shushed, 'Be quiet.'

'I only asked,' Lloyd replied peevishly.

'I'm taking you to a special place, to get you another bottle of brandy. We will be there in a moment but you must be quiet. Do you understand?'

Lloyd nodded.

Reaching the stone built banks, Tommy looked across to the west side of the river where haloed gas lights glimmered at Birkenhead Docks.

'We nearly there?' Lloyd mumbled.

'Shush,' Tommy sighed.

The night oozed rain, the lowering clouds banked in a moonless sky. Ink black waves surged along the dockside's granite face, hissing and tumbling, shedding arcs of cold spray into the drizzle. A gull called; the cry startled Tommy and he looked around quickly, listening intently for the approach of a passer-by, but there was no one there, the night was too forbidding to be walking along the banks of the Mersey.

Suddenly confused, Lloyd looked blearily at Tommy. 'Why are we here?' he mumbled drunkenly.

Tommy gripped his arm more firmly. 'Remember I told you not to drink.'

'You sound like my wife,' Lloyd sneered.

'Did she also say that drink would be the death of you?'

'She says it all the time,' he muttered belligerently.

Tommy shifted his weight, getting a good balance, his entire body tense. 'Well, she is right,' he said, flinging Lloyd forward.

The lightweight man tottered, dropped the bottle with a crash of splintering glass, teetering, his footing precariously balanced on the edge of the paving slabs.

Raising his leg, grunting with effort, Tommy kicked his rump viciously.

Lloyd fell forward landing in the water with a loud splash.

Several gulls took to the air, squawking with alarm, their cries concealing the drowning man's shouts of panic.

Tommy caught a glimpse of Lloyd's head going under before he was swept away, the incoming tide carrying him fast up to Seaforth and beyond.

Job finished, he brushed his hands together. Lifting the sack with its valuable cargo, he set out to walk into the city.

Chapter 14

Two uniformed constables walked along the avenue in the cool shade cast by the twin line of lime trees, the green arc of the branches forming a near perfect frame for Plas Mawr in the near distance. As there was a probability that Tommy Standish was skulking in the parkland they were watchful, glancing from side to side at the slightest disturbance, and witnessing an occasional rabbit or bird fleeing from the beneath the orderly bushes.

Four of their comrades had drawn short straws and were now searching the Garddryn and Ruby quarries and the surrounding district for the fugitive. Not that anyone actually believed they would find him hiding in the vicinity of Caernarvon but they were following the orders of the Police Captain, Cameron Chamberlain.

On reaching the grand house they climbed the steps to the imposing entrance and the elder, Constable Humphrey, tugged the bell pull. A peal sounded indoors and a moment later the door was opened to by a smartly uniformed footman.

'We wish to see the master of the house, Mr George Bellamy,' Constable Humphrey said with as much authority he could muster with his coat collar rubbing his sweaty neck sore, and his swollen feet aching.

The footman looked down his long nose. 'Please wait, I will ask if Mr Bellamy is at home.'

Irritated, Constable Jones shoved the door with his boot. 'We are here to search the house and we are coming in now.'

The servant bowed, standing aside to let them enter.

'Mr George Bellamy may be on the breakfast room terrace,' the footman said stiffly, looking down his long nose at the intruders. 'I will inform him of your visit.'

'You do that,' Jones answered, his head swivelling to take in the grandeur of the Great Hall.

The footman went almost silently down the long corridor to the door of the breakfast room; entering, he crossed the silk carpet on rabbit skin slippers. The French doors were open and he saw the new master and his wife sitting together on a wooden garden bench discussing the merits of the red geraniums blooming in terracotta pots on the borders of the stone terrace.

Mary was dressed plainly in a long sleeved grey dress, a simple row of pearls at the white lace collar. Hearing the servant's approach, she turned and watched as he came out of the shadows. George, partially deaf as a result of the attack, was unaware of him until the man stepped over the threshold and onto the terrace.

The footman gave a precise little bow. 'Mr Bellamy, two constables are here to search the house.'

'Why ever do they wish to do that?' Mary said, standing.

'I am afraid I do not know, Mrs Bellamy. I thought it impertinent to ask.'

George started to rise, and Mary put a gently restraining hand on his shoulder.

'George dear, do not be alarmed. No doubt they are looking for something of Tommy's. There's nothing for you to worry about.'

She turned her face to the footman. 'Don't let them roam around, bring them here. There's no necessity for us to go indoors and miss the glorious weather.'

The constables came through the open French doors and out into the sunshine, looking awkward and out of place dressed in dark uniforms in the pleasant and sunny garden.

Mary looked at the pair quizzically. 'How can we assist you?'

Humphrey gave a short cough. 'It's about Tommy Standish.'

'Yes,' Mary said, shading her eyes from the sunlight as she looked up into his red and hot face.

'He's escaped,' Humphrey said, trying hard not to be too dramatic.

Shocked, George staggered to his feet. 'Standish has escaped? How? When was this? He's a dangerous man, how could you be so careless as to let him go? He'll come looking for me and Mary,' he said, visibly distressed.

Mary put out her hand and touched his shoulder. 'George, try to be calm.'

She glanced at Constable Humphrey. 'We will go indoors.'

The two men stood aside as she led George through the French window and into the breakfast room. With Mary's aid George was handed into a comfortable chair, and she anxiously glanced at him as she tugged the bell-cord to summon a servant.

The door opened almost immediately and a maid came in

'Bring tea for four into the library. Make sure the windows are open. We will follow in a moment, Sarah,' she said, addressing the girl.

George started to come out of the seat and Mary came to his assistance immediately. Taking his arm, she steered him slowly towards the door. 'It will all work out, George. Tommy will be found quickly and once again be put behind bars. You really must not upset yourself, darling.'

She gave a sidelong glance at the constables following at her own slow pace.

George was trembling. 'Mary, he's dangerous and he will

come to Plas Mawr and hurt us.'

'That is not going to happen. We will send for the quarry manager and ask him to find strong men to protect you and the house.'

'Oh Mary, there has to be another way. I don't want strangers wandering in and out. It's unsettling.'

Worried for him, she smiled encouragingly. 'We will make arrangements that suit you, George. Please do not fret.'

Reaching the library, she helped in him into an upholstered chair beside the fireplace, where he sat looking fretful, slowly spinning the gold wedding band on his finger.

Without moving from George's side, she gestured to the two leather seats near the open window. 'Please make yourselves comfortable.'

The door opened and a maid carried in a tray and placed it on the desk. All four remained silent, watching as she poured the tea and handed it around. Making a perfunctory curtsey in Mary's direction, which Mary acknowledged graciously, the girl went through the open door and out in the hallway and the door closed behind her with a small bump. For a moment the only sound in the library was the chink of china and the song of a thrush in the garden.

'So please explain exactly what has happened,' Mary said, addressing the younger constable who appeared more alert than the other man.

Jones put the fragile cup and saucer carefully on a side table. 'During the night, or first thing this morning, Standish escaped from his cell and left the building. His absence was not noticed until after eight o'clock today. The keys had gone missing, and we suppose that Standish made off with them to create even more havoc and disturbance.'

Mary looked baffled. 'But how can it have happened? Surely the door was securely locked.'

Embarrassed, Humphrey explained, 'We believe the constable on duty last night may have let him out. That man has also disappeared. We have started enquiries and hope to apprehend the fugitives quickly.'

George cried out fretfully, 'Impossible to catch them when you do not know where they may be hiding.'

The grandeur and obvious wealth on display made Jones feel unkempt and his uniform cheap and of inferior quality; normally he wore it with pride and the authority it gave him placed him head and shoulder above the working man. It had been years since he felt inferior and of a lesser class, and he cursed Lloyd for snatching away the image he had of himself. He felt no sympathy for the spoilt man and his fussing wife, who only had to snap their fingers and others would come running to do their bidding.

In a clipped uninterested voice he said, 'At the moment we do not know, but we are investigating.'

George tut-tutted with frustration.

Mary touched his hand to reassure him. Then, turning her face to the two men, she said, 'How do you propose to protect us from Tommy Standish?'

Neither one had considered the problem. Remaining silent, they both stared into the white and gilt rimmed china cups.

George clutched Mary's hand. 'Mary, we go at once to our old home in Chester. Standish does not know the location. We will be safe there.'

With no other suggestion to hand, Humphrey nodded in

agreement. 'It's the best idea. Who knows what Standish may do to silence a witness?'

George flinched.

The reaction was all Mary needed to make a quick decision. It was important to get George away from Plas Mawr as swiftly as possible; remaining in the house may very well jeopardise his recovery. Without a second's hesitation she rose and went to the bell-cord, and giving it a tug she summoned a servant.

Coming into the room, Sarah gave a little curtsey.

Mary spoke quickly, convinced there was not a moment to lose. 'I wish you to pack our essentials and call for the carriage to be brought around to the door. But before you do, I want you to find Miles and send him to me.'

The door had not quite closed behind the maid when the constables rose.

Humphrey ran his index finger under the sweaty collar of his coat. Decidedly uncomfortable, he hoped the cellars would be considerably cooler than the room they were in.

'We will begin our search in the cellars and work our way up to the top of the house,' he said, trying to hide a sigh.

Mary was aghast. 'Surely you don't think we would give Standish refuge and an opportunity to kill us.'

'No, Madam. But we must follow orders.'

Mary bristled at the idea that she, or George, were capable of harbouring the monster, Tommy Standish.

'I expect you to go about your business carefully and don't disturb poor Edward,' she said. 'The boy has suffered enough these last few days.'

Miles came in, slightly flustered.

Mary was curt. 'Please show the constables to the cellars and then come back here for instructions.'

Though curious, Miles hid it well. 'Yes Madam,' he said in a clipped tone.

With the exit of the three men the room fell quiet.

Mary sat on the arm of George's chair and ran her hand through his sparse hair. 'We will be gone very soon. Please try not to get too upset, George dear.'

'But it's so frightening thinking that he could be close by.'

She kissed the crown of his head. 'He'll be long gone. Standish wouldn't risk coming too close, he'll know the police will be searching for him. They'll go to all his haunts.'

Miles came back in and stood in the centre of the Turkey rug.

Mary rose from the arm of the chair. 'Tommy Standish has escaped custody and is on the run. We are leaving at once for our home in Chester. We feel that Standish may come here and seek revenge for the loss of his home and freedom besides many other things. We will be in touch with you and may return when he is recaptured.'

'Oh no, Mary,' George pleaded. 'I never wish to come back to Plas Mawr. I'm happier in Chester in our own little home.'

She smiled. 'Then that is where we will stay.'

George visibly relaxed. 'We must speak to Edward before we go.'

'Yes of course. Will you find him, Miles?'

'Yes, at once, Mrs Bellamy.'

Within an hour a carriage bowled down the avenue heading for the railway station.

Sitting on the leather seat, George looked through the small open window to the parkland and woods beyond, saying a final farewell to his boyhood home.

Edward was upset by the news of his father's disappearance but not upset that his Uncle George and Mary had taken their leave of the house. It had seemed very odd having two complete strangers in his home, and for the past days he had been confused to his own position in the house.

From his bedroom window he watched the carriage drive into the avenue, losing sight of it when it went under the canopy of the lime tress.

All fingers and thumbs, he changed into his riding gear. Carefully picking the puppy up off the bed, he held it gently in the crook of his arm, and leaving the room he trotted down the stairs in search of Miles. Discovering him in the butler's pantry, he explained that he would be out of the house for a while visiting his grandparents at Corn Cottage.

Miles looked at the puppy already sleeping. 'Would you like me to take care of the little chap whilst you are out, sir?'

'Oh he would love that, and perhaps you could play with him in the garden until I return.' Edward smiled.

Scooping the droopy animal up, Miles held it close to his chest. 'We will see you later.'

'Thank you, Miles.' Edward grinned.

It had become a habit whilst at home, much to his father's chagrin, to take his leave of the house via the kitchen and the back door leading into the yard.

Unencumbered, Edward made a dash for that part of the house.

In the kitchen, Cook waved a cloth at him as he snatched a jam tart from the plate on the table.

Darting through the open door, he headed for the stable block. The head groom tacked a mare and in moments Edward was trotting down the avenue, beneath the leaves of the lime trees splattering sunlight.

The ride gave him time to think; it was incredible that his father was charged with attempted murder, though he didn't doubt that he had struck the blow that felled his Uncle George. Mary and George had made that quite plain to him. It had angered and upset him to discover his father was capable of such heartless cruelty, but he was saddened that he should languish in a prison cell. The revelation that he had escaped brought mixed thoughts into his mind and he felt confused, not understanding if he should be happy or sad at the turn of events. He didn't want his papa locked up, but neither did he want him on the run and never likely to see him again.

Coming to Corn Cottage, baking in the sunshine, he dismounted and went through the wicket gate.

Hearing the latch rise and fall, Emily came from the back of the cottage where she was tending a row of lettuce.

Edward's eyes filled up on seeing his grandmother and he ran into her arms.

Emily held him close, wondering what new turn of events had made the lad so unhappy.

'Where's young Scamp?' The moment the words were out of her mouth Emily could have bitten her tongue. For Edward to be so sorrowful something must have happened to the puppy.

'Oh, he's fine. Miles is taking care of him for a little while.'

Emily breathed a sigh of relief. 'So what has Scamp been up to since we saw him last?' Taking Edward's arm, she steered him into the cottage.

'He's chewed Cook's slippers, they are ruined, also the hem of the curtains in the dining room. He is quite naughty, Nan. But he's great fun. I don't know what I would do without him now.'

His eyes filled with tears again and he began to cry.

'Oh, Edward lad, whatever is the matter?' Emily said, her eyes watering.

'Papa has escaped from gaol. He left this morning. I know he will never come back. What he did to Uncle George was terrible but I still miss him dreadfully.'

The news floored Emily, and it was a struggle to remain calm and cope with the boy's distress.

With no solution to the problem but the offer of a treat, she said, 'We will take a jug of lemonade into the garden and sit under the apple tree. We can try to make sense of all of this. Your grandpa will be home soon, he'll know what to do.'

'I have thought things through and have come up with a plan,' he said sniffing. 'But I'll wait until grandpa is here before I explain everything.'

Emily looked at the mantel clock, willing Joe to come early and help the poor boy.

It was inevitable that Joe would be late in. Dawdling along the lane, seeing the mare tethered at the garden gate, he picked up his step and came into the cottage smiling and cheerful.

The look on Emily's face told him that all was not well.

But by then the lad was in his arms, clinging to him.

Learning the news, Joe kept his anger under wraps. It was Edward he had to consider, what became of Tommy was Tommy's affair. Part of Joe wanted to say good riddance, but the father in him felt bereft for never again would he set eyes on his son, once a little lad that had clutched his hand tightly fearing he would be lost.

'I have an idea I wish to talk to you both about,' Edward said, a little more brightly.

Nora and Frank sauntered into the kitchen-cum-parlour, each carrying a dirty, sticky baby. Caleb, the elder by three minutes, screamed to be put down. Sighing, Nora put him on the slate floor where he crawled over to Joe. Bending down, Joe picked him up and put him on his lap. Abel beat his father's chest with his tiny hands until Frank let him join his twin brother. Edward was delighted with the pair and in minutes he was on the floor playing with them.

Emily put a pan of water on the hob to heat for their bath. Nora, sighing with tiredness, took dirty outdoor clothes into the scullery to wash.

For the next hour it was bedlam: crying children, Nora anxious, and Emily trying to find a space to prepare the rabbit stew for supper. Eventually when the babies were clean and fed, Nora put them down for their afternoon nap.

'Peace,' Joe said, taking his pipe from the mantel and lighting it with a spill.

Standing in the middle of the cluttered room, Edward said, 'Can I tell you my idea now?'

Emily sat on a wooden chair at the table to peel potatoes. 'I'm all ears, Edward.'

'Aye, and me,' Joe said, sucking the end of the pipe with little popping sounds.

Frank slumped in the only comfortable chair in the kitchen, with his long legs straight out and likely to trip anyone trying to get to the cooking range.

Nora came back brushing her untidy hair off her hot face. 'They've gone off,' she said, sitting on the arm of Frank's chair.

Edward was fully aware that what he had to say would be life changing for his grandparents; it was equally important to him, for he needed his grandfather's help more than he had ever needed anything before.

Hands folded at his waist, he stood in the centre of the room very much like he had seen his school headmaster stand when he was to impart something of great importance. He started with a small nervous little cough. 'When we heard the news about Papa this morning at Plas Mawr, Uncle George and his wife Mary left to go back to their house in Chester. So there's only me there now, and Scamp of course.'

'And all the servants,' Nora said unhelpfully.

'Yes, those people too. But it's not like having family there,' he said innocently.

'Go on lad,' Joe said softly.

'Papa will not be coming back.'

For a moment, Joe thought the lad was going to well up again, but he managed to go on.

'It has been decided by Madoc and the quarry manager that the quarry will be managed until I have reached my majority, whenever that is, but I expect that it's a long way off. So what I would really like is for you, Grandpa and Nan, to come and live with me at Plas Mawr. Nan can keep the servants in order, she would be good at that, and you Grandpa, I want you to help me with Ruby and the Garddryn. You can advise me on safety and fair pay for the workers. I also wish to build a hospital for the quarrymen and their families.'

Joe was silent, seeing all the things he had hoped and worked for coming to fruition through his grandson.

'There could be a union office in the main building for Frank. It would be a place for the quarrymen to go to for advice and support.'

He glanced pleadingly at Joe. 'Will you help me make the Garddryn and Ruby the safest quarries in the county and beyond, Grandpa?'

Joe was flabbergasted. 'It's incredible that you have thought all this out in such a short time, Edward.'

Edward looked down at the blue-grey floor, knowing instinctively that the slate came from Garddryn quarry.

'It has been in my mind for quite a long time. But I hadn't anticipated that the changes could be made so early, I expected to have to wait until I received my inheritance.'

He glanced anxiously at Emily, sitting bemused with a half peeled potato held in one hand and a small knife in the other.

'Nan, I know how much you love Corn Cottage but do you think you could give it up and come and live at Plas Mawr? I really want you there.'

'I don't know what to say, lad. The cottage has been my home for a long time, it would be hard to part with it.'

Edward stepped to her side and took her hand. 'But Frank's family would take it over and they would have much more room for the twins.'

'Aye, there is that. Since the boys have started to crawl there has been a terrible lack of space. The noise the two bairns make...' She tut-tutted for effect.

'It's worth thinking about,' she said, her eyes roving over everything familiar.

He tried another tack to convince her that the move would be good for everyone. 'If you do not wish to part with the boys, Frank and Nora could come to Plas Mawr too.'

Joe spoke quickly. 'No, that will not do, Edward, we lost one son to Plas Mawr when his head was turned by wealth and position. I'll not risk our grandchildren going the same way. They belong in a cottage like this one, where they will grow up to be working men with sensible ideas in their heads.'

Nora thought it very presumptuous of Joe to speak for her and Frank,; she would like nothing better than living in a grand mansion with servants running to her beck and call. She pouted with annoyance.

Joe filled his pipe, sucking at the stem. 'Frank and Nora would be pleased to have a cottage such as this to bring up their family, and without us two old ones getting under their feet.'

He hadn't missed Nora's cross look.

Putting a flame to the bowl of the pipe, he sucked the tobacco to life.

He glanced at Edward's worried face. 'I see that we would have more time to spend on the plans for the quarries, working with an architect over there would be easier than asking the man to come here. Madoc and Rees would be more at home at the mansion too. I see your reasoning plainly, Edward, but it's a big step, especially for your grandmother.'

Emily saw that in reality the decision was hers. Tommy had cost many quarrymen their lives. Widows were raising children alone and living in terrible hardship. Whereas she was only being asked to give up her cottage to her youngest son and his family; what sort of woman would she be if she didn't give this small part of herself for the benefit of the hundreds of men toiling all hours in atrocious weather?

Joe had worked tirelessly for years to see a union thrive in the quarry and had dreamed of a hospital for the men and their families.

Tommy had cost the village dear, wrecked lives, put families in the poor house, and forced men to work in the copper mines when he banished them from the quarries for a lifetime. The injuries some of those men suffered were horrendous: burned, maimed and blinded when red rivers of molten copper exploded and sheathed their flesh with burning liquid, dying horribly when it hardened to a coat of armour.

If the cottage was the price she must pay for bearing Tommy, fruit of her womb, an evil human being to walk amongst them, then she would do it with as much grace as she could muster.

Thoughtfully, all eyes upon her, she finished peeling the potato and dropped it into the water in the pan; it fell with a plop.

Wiping her hands on the skirt of her grey apron, she said with a smile, 'I suppose there's time to finish cooking supper before we flit Corn Cottage.'

Edward grinned. 'Sunday would be fine, Nan.'

Resigned not to be going to Plas Mawr, Nora decided that she would get Frank to paint the cottage at the first opportunity.

The following days were filled with cleaning and packing. Emily refused to leave until every article had a proper scour. When she handed Corn Cottage over to Frank and Nora it would be as pristinely clean as the old place could be.

Joe was glad to have the opportunity to leave the cliff-face and the treacherous galleries. The cold weather and hard manual work played havoc with his rheumatics.

The quarrymen cheered on hearing that Tommy Standish's malicious rule had come to an end and the constant threat of lock-outs and strikes was over. Negotiation became the most used word on the galleries and in the cabans.

The following Friday, Iwan Rees, the quarry manager, called a late afternoon meeting. Many hundreds of quarrymen gathered on the quadrangle outside the office building expecting to hear bad news, that the quarry was to close, or that new owners were taking over. Instead they learned that Joe Standish had been appointed to instigate new employment conditions, fair pay for a day's work, safer working conditions. Men were to be encouraged to join the Quarrymen's Union, and a site for the new quarrymen's hospital had been chosen. The resounding cheer that followed the announcement was heard in the valleys and far mountains.

Busy packing the old carpet bag, carried from the slums of Manchester so very long ago, Emily heard it and knew that the cheer, like water rushing down a mountainside, was for Joe. The man that had worked and risked his life on more than one occasion, to bring justice and safer conditions to the men that toiled in the dangerous quarries. She was proud, prouder than she had ever been, and the pride destroyed the shame she endured for bringing a ruthless and hateful man into the world.

For several mornings following the meeting, Joe went to Plas Mawr to write reports and give Edward a better insight into the working of the quarries. The lad was enthusiastic for change, and saw that with the new improvements the business, going through an incredible upsurge through world trade, would grow and prosper everyone, quarrymen and management.

Frank was working hard for the union, signing up members until late into the night now that the workers were no longer threatened by the sanctions that Tommy Standish had imposed if he discovered anyone in Ruby or the Garddryn were paid up union members. For Joe it was like a breath of fresh air blasting through the galleries, sweeping away everything that made working in the quarries hateful and menacing.

Edward was learning the business and devoured every bit of information that Joe brought forward. There was no doubt in Joe's mind that the lad would grow into an impressive and respected master, a man that would far exceed his father in profits and good management of the company.

Edward made an appointment for his grandfather with a Caernarvon tailor, requesting that the man make several suits, coats and shirts and all to be made as quickly as possible. Joe attended the shop and returned to Corn Cottage with two new work trousers, and a few baggy shirts fit for a quarryman. Insisting he didn't need fancy clothes to do a job right, he did not want the workers to see him differently than he had always been to them, but promised faithfully to shine his boots more often if it pleased Edward.

On Sunday morning Edward drove a carriage to Corn Cottage to collect Joe and Emily.

Standing at the range, making a brew, Emily heard the rumble of wheels.

For almost a week she had thought of little else but the moment she would say goodbye to Corn Cottage. The sands of time were now run out, and in moments she would go away from her home and into a strange place, though Plas Mawr had been part of her world since little Tommy went there for his lessons so very long ago.

Outside a bucket rattled, and she knew that Joe was returning from feeding the two pigs.

There were so many day to day routines that she would miss, like feeding the pigs, Joe coming home whistling, tramping his boots outside to shed the shale of the quarry. Frank breezing in a rush, driving smoke down the chimney and for minutes after his arrival there was usually a grey haze hanging in the air. She sighed. The garden would be a big loss.

'Listen to me,' she said aloud. 'Anyone would think someone was dying, not going off to a posh house where servants would be happy to wait on them. Pull yourself together, Emily Standish. Make the brew. Sit down and enjoy a cuppa.'

Joe's laughter filtered in through the open door.

Joe's happy to be going, she thought, taking a sip of the hot tea. He loves young Edward and together they would make the quarries places to be proud of, not feared and hated as they had been for many a year.

Putting aside the mug, she untied her green apron and folding it neatly placed it on the table top. 'Shan't need a pinafore where I'm going,' she muttered unceremoniously.

Hauling the tin bath into the kitchen would be a thing of the past. Edward had said that Plas Mawr had baths with hot water taps. Emily tut-tutted. Could anything get more posh than that? She was looking forward to seeing the contraptions. Tomorrow she would try it for herself.

Joe and Edward came in through the front door.

Edward's grin spread from ear to ear. 'Are you ready to go, Nan?'

'As ready as I'll ever be.'

With the palms of her hands on the table, she rose from the wooden chair a little arthritically.

Joe was by her side in an instant, looking worried. 'You do want to go, Emily?'

'Aye, of course I do, Joe.'

Edward breathed a sigh of relief; for a moment he thought that his plans were going to fall apart. 'Let's go, Grandpa. Before Nan changes her mind.'

Emily threw a green shawl over her shoulders and tied it at her waist.

'Joe, go into the bedroom and fetch the carpet bag, it's on the bed.'

He was back in a moment, carrying the bag and looking flabbergasted. 'Emily, this old thing can't be the one we brought all the way from Manchester decades ago?'

'Course it is, Joe,' she said, pulling on a pair of white gloves.

'Well, I'll be damned. I thought you kicked it out long ago.'

She frowned. 'Why would I do that? It may have come in useful.'

She grinned. 'And I was right, it has.'

Joe shook his head slowly from side to side. 'Emily, you never cease to amaze me.'

'I know, Joe. That's why you have stayed around for so long.' She smiled cheekily. 'Now get a move on, we've a new home to move into. And we haven't begun to say our goodbyes to the little boys and Nora.'

It all took longer than Edward expected and he breathed a sigh of relief when his Nan climbed into the carriage and waved a final farewell to the twins.

The groom, waiting patiently at the mare's head, climbed onto the driving seat and the vehicle bowled down the lane.

It was Emily's first experience in a carriage and she liked the quickness of it, so much better than swaying from side to side on an old farm wagon with which she was familiar.

In minutes they were turning into the avenue and under the green canopy of trees.

Emily remembered her last and only visit here, a terrible wet day when the sky was filled with gales. Henrietta's funeral and Tommy had turned away from his own mother pretending not to know her. It still hurt, a physical pain in the region of her heart, when she recalled that moment.

Today, she wasn't going to think about it; she was determined to enjoy the ride, the sunshine, and take pleasure in Edward's delight that his grandparents were really coming to Plas Mawr to live with him.

Edward took her hand and held it tightly; his china blue eyes, identical to Joe's, shone with delight. 'Nan, I don't think I have ever been happier that I am at this moment. Thank you for agreeing to come.'

Emily's eyes filled with tears. The lad was so like his mother, and she had loved Henrietta like a daughter. She would have been so proud of her fourteen year old son.

Emily's mind went to Tommy's confession that he had killed Henrietta, but she made an immense effort to shun the cruel words he had uttered in his prison cell. Determined that the ugly memory would only surface in her mind in the dark shadows of the night, she would not sully a happy day or God's sunshine with Tommy's evilness.

The servants, on Edward's suggestion, were waiting on the steps of the house to greet the new arrivals. A stable lad with the fastest legs had been waiting in the avenue; when he spotted the carriage turning into the gateway, he flew back to the house and clanged the entrance bell with all his might to gather everyone together.

Though Miles had ordered everyone not to fidget, and instructed them how to correctly address Mr and Mrs Standish, firmly reminding them that the two people concerned were the much loved grandparents of the young gentleman, there was still too much staring and a few open mouths when Emily and Joe descended the carriage.

Edward's enthusiasm was infectious and the welcome from everyone present was natural and warm.

A celebratory luncheon was served on a beautiful terrace in the Italianate gardens overlooking the Menai Strait. Emily and Joe had seen the particular stretch of water on many occasions, but this vantage point, and the wonderful weather, made it appear tranquil and an exquisite backdrop for the special occasion.

The chicken was roasted to perfection, and the little bits of greenery, which only Emily nibbled, were a work of art on the plate.

Miles brought a bottle of chilled champagne to the table and when his back was turned, Emily giggled like a girl as the bubbles tickled her nose.

Ice cream, Cook's very special dish, followed and Edward took delight in explaining the workings of the ice-house. Joe said it was his intention to visit the tower before the end of the day if Edward would point him in the right direction.

The day went exceptionally well and going to bed that night Edward congratulated himself on a job well done. Nan loved the bedroom he had chosen for them and the adjacent sitting room was met with great approval. He didn't mention that the rooms had once belonged to his mother, as his grandmother was always sad when Henrietta's name was mentioned. He wanted very much to discover more about his mother, but was prepared to wait until his grandmother had settled into Plas Mawr and felt at home.

Tomorrow he would take her to meet the head gardener, as she loved gardening and had offered to help wherever she could. He made a mental note to make his grandmother her own rose garden, a place where she could choose every variety her heart desired and tend the roses alone or with help.

For Joe the day had been momentous and lying in bed, Emily asleep beside him, he decided that tomorrow he would really get stuck into work. The architect was arriving at ten o'clock and before the man left that afternoon the outline of the hospital would be on paper. Frank was due at five o'clock on union business and he was to have his supper with them. It'd be a full day, but by heck it beat swinging on a hemp rope over a quarry terrace, the rain lashing, and water trickling down the back of the collar of his old fustian coat.

Tuning onto his side he closed his eyes; the smile remained on his face until he finally fell into a deep sleep.

Chapter 15

Tommy woke in a strange bed, his head on a grey pillow and even greyer sheets beneath his chin; there was a definite and suspicious odour trapped in the cheap cotton.

Recall came back to him slowly, but then he remembered that on the previous night he had fled the banks of the Mersey and fetched up in a whorehouse in the docklands of the city. Immediately following the tipping of Constable Lloyd into the water, he had crossed the docks and taken hasty refuge in Dirty Mary's; he had been told by a customer that the establishment was so named for the sexual proclivity of the female proprietor, but the state of the linen could also be a reasonable motive.

Throwing his legs off the lumpy mattress he sat on the edge of the bed, elbows on his knees and head in his hands. The room was dreadful, but then he hadn't chosen the house because of the furnishing or cleanliness; it was his first choice because women that had chosen to be whores were less likely to be scrupulous citizens intent upon obeying the law, they had too many secrets of their own and other people's to be worried about a nameless man taking a room for a few nights. If he paid Mary well, and didn't expect sex in return, she would run errands for him, discover which ship was leaving the docks for America or Australia in the next few days.

There were no regrets about Lloyd, the man had been a dangerous menace and likely to get them both locked up; his drinking was out of control just as his tongue had been. He gave a grim smile. At least he didn't have to pay the man now.

Lifting the portmanteau onto the bed, he opened it, and tipping it upside down emptied it of the money hidden there. It took him a while to count and stack it. When he had the exact figure he put the cash back into the bag and pushed it under the bed. It was safe enough as he had no intention of leaving the room until he departed for good to climb aboard a ship heading across the sea.

There was a light knock on the door. Tensing, Tommy climbed off the bed, and silently on bare feet he went to stand beside the door frame.

'Who is it?' he whispered.

'Only Mary, I thought you might like a glass of ale or a brandy, it's past ten o'clock.'

Opening the door carefully, he gave her just enough space to pass through and come into the room.

She smiled winningly. Tommy noticed that she looked a lot more haggard by daylight than the flame of last night's lamp.

She put two glasses down on the meagre side-table beside the bed.

'Do you want food brought up or are you coming down?'

'Here will be fine, I have no need for social gatherings,' he said stiffly.

She smiled, showing crooked and stained teeth. 'I like a man of mystery,' she said, trying her hand at coquettishness.

She had already decided that the man was one of the gentry, and it would be worth her time and trouble to suck up to him, one way or the other.

'Beef steak and bacon do for you?'

His eyes raked her blue brocade bodice; her décolletage was showing signs of age, but her breasts were round and full. He gave a thought to the name of her establishment, and as he hadn't caught a whiff of body odour from her flesh or clothes, he assumed it was a sexual connotation which was intriguing. As he hadn't lain with a woman since ravishing Sadie at Penrhyn Castle, he decided to waste an hour or two in the woman's company. But food first, he was hungry.

'Rare beef steak,' he said, using his eyes to send a sexual message.

Her response was a grin and he saw the stains on her teeth for a second time.

Slipping out of the door, she said, 'I'll be back with the steak and fried potato.'

Tommy closed and locked the door behind her and for a moment he listened to her small feet tripping down the uncarpeted stairs.

Another reason for him to hole up in a dump such as this: no one would think to look for a man familiar with wealth and luxurious splendour to endure a hovel like Dirty Mary's.

Tommy caught the aroma of hot beef fat as Mary carried the meal up the flight of stairs, crockery rattling on a tray. She knocked once, said her name, before he opened the door to let her in.

'My word,' she chuckled cheekily, 'you're a cautious one.'

'My business,' he answered surly.

'Of course it is,' she placated.

The smell of the food made his mouth water and he sat on the bed, tray on his lap, to eat.

Mary had brought a bottle of wine and two short stemmed plain glasses. 'I thought you might like to share this. I've put it on your bill, so you might as well.'

His mouth full, he held out his hand to take a glass as she poured it out. He took a slurp. The quality was inferior but tasted like nectar after the abstinence of the last days.

'You'll get bored just sitting here. Why don't you come out tonight? I could show you some lively haunts in the city, beyond the docklands.'

'No thanks,' he said, shovelling another fork of potato into his mouth.

Mary chuckled. 'You are a real dark horse. But never mind, we can have our own fun here. Can't we?'

Her dress rustled as she sat beside him on the bed.

He glanced sideways at her but said nothing.

To entice him she stroked the skin of his chest through the opening of his white shirt. Getting no response, she lifted the glass to her lips again and took a long swallow.

Finishing his meal, he put the tray down at the side of the bed, and taking the glass from her hand he placed it beside the tray.

'So Dirty Mary,' he said, deep from his throat. 'What new lessons can you teach me?'

She giggled girlishly. 'Plenty to show and teach,' she said, dark eyes flashing with interest.

He undid the top button of her dress, his fingers lightly touching her flesh; she shivered at the contact.

'Someone just walked over my grave,' she said, giggling again.

Dipping his head he kissed the hollow at the base of her throat, his tongue making a damp circle there.

With fast nimble fingers she began to unbutton the bodice of her dress; it fell to the floor and lay like a blue puddle at her feet.

She wore no drawers, and the palm of his hand stroked her warm rump. Aroused, his penis hard against the restriction of his trousers, it was difficult to restrain the urge to slap her flesh beneath his hand and feel her body flinch against his, her short sharp cry breathy and warm in his ear.

It was almost dark outside when Tommy climbed off the bed. The woman was still sleeping so he gave her rump a clout, and she turned over bad-temperedly, her hair dishevelled and make-up ruined.

'How far is it to the closest shipping office?' he asked, striking a match to light a cigar.

She brushed hair off her face. 'Not far.'

'It's not what I asked. I said how far.'

Grumbling she climbed off the bed, her limbs aching, and between her legs was sore and sticky. She hoped to God the bugger had enough money to pay for what he'd taken. Even in her trade, which was rough by any standard, the bastard was vicious. It'd take a week before she was any use to another man unless she was prepared to suffer for the pennies the sods threw her way.

'Three in the next street,' she said belligerently.

He pulled the curtain back an inch or two and glanced through the gap onto the street. Three drunks were coming up the road, bags slung over their shoulders, their walk giving them away as sailors.

He half turned to her. 'Do they have timetables in the windows?'

'Not really sure, but I suppose so. It's never interested me. There's no chance that I am going to get away from here in a million years, Liverpool born and bred and likely to die and be buried here too.'

He was back at the window, the curtain shoved a little to the side.

The peal of ship's siren pierced the night, reminding him that

254

he should have been out as soon as it was dark, searching for the first ship sailing out of the docks; its destination was unimportant, he just had to get away from here before someone in Caernarvon caught on that he may have headed for Liverpool.

'Do you have any idea of sailing times?' he asked, expecting no help from her whatsoever.

'Yes.'

Dropping the corner of the curtain, he turned to her. 'Is there a sailing tonight?' he asked, a bubble of excitement worming its way into his mind.

'Yes, there is.'

'How do you know?' He didn't trust her. The whore was only out to make money.

'Me brother's a sailor. He goes and back and forth to America. It wouldn't suit me, back and forth, back and forth.'

He was churlish. 'I thought you said that you wanted to get away from here.'

'I do. But I want to go once, not keep coming back. What bloody use is that?'

She grinned. 'Are you thinking of asking me to come with you?'

His eyebrows rose. 'What do you think?'

'Suppose not. But you owe me.'

'I'm aware of that. When does your brother next leave for America?'

Stooping, she picked her dress up off the floor and stepped into it. 'Tonight,' she said, half turning towards him.

He seized her shoulders. 'What time?'

She shrugged him off. 'Hey, watch who you're grabbing.'

'There's money in it, if you tell me the truth.'

255

'The ship leaves at two o'clock. He came in earlier to say goodbye. That's how I know.'

He released her and paced back to the window. 'How do I get a ticket?'

'Don't need one. The ship's half empty. They'll be glad to take your money if you turn up on the dockside.'

Crossing to the door, he turned the brass knob. 'Wait on the stairs for a few minutes. When I call you, come back and collect your money.'

Truculently, she went through the door and stood on the top step.

Tommy pulled the portmanteau from under the bed. Hurrying, he changed into respectable clothes, and wiped the stains off his shoes with the bedclothes. Carefully he counted out enough cash to appease the woman and buy her silence if the law should come looking for him. It was a guess to how much it would cost to sail tonight. To be on the safe side he put a small wad of cash into his coat and another into his trouser pocket. Checking that he'd left no items, he picked up the bag and went out.

The woman was sitting on the top stair.

Tommy handed her a small pile of notes. 'There's enough here to pay for the afternoon fun and the meal and still plenty left over to guarantee that if anyone comes looking for me you'll remain silent, if that's too difficult just say that I went to Ireland and you saw me leave on the Irish ship.'

She looked up at him, wide-eyed. 'You've got me silence and me blessings for as long as I live mister. Just get the hell out of here and find somewhere safe. You are not like mortal men, you're a bloody angel.'

Tommy smiled for the first time in days. 'Take care, Mary.

Try and find yourself a regular man.'

She grinned. 'The only one I want is leaving on the night sailing.'

Passing her, he trotted down the stairs and into the night.

The siren pealed again and he headed in the direction of the sound.

The dockside was alive with swinging lamplight as dock workers and the ship's company went about the last minute business.

Tommy passed a notice board advertising Pacific Mail Steamship Company and knew that he was heading in the right direction.

The buildings were now behind him, and passing an old three mast schooner he saw the *Pegasus*, a new sail and steam ship, her three masts rigged. The paintwork new, she was elegant and she looked fast.

Several passengers were being escorted along a gangway into the ship. Tommy went to the man standing at the walkway, a passenger list in his hand.

Displaying his most charming smile, Tommy said, 'I'm afraid I have mislaid my ticket.' He made a show of patting his coat pockets. 'But I am prepared to pay again if it is necessary.' He smiled again.

'What name was the ticket booked to, sir?' the young man asked politely.

'Thomas William,' Tommy smiled again.

'I'm sorry sir, but I don't appear to have you on my list.'

Tommy pretended surprise. 'Oh, there must be some kind of mistake. I asked my secretary to make the booking a few days ago and she assured me everything was in order.'

The steward checked his list again, and then said, 'I'm so sorry, sir.'

'It's not your fault, young man. There must have been a mix up in my office. Is there a way I can board and pay for the ticket once I am inside?'

'Yes sir. If you go to the main deck you'll see the ticket office there.'

Driving quite close, a smart Landau came to a halt and an elderly man stepped down, and then assisted a heavily jewelled woman out. Following the woman was a plain girl, built a little solidly.

Tommy noticed the string of pearls around her neck, and was reminded of the lovely gems he had given to Lady Isabelle when she had been just past the height of her beauty. A pang for the lost days wormed its way into his equilibrium.

'Young man,' the elderly man shouted, waving a cane. 'Our luggage needs your attention.'

Looking slightly harassed, the man once again checked the passenger list. 'What name is it, sir?'

'Sir Humphrey. Lady Felicity. Harriet.'

Tommy made a mental note of Harriet Humphrey, he would look out for her later, and maybe spend some time with the young woman whilst aboard. Loyal and unstinting attention would work wonders with a plain woman like Harriet. In no time at all she would be opening the door to her father's obvious fortune.

Pleased, he picked up the portmanteau and walked towards her mother. 'Madam, perhaps I could carry your smaller bags aboard.'

Lady Felicity chortled. 'Oh what a charming man, but my

husband will organise the luggage. Perhaps you would be so kind as to help me aboard. I do not have sea legs and always fear I may trip.'

Tommy smiled. 'Please take my arm.'

Half turning, Lady Felicity called to Harriet, 'Don't dawdle. Your father will attend to everything. Come along and meet this most charming gentleman.'

Turning back to Tommy, her jewels glinting in the lamplight, she said, 'I'm so sorry, I didn't catch your name.'

'It's Thomas William, Lady Felicity.'

'Oh I do so hope the ship is not crowded, Thomas. When we sailed from New York the ship was very crowded and the second class passengers were such a bore.'

'I do believe that there is a shortage of passengers on this sailing,' he said to please her.

'Oh look, Thomas, we have arrived. I will just sit there on the sofa and wait for my husband. He is sure not to be too long.'

'Perhaps I will have the pleasure of your company later,' Tommy said, taking her hand and placing an imaginary kiss on the white kid glove.

'That would be delightful, Thomas.'

Backing away, he made it to the onboard ticket office. Behind him he heard Lady Felicity chastising poor Harriet for not taking more of an interest in a possibly eligible bachelor.

Tommy smiled.

The first class ticket was expensive, but he considered it money well spent if it got him into the society he needed to break into in New York.

A steward carried his portmanteau to his suite, and opened the door. Tommy went in. The cabin was small, almost as small as the prison cell he had so recently vacated. Tipping the steward, he closed the door on the long carpeted corridor.

There was still more than an hour before the ship steamed out of the dock, time enough for the police to come aboard and arrest him; the safest thing to do was to while away the time in the suite. Once the ship was out at sea he would go on deck and check there was no policeman awaiting him. Impossible to stay holed up in the small suite; his absence in the dining room or on deck would arouse interest and that was the last thing he needed.

Weary, he had lost two nights' sleep. He lay with his head on a pristinely white pillowcase. The ship was moving when he awoke; with no idea of how long it had been steaming towards the open sea he tried to judge the movement of the hull to decide if they were in deep or shallow water. A hopeless task, and although hungry and thirsty he slept again.

Sunlight falling on his face woke him, and for a dreadful moment he thought he was back in the cell, a prison guard shining a light in his face. His eyes quickly scanned the cabin and it took a second to remember his location.

Throwing his legs off the bed he went to the tiny bathroom to relieve himself. Washed and dressed, he was ready to look over the ship and check that it was free of officers of the law.

Standing at the cabin door, staring at the varnished wood, he made two false starts before he gathered enough courage to open the door and walk out of the suite and into the corridor.

He passed a steward and the man smiled; it was a good omen.

Going forward he climbed a companionway up to the open deck.

Outdoors, breathing clean salty air cleared his head from the fug of the suite.

He took a cautious look around; many of the passengers were nonchalantly strolling around the deck, and the less energetic were sitting in the sunshine reading, chatting, or just looking out to sea with contented expressions.

All seemed perfectly normal, but he was still uneasy, wondering if he should have stayed below until nightfall. After dark, if the police tried to apprehend him, there was a better chance of evasion. He was perfectly prepared to tip anyone overboard if they tried to take him. There was nothing to lose by committing another murder. Take one life and the hangman's rope is a certainty, take two or more and the same applies.

The disquieting thought was driven out of his head by the strident call of Lady Felicity.

'Thomas, we were beginning to wonder what had become of you, we thought you may have fallen overboard,' she chortled.

Automatically, Tommy put a carefree smile on his lips. The woman was sitting on what looked to be a bath chair, a tartan rug almost covering a green taffeta skirt. She sported a hat of the same shade of jade, the long feather attaching fluttered like a beacon in the sea breeze.

Tommy strode towards her as though his sole intention was to sit alongside and amuse her, as though he were an old friend.

From the corner of his eye a steward saw Tommy's intentions and was quick to draw up another chair beside Lady Felicity.

'My dear lady, what a wonderful way to begin my day,' Tommy said gallantly on being within hand's reach.

The corners of her eyes crinkled as she smiled, the brown pupils glistening like cut topaz. 'Near perfect weather, Thomas,' she said, shading her eyes with her bejewelled hand and looking out across the water.

'Steaming along nicely,' he said, sitting down beside her.

'Oh, look, here comes my husband.' Lady Felicity waved frantically to Sir Humphrey as he came striding towards them in clothes that were better suited to a country walk than an ocean voyage.

Another chair was brought by a steward and Sir Humphrey 'Umphed' loudly as he slumped upon it.

'Steaming at about ten knots,' he said certainly.

'However do you know that?' His wife said, glancing at him.

'Asked the purser, just passed him now as I was coming to find you, my dear, but I see that you are in good company.'

He smiled at Tommy. 'We couldn't ask for a better day.'

'Absolutely perfect sailing weather,' Tommy agreed.

It had been some time since he had eaten and his stomach clenched with hunger pains. It was in his mind to abandon the pair and go in search of a late breakfast or early luncheon when Harriet, dressed in a navy blue dress with a sailor collar trimmed in white, headed towards them.

She looks hideous, Tommy thought ungallantly.

Seeing Tommy with her parents, Harriet thought to retreat but her mother had already noticed her approach so the girl had no choice but to join them.

Tommy leapt up offering her his seat, but just as before a steward stepped forward with another chair and Tommy sat back down again.

'Where have you been?' Lady Felicity said a little peevishly.

Harriet's face pinked. 'Oh just here and there, wandering about.'

Sir Humphrey spoke over the two women. 'What is your line of work, Thomas?'

'Company solicitor but I have interests in mining. Australia mainly,' Tommy lied.

In the early hours he had remembered that he had seen Sir Humphrey's name in a business portfolio; the man was heavily involved and invested in mining in Victoria, Australia. By inventing a shared interest Tommy hoped that it would lever him into the man's business and family life, though using the same method as he had with the Bellamy family to acquire Plas Mawr and the Garddryn had a certain déjà vu.

Harriet began to fidget but as her father totally ignored her, Tommy glanced her way giving a secret smile.

Harriet blushed to the roots of her brown hair.

In the hour before luncheon Tommy gathered many facts and figures and now had an excellent insight into the workings of Sir Humphrey's mining interests. The Aborigines, the immigration of the Chinese, brown coal, gold, tin; Sir Humphrey had an interest and opinion on the subject that shaped and changed his business interests and fascinated, his mind whirling with the possibilities opening up, Tommy not only relaxed but the loss of Plas Mawr seemed much less important. In his bones he could feel his life broadening, North Wales had been too provincial, and not the right location for him to spread and realise his great ambitions.

Harriet whispered to her mother that she was hungry. Ever attentive, Tommy suggested they go to the dining room for luncheon. Grateful to him, Harriet put her hand on his arm, allowing him to escort her.

Tommy chatted inconsequentially until they entered the dining room and he handed her into a pale blue dining chair. Though Harriet spoke little during the first course of clear soup,

Tommy felt her eyes upon him on several occasions, but instead of returning her glances he concentrated almost entirely upon Sir Humphrey, only turning away for a moment to Lady Felicity to remark on how delicious the fried soles and caper sauce looked upon the serving dish. Sir Humphrey said little until the soles were demolished and only a vein of fragile bones lay on the luncheon plates. The third course of roast beef, beetroot, and mashed potatoes caught the elderly man's interest and he relayed a story from his boyhood when exactly the same course had been served when a member of the royal family paid a visit to the family seat in Berkshire. Tommy had never really cared for pheasant and was disappointed that it came to the table, though out of politeness he picked at the aromatic flesh. A sweet omelette served with stewed prunes and cold rice followed before the cheese and celery was brought to table. Throughout the luncheon a wine waiter had replenished Lady Felicity's long stemmed glass with champagne, and her ladyship was somewhat tipsy when she rose from table.

'I do think the sea is less calm,' she said, steadying herself on the rim of the table.

Moving from his chair, Tommy gallantly went towards her. 'I believe you are correct, Lady Felicity. Do take my arm.' He smiled at Harriet. 'Nothing would please me more than escorting two delightful ladies.'

Sir Humphrey remained where he was. 'I'll have a glass of port,' he said, stifling a tiny belch. 'Thomas, when you have taken the ladies wherever they wish to be, perhaps you could join me.'

'I would be delighted to,' Tommy said, happy to oblige.

As Lady Felicity wished to go to her cabin, Tommy took both

mother and daughter there. Coming away, walking down the long carpeted corridor making for the companionway that would take him to the upper decks, Tommy didn't think he was mistaken in believing that Harriet was already blossoming under his influence.

An onboard routine was established and for the next few days Tommy spend most of his time with the family. Harriet certainly chattered more and Tommy often caught her looking at him. Sir Humphrey began to see him as a potential son-in-law and he thought that he couldn't do much better for Harriet than pay for an expensive wedding and buy a sprawling apartment for the couple in the best district in New York.

When the tragedy unfolded it came with nightmare speed.

The group had already arrived in the dining room and were sitting at their usual table.

Lady Felicity dressed in a red silk gown, the design and décolletage somewhat too young for her, but the incorrectness of the ensemble ably compensated by her jewels; exquisite rubies and diamonds sparkled at her neck, a matching tiara nestled on her grey hair, and her long lobed ears rained diamonds speckled with pigeon blood red stones. The display was magnificent and Tommy wondered what had sparked the idea for such a show. Perhaps Lady Felicity was expecting him to propose to Harriet and thought that a show of the family assets would tip the matrimonial balance; he would propose tonight, had he not considered that it was too soon for Harriet's papa.

A silver champagne bucket was brought to the table and a waiter poured into Lady Felicity's glass.

A delightful dinner followed, the conversation intermittently interrupted by a long mournful drone of the ship's foghorn.

Dining so extravagantly on rich food Tommy was beginning to feel bloated, and when the dish of crayfish soup was brought to the table he had very little.

Sir Humphrey dined well on salmon, whitebait, fricassee of chicken, fried sweetbreads, and haunch of venison.

Harriet ate very little as she wished to watch her figure. Tommy was amused, for he would marry the woman whatever her shape.

The foghorn wailed into the night.

Tommy took his eyes off the plate and glanced to the window and portholes and saw only thick grey fog swirling by. The room was chill, as though the cold grey had seeped in through the glass like an ethereal ghost.

Lady Felicity raised her glass to the lips to take a sip when the ship lurched violently, throwing her chair backwards. Tommy slammed into the table and it went toppling over. Screaming, Harriet clutched at Tommy. Sir Humphrey, thrown to the floor, climbed to his knees wheezing, his face the colour of a beetroot. Still holding onto Harriet, Tommy stooped to help Lady Felicity up. A steward knocked to his knees rose, staggering, a trickle of blood seeping from a cut above his eye.

There was pandemonium, people screaming, a child crying hysterically. The floor, now listing sinisterly, was littered with broken glass, chinaware, scattered cutlery and the remnants of dinner. There was hardly a piece of furniture standing, and the blue carpet was stained with pools of water from broken flower vases. Some of the candles in the candelabras had survived and were burning, threatening to set light to the carpet. The stewards began to stamp on the small flames.

Tommy got Harriet, Lady Felicity and Sir Humphrey together

and suggested they remained where they were until he went to see what the situation was on deck. Lady Felicity was crying quietly and Harriet tried to comfort her but to no avail, the woman was terrified.

Through the dense fog Tommy saw the outline of another ship; obviously there had been a collision, the old sailing ship had come off worse in the accident and was listing dangerously, the main mast had collapsed and dark sails hung in the rigging and across her portside. Dark figures at the rails were screaming hysterically; some people, either thrown or who had jumped, were in the black water thrashing aimlessly, calling and pleading for help. A scene from hell shrouded in grey swirling murkiness.

There was confusion and panic on the *Pegasus*. The decks were listing slightly. Several people who had been on deck when the accident happened had fallen badly and one woman was screaming for her husband who had fallen overboard.

The crew, as startled by events as everyone else, were trying to get passengers inside but for what purpose mystified Tommy. Ignoring them, he went towards the bow of the ship where the collision had occurred and looked over the wrecked rails. *Pegasus* was holed extensively, and the opening went below the waterline. Icicles of fear seeped into his veins. If they couldn't get everyone onto the lifeboats they would die in the water.

Pegasus was going no further; in hours she would lie on the bottom of the ocean. The ship lurched with a dreadful cracking and grating and the slope of the deck increased.

Hurrying, Tommy went back into the dining room and went to where he had last seen Sir and Lady Humphrey and Harriet. They were still in exactly the same place, frozen with fear.

'We have to go to the lifeboats,' he said urgently to Sir

Humphrey. 'There's no chance that the ship will survive for very much longer. There's another close by, also sinking. There will not be enough life boats for everyone and even if we do get into one, the chances are that it will be so overcrowded it will sink. Our only chance is to get in one now and get away from the people already in the water. Do you understand?'

Sir Humphrey nodded that he did. He clutched Tommy's coat sleeve. 'Tommy we will not make it, my wife and I are too old.'

Tommy tugged at the man, trying to make him rise. 'You must try.' He could see his chances of a wealthy life with the family slipping away. If the man didn't make it then there was nothing, and it was probably too late to rescue the portmanteau from his suite. Even if he did survive he would be destitute.

Sir Humphrey's colour worsened. He clutched frantically at Tommy's clothes. 'Please, Thomas, save Harriet.'

Rallying, he found the energy to move on his backside to come alongside his wife. 'Felicity, take off your jewellery.'

She was reluctant and he began to snatch at the clasp on the ruby and diamond necklace. 'Hurry woman, we don't have much time.'

Harriet began to wail, her despair lost in the clamour of the other passengers' misery and fear.

With the necklace glistening in his hand, he snatched at her tiara. Lady Felicity gave a sharp shout as he tugged off her hair.

'The earrings, the earrings, hurry Felicity,' he urged, his fingers already on the clasp of one of them.

With the prizes in his hands, he shuffled on his bottom to get to Tommy again.

The glittering bundle held against his shirt front, he said, 'Take this Thomas. Take it all.'

He pushed the precious load into Tommy's coat pockets. 'All I ask of you is that you save our girl. Take the gems as a reward. Harriet will give you much more when you are both safe in New York.'

Tommy ceased to hear the crying and wailing, his entire being centred on the noises of the dying ship, and when a grating noise like broken bones sliding one against another, he rose fast to his feet, grabbed Harriet's hand and ran out onto the sloping deck.

Tears wetting his face, Sir Humphrey waved a last farewell to his girl.

Then with his back against a metal stanchion he waited for the water to claim him and his poor wife, Felicity. Taking her hand, he held it tightly against his chest.

Tommy knew that there was no time to retrieve the portmanteau and the treasure within it; he would surely be trapped down below when the ship made a final lurch to the bottom of the ocean. Still running, he made for the lifeboats but every cradle was empty; pulling Harriet he went to the other side of the ship and ran the length of it, sure that he would find one last boat hanging there, but every cradle was empty, slipped overboard by well-meaning *Pegasus* crew in an attempt to save the passengers from the other ship already in the water.

The bow dipped and the new ship slipped under the waves quickly; her stern rose to the sky and she was sliding in fast. There was no time to lose and Tommy, leaving Harriet, jumped.

Alone and terrified, Harriet gripped the rail and then, losing her hold, she slid towards the bow, now sunk below the waves.

As he swam frantically away from the hull that would surely drag him down, Tommy heard her final scream.

He didn't stop swimming until he realised that the only sound was lapping waves; treading water he turned to look back, and all he could see through the swirling fog was the mast of the sailing ship, like a sword piercing the grey.

He listened intently for the sound of oars, and the cries of other people in the water, but there was only silence. He wondered how long he had actually been swimming, for fear had driven him on to the ultimate of his energy. But now he had reached the end of that, his arms were no longer moving with any strength.

He was cold, colder than he had ever been. Turning slowly on his back he looked up into the fog; there was chink in the grey and he could see a patch of ink blue sky.

The gems in his pockets were pulling him down but he hadn't the strength or the will to discard them, rubies were too precious.